M000087958

THE WOMAN IN THE YELLOW DRESS

Robert Forte

Copyright © 2016 Robert Forte
All rights reserved.

ISBN: 0692756205
ISBN 13: 9780692756201
Library of Congress Control Number: 2016912174
Robert Forte, Johnstown, PA

To Evelyn

CHAPTER ONE

The first thing she noticed was her left hand shaking uncontrollably. No matter how hard she tried, she couldn't make it stop.

The fear of it all finally happening had manifested itself right down to the tips of her fingers, and it became quite clear to her that the shaking wasn't ever going to stop until this was over.

Until it was really over. Finally over.

She had started secretly drinking and smoking several weeks ago but nothing helped. The fear was too overwhelming. It seemed to wash over her like ocean waves crashing on a shore at the onset of a raging storm. The storm was about to begin and she knew there was no turning back.

Not this time. Her left hand shaking and the foul taste of cigarettes and alcohol were small prices to pay. She was ready and well prepared.

She never dreamed that the man who had once stolen her heart, held her close every night and made her feel safe, would become a vile and cruel monster, not only to her, but to both of their teenaged girls.

She wanted to blame the war. People said it changed good men into bad but she had seen signs long before he went off to fight the Germans.

She and Stanley met in high school and couldn't wait to run off and get married, which is what they did exactly three days after graduation. She was two months pregnant with their first daughter, Elizabeth, and Stanley wanted to do the right thing, stand by her, and be the best husband and father he could possibly be.

That was his promise to her. Three years later Sandra was born and family life was good. Stanley had a good steady paying job working as a mechanic at the Los Angeles airport. They managed to buy a house in a very nice, quiet neighborhood in Van Nuys, and life for the most part was good.

Time passed. Good time.

About eight years into the marriage, Stanley began to change. He became short tempered, disagreeable, kept telling her to be quiet and leave him alone with his thoughts or his cold beers and his hard pretzels.

They made love only when it was his decision and it was always too quick, too rough, and never satisfying for her.

Stanley was a mountain of a man. Broad shoulders, large hands and feet, standing about six foot four, and a well-muscled body. He always had dreams of maybe playing football, although he never actually played in any sports growing up. His size also, at first, always made her and the girls feel safe from anyone or anything that might ever threaten them.

But now the threat wasn't outside. The threat was right in front of their faces sharing meals, talking uneducated politics, and sometimes even sharing a laugh over some joke one of the girls had heard at school.

The first time he hit her changed everything.

For months she kept telling him, they needed a new refrigerator. One morning she stood at the kitchen sink washing the breakfast dishes and again, casually mentioned the possibility of buying a new fridge. Suddenly, he stepped up to her from the kitchen table, turned her around and slapped her face so viciously that she fell to the floor. The girls had already gone off to school and were spared the ugly transformation that had finally bubbled up inside their father after so many years of marriage.

That ugliness would show itself again much sooner than later.

Always, she blamed herself for his bad behavior. Maybe she was too demanding, too talkative, always making suggestions for ways to invest or spend their hard-earned money.

Although always calling it his money.

When the war ended and Stanley returned home from Europe as so many other young men, he no longer resembled the Stanley she had married all those years ago.

He was much thinner, and he carried a look in his eyes she had never seen on any man or woman in her entire life.

Stanley went back to his aircraft mechanic job and began to settle in to a weekly routine working Monday through Friday, and performing weekend outdoor house chores. He even bought her the new refrigerator she had so desperately kept asking for. She accepted it as his way of apologizing for the hard slap, but the damage had been done. The look in his eyes intensified, and the crippling fear also kept nagging at her, day after day, night after night.

Stanley had clearly changed, and not for the better. He grew angrier as days became weeks, and weeks turned into months. He became more and more controlling over her and their daughters.

More than ever before.

The fear began, and grew with such intensity that it finally broke her heart, snapped her soul, and completely changed her feelings towards Stanley.

Forever.

Anything and everything bothered him.

Work pushed him too hard, everything seemed to cost more, and at the end of the month there never seemed to be enough money to get ahead.

The girls were always getting on his nerves. She could never do anything right, anymore, and their sex life was nearly nonexistent. Stanley clearly was a changed man; his entire demeanor shifting from a loving husband and father to a human volcano that would erupt at any given moment.

But when Stanley began taking his anger out on the girls too, she knew she had to act. She had to do something, and do it quickly.

Unfortunately, she wasn't quick enough.

They had made love one night and she thought there might still be a slim chance for her and Stanley to possibly turn things around. He acted like his old self. He was kind and sweet and once again made her feel safe.

But it was all an act.

His loving kindness was a false mask hiding the true monster Stanley had allowed himself to finally become.

A monster that had to be destroyed.

Thinking she had fallen asleep, Stanley quietly got out of bed and closed the door to their bedroom.

Her first signal that something wasn't right.

He never shut the door, even if he was going to the bathroom or decided to get a drink of water or something to eat.

In her broken soul, she felt something wasn't right, and that feeling made her suddenly sit up in bed and listen to the dark.

And when the dark spoke she became terrified and felt horribly alone.

There were muffled voices. Someone was talking, but she couldn't quite make out who was being spoken to or what was being said.

Quickly, Grace got out of bed, put on her robe, silently opened the bedroom door and looked down the hall.

Everything was quiet and dark. Too quiet. Too dark.

And then she heard a familiar squeaking sound. Her heart seemed to fall right out of her chest.

She ran down the hall and burst into Elizabeth's room and turned on the light. Stanley was lying naked on top of Elizabeth with one hand holding her arms above her and the other over her mouth.

He was inside her and Elizabeth's eyes looked to her mother, silently crying out to her in desperation.

Grace froze in the doorway, not believing what she was witnessing. Before even realizing how she was reacting, she was standing next to him, pushing and clawing at him, screaming at the top of her lungs to stop!

"Get off of her and move away you monster!" she cried. "You get the hell out of here right now! You sad, sick, son of a bitch! Leave Elizabeth be! What in God's name is wrong with you?"

"Back off me, Grace!" he said pushing her slightly with his right arm.

"No! I won't, God damn it!"

"You and these girls belong to me!" he screamed. "I own you! All of you!"

"She's a child! She's our child! Get out! Now!" she screamed, crying hysterically.

Stanley stood up, looked at her, and punched her squarely in the face.

Instantly everything went black.

When she came to, both girls were lying next to her on the floor, still in Elizabeth's room.

She quickly checked the girls terrified faces and tried to calm herself for their sake.

"Where the hell is he?" she asked.

"Back in your room, Mama. Sleeping," Sandra replied and lightly brushed some hair from her mother's swollen, bloodied face.

Grace's nose was clearly broken and her left eye began to puff up dramatically. She looked at Sandra and tried to smile a motherly smile.

"Get me the phone book," she whispered. "Do it quietly."

She watched Sandra leave the room and then she looked directly at Elizabeth, touching her hand.

"Are you all right?" she asked. "I'm fine Mama. I am."

"How long has he been doing this?" she asked.

Elizabeth tried to hold back her painful tears but they rolled down her face as she stared back at her mother.

"This was the fifth time, Mama."

Her daughter's words made her gasp.

"And your sister?"

"Once. Last week."

The horror of it all pulled her face down into a saddened frown of misery that she had never experienced before. She reached out and grabbed her daughter, holding her tightly in her arms.

"I am so sorry, Lizzie baby. I am so, so, sorry."

"It's not your fault, Mama. It's not your fault."

Elizabeth and her mother sat clinging on to each other as Sandra returned with the phone book.

"He is never going to hurt any of us ever again. Never," she proclaimed. "I promise you. It's my promise to both of you."

Sandra sat on the other side of her mother and the two girls put their arms around her.

"Who are you going to call, mama?" Sandra asked.

"Someone who can make all of this go away. Someone I should have called months ago," she replied as she leafed through the phone book.

"Who is it?" asked Lizzie.

"He's a man who can protect us," Grace replied and wrote down a phone number. "Shut the door honey. Quietly. We'll stay in here together tonight."

Lizzie smiled and closed the bedroom door.

The next morning Stanley got up, made his own lunch, and without seeing or speaking to anyone, left the house and headed to work.

Grace made the call the moment he was gone, and her plan to end the horrific damage he had done was immediately put into motion.

Still very shaken and afraid, she knew she was at last doing the right thing. She hoped and prayed this new plan would work out the way she was told on the phone that it would.

She wanted to believe. Had to believe. Someone had to slay the monster.

For her.

And for her girls.

Now there was no turning back. Her life and the lives of her two girls were clearly at risk. Grace was not about to spend another day with this sick and deranged, angry monster pretending to be a doting father and loving husband whenever the mood suited him.

That night when the soft knock at the door came as she expected, she still jumped fearfully. Taking a deep breath and blowing it out ever so slowly gave her a sense of false strength, and she marched purposefully to the door and opened it.

Standing in the doorway was the man who promised her the moon. He told her to trust him. He told her what she needed to do, and he had come to make that all happen for her and the girls.

Her knight in shining armor had arrived to save them.

Standing outside her broken screened door was Patrick Miles Atwater. Private Eye. Just shy of six feet tall, with dark brown hair and eyes, he too had just recently returned home from the war, and also trying to get his life and his business back on track.

Patrick had seen a lot of action, more than he cared to remember, and felt in his heart that he had fought the good fight in defeating the Axis Powers. Now it was time to turn his attention back to the home front.

Do some good in the world.

A man of high integrity and strength of character, Patrick knew when something was not right and he would do whatever needed to be done. Change it, fix it, make that wrong disappear.

"Hello Mr. Atwater." Grace greeted him.

"Hello, Mrs. Clifford."

"Please. Call me Grace. Come in."

"Thank you," he replied.

Nervously she opened the screen door and let him in.

They crossed the small living room and sat down at the large dining room table. Patrick felt the tension throughout the house and sensed her nervousness.

"We haven't much time, Mr. Atwater," she said.

Noting the urgency in her voice, Patrick calmly took out a paper and placed it in front of her.

"This is it?" she asked. "This is the paper?"

"Yes, Mrs. Clifford, just as I explained to you on the phone."

She focused on reading the entire paper, word for word, and the light from the ceiling fixture above allowed Patrick to see the damage Stanley had done to her face.

The extra make-up she had applied to hide the bruising was clear to him, and he noticed her left hand trembling slightly.

"Are you all right?" he asked. "I've been better."

"When did he do that?"

Without thinking, she instantly touched the bruised side of her face. "Last night."

"Were you arguing?" he questioned.

"No. I was trying to protect my daughter."

"Protect her?"

"Yes."

"Before or after?"

She stopped reading and looked directly into Patrick's face.

"After. Is everything worded here correctly?" she asked. "I want no mistakes. I can't afford to make any more mistakes, Mr. Atwater."

A wave of emotion suddenly came up over her and she fought back tears. Reaching out, she grabbed one of Patrick's hands with both of hers and tried to form a smile.

"I understand completely, Mrs. Clifford. Don't you worry about a thing. It's all worded properly and correctly. I just need you to sign it."

"Sign it?" she asked. "Yes," he said.

Patrick took out his pen and placed it on the table beside her.

"You are certain this is all I need to do? All I have to do?"

"For now? Yes. You sign there. And initial. Right here. And right there."Her fear kept holding on to her, making her hesitate. Patrick leaned his head down to catch her eyes.

"If you don't sign this paper, Mrs. Clifford? I can't help you. And the courts? The police? They won't be able to help you either. You have to sign this and you have to sign it right now. As I explained to you before."

"I know. I know," she replied.

"You have to sign to make it all work. Please? Mrs. Clifford? I know you're scared. Trust me. You sign this? And everything will change. Everything will be fine. I promise you."

Patrick pointed out again to her the last three steps on the paper to make it all legal and official. Grabbing up the pen, she quickly signed and initialed in both necessary places, then gently put his pen down with a deep added sigh. Grace suddenly realized her left hand had stopped shaking.

She looked up at the clock.

"Oh my God, Mr. Atwater. It's almost six o'clock. He's going to be here in a few minutes. This? Is not going to sit well with him. Not at all. Not one bit."

A slight grin came over Patrick's face, but for her sake he kept it in check.

"I'm not here to make him happy. I'm here to help you. Help your girls. As I said? Trust me, Mrs. Clifford. Your husband will never hurt you or them again. My word on it."

Sandra and Elizabeth, listening from the kitchen, slowly walked into the dining room and looked at their mother.

"Did you do it, Mama? Did you sign it?" Elizabeth asked.

"I signed it, Lizzie. It's all done."

Both girls smiled and Patrick put the paper in his jacket pocket.

"What now?" she asked.

"Now? We wait. We sit. Calmly. And we wait." Patrick answered.

"Are you serious? We can't just sit here and wait!"

"Yes we can, Mrs. Clifford. I have police on their way here. Everything is going to be fine."

Patrick looked over at the girls and smiled assuredly.

"How many police do you have coming here, Mr. Atwater? How many? Because when Stanley walks through that door? And he sees you? Sitting here? At our table? Sees that paper you have in your pocket? He is going to explode. I know how he can get. We all do!"

"Stay calm, Mrs. Clifford. I will handle Stanley. I promise. He can do all the exploding he can muster. It won't matter and it won't jeopardize your safety or the safety of your two beautiful girls here."

She wanted to believe him, but before she could form any new opinions, Stanley came through the front door, put his jacket and lunch pail down and stared hard at Patrick.

"Who the hell is this, Grace," he demanded.

Grace stiffened with fear and looked at Patrick.

"This is my husband, Stanley Clifford."

Patrick calmly stood up and placed his left hand through the brass knuckles he carried in his pocket, keeping them hidden behind him and out of Stanley's sight.

Stanley was a big brute of a man, but Patrick remained calm and was well prepared for anything Stanley might have in mind.

"I'm Patrick Atwater," he answered.

"What are you doing here in my house? Patrick Atwater?"

"It's a simple thing, Stanley. I'm here to protect your family," Patrick replied.

"Protect my family? Protect my family from what? You some kind of insurance salesman?"

"I don't sell that kind of protection. I'm here to protect your family from assholes like you, Stanley."

Patrick knew his tone should have triggered an immediate response but Stanley didn't give him the reaction he was expecting.

Not at first.

Patrick stood his ground and was ready, knowing in a very short time the reaction he expected from Stanley would be coming in spades.

At first Stanley only took a large step forward and looked directly into Patrick's eyes.

"Asshole? You are here in my house and just called me an asshole?"

"I did and you are. A major asshole."

Stanley smiled slightly.

"Let me tell you something. My family doesn't need any protecting. Not from me! What the hell have you done here, Grace? Who the hell is this guy really?"

Patrick quickly took a step forward, standing in front of Grace and completely blocking Stanley's view of her.

"Your wife has done something tonight she should have done a long time ago. Living here with a man like you."

"A man like me? You don't know me!"

"Oh, but I do." Patrick answered. "I've met a lot of men like you. You're big. You're strong. You also think you're tough. So tough you think you can slap your wife and your children around to keep them in line. But a big guy like you doesn't just stop with the occasional slaps now and then. No. Or the bloodied lips? Or even a blackened eye? No. You don't stop there. Do you, Stanley?"

Patrick wiped his bottom lip with his pointing finger. He could tell his words were hitting their marks; hitting them hard.

Stanley took another step forward, stretching his neck to make eye contact again with Grace.

"What the hell did you do here, Grace? What did you tell this man?"

Once again Patrick stepped between Stanley and Grace and decided to provoke the man a bit further. He knew it wouldn't take much and clutched the brass tighter.

"Don't look at her, Stanley. Look at me. Your wife told me the truth. So listen up. Pay close attention. I don't want you to miss one word of what I am about to tell you."

"And what's that?" Stanley asked.

"You are leaving this house tonight. You're leaving it now. Right now!"

Stanley's blood began to boil. Patrick could see it in Stanley's face and set his feet squarely on the floor.

"Who the fuck do you think you are? This is my house! My house! This is my family! You don't come in here and tell me what to do! I'm not going anywhere!"

Patrick stepped in closer, keeping his eyes locked onto Stanley's. The brass around his knuckles began to feel heavy and cold. Grace and the girls held on to each other and stood in the kitchen doorway.

"Yes you are, Stanley. You're going out that door. You're going out tonight and you're never coming back."

"Never coming back?"

"That's right."

Stanley looked at Patrick and laughed.

"No, I'm not," he said.

"Yes, you are," Patrick replied.

"Who's going to make me? You?"

"It's not me, you sap! It's the state of California kicking you out of here. Away from your wife and especially away from these girls. And you know why that's happening? Do you Stanley? Well? Do you?"

Patrick took one more step towards Stanley. He knew now it was just a matter of seconds before the real confrontation erupted.

Stanley was starting to breathe heavier as his anxiety increased. Patrick could see he was becoming extremely nervous and highly agitated.

Stanley tried to calm himself by giving Patrick a warning.

"You listen to me. Nobody's kicking me anywhere! And if you don't back up and get out of my face...?"

There it was.

Patrick had him now. First the threat and then the action. Patrick pressed in harder with an abrupt interruption that put a shocked look on Stanley's face.

"Or what? What are you going to do to me, tough guy?"

"You get the fuck out of my house right now or I am going to put parts of your face, most of your teeth, and big chunks of your brains all over my dining room wall! Do you understand me? My dining room wall!"

Stanley stood pointing at the wall and Patrick knew all that had to be done now was to take that one more defiant step forward instead of going back.

Patrick was right.

As Patrick accepted the challenge, Stanley's eyes widened and he suddenly sent a long wide round house right at Patrick's face. Patrick quickly ducked down, returned it with a fast short left and pounded the brass knuckles hard and deeply into Stanley's ribs.

A muffled quick cracking sound emerged from Stanley's right side, and he instantly winced with pain, gasping for breath as he felt a rib snap from the blow.

The punch took Stanley by complete surprise.

He turned to look at Patrick still crouched below him as another left came flying straight up into Stanley's face, breaking his nose with a loud dull crunching sound and sending Stanley down onto the floor.

Stanley grabbed at his bleeding face but before he could say a word, Patrick was over him again, hitting him with three quick lefts to his face.

The brass had done the job.

Stanley was sprawled unconscious on the dining room floor. His eyes were already turning black and blue, and his nose squirted a significant amount of blood onto his face and chest before finally stopping.

Stanley slowly regained consciousness as the sound of two car doors closing echoed from outside.

"The police are here," said a shaken Grace Clifford, but a new tone was now in her voice.

It had a tone of hope.

Her voice carried a tone of a whole new beginning for her and her girls.

Grace took Patrick at his word and Patrick delivered on his promise. She was glad to have this nightmare end and she was glad to have witnessed the beating Stanley took before her eyes and in front of her children.

Patrick was acquainted with the policemen that entered the house.

"You're late, Hanks," Patrick said.

"Sorry, Patrick. I missed a block racing to get here on time," said Sgt. Hanks.

"Better late than never."

Sgt. Hanks looked down at Stanley, impressed that the situation wasn't reversed.

"Whoa! We got us a big one here. Let's get him up and cuffed. You got the order?" he asked.

Patrick reached in his pocket and handed Sgt. Hanks the signed piece of paper. Officer Kramer got a dazed Stanley to his feet and secured the cuffs on his wrists.

"Here it is," said Patrick. "Signed and delivered."

Sgt. Hanks read the order and Officer Kramer noticed Stanley's face.

"This man's nose is broken," said Officer Kramer.

"He might have a rib or two broken also," Patrick said.

"A rib? Or two?" Officer Kramer questioned.

"Yes. He, uh, tripped and fell down over there trying to run away when he heard you guys driving up," he lied. "He must have hit his face and side against the wall there."

Sgt. Hanks nodded his agreement.

"I can see that. Do you see that, Officer Kramer?"

Officer Kramer looked at Sgt. Hanks and nodded yes.

"Yes sir. I do. This man clearly fell down and hurt himself attempting to escape. Obviously."

Officer Kramer grinned broadly.

"He looks like the clumsy sort. Doesn't he?" Officer Kramer said.

"I'll make sure to note that in our arrest report," answered Sgt. Hanks.

"Thank you, Officers," said Patrick.

Sgt. Hanks shook his head back and forth, grinned broadly and assisted Officer Kramer in walking Stanley slowly out of the house.

Still dazed, Stanley tried to protest.

"What the hell is going on here? Somebody want to tell me what this is all about? What arrest report? I ain't done nothing," whined Stanley. "This man attacked me in my own home! Look what he did to me! Tell them, Grace!"

Sgt. Hanks looked at Stanley.

"Stanley Clifford? You are under arrest for domestic assault, spousal abuse, and rape."

"Rape? I never raped my wife! Never!"

"But you did rape your daughters? Didn't you?" asked Sgt. Hanks.

"No! That is crazy! Tell them, Grace! Tell them it isn't true! Lizzie? Sandra? Don't let your mother do this!"

Grace stepped forward and stared hard at Stanley.

"It is true! Everything in that report! Every word! You're going to prison, you rotten bastard! I never want to see you again! Your girls don't want to see you again! Ever!"

Elizabeth and Sandra stood beside their mother and watched as the policemen marched Stanley toward the patrol car.

"Grace? Tell them you made a mistake! You were just upset because I slapped you around a little. She doesn't listen good! Tell them, God damn it!" he cried.

"Rot in hell you son of a bitch! You rot in hell," Grace screamed.

She put her arms around the girls and held them both tightly. Sgt. Hanks looked at Patrick.

"Have a good night, Patrick" he said.

"You, too. And thanks."

Stanley suddenly turned and tried to move towards Grace. Officer Kramer and Sgt. Hanks held Stanley back.

"Don't let them do this, Grace! You fucking bitch! I'm warning you. I'm warning all of you! I want a God damn lawyer! I'm going to sue this fucking state! I'm going to sue the entire police force! And then I'm coming back here, Grace! You can't do this to me and think for one God damn minute you'd get away with it! You bitch. You fucking bitch!" snarled Stanley.

Officer Kramer purposely pushed Stanley into the door jamb, bonking his broken nose a second time.

"Hey! Watch it," Stanley whined.

"Don't be so clumsy, sir. I'm just trying to do my job here," said Officer Kramer.

The policemen bundled Stanley into the squad car and drove away. Grace and the girls turned their attention to Patrick.

"Thank you, Mr. Atwater. I couldn't have done this without your help."

"The worst is over now, Mrs. Clifford. Stanley can't hurt any of you ever again. He'll be arraigned in about a week or two and sent away from you and your daughters for a very long time."

"How long, Mr. Atwater?" asked Elizabeth.

"My guess? Five years. Maybe even ten or more."

"Can't we ask the judge to give him life?" she asked.

Patrick looked at her and smiled.

"Trust me. Whatever sentence he's given is going to seem like a lifetime to him. My word on it. You stay happy and you stay safe. Okay?"

"We will," said Grace and held her daughters closer. "We will."

Patrick gave one last smile goodbye to Mrs. Clifford and her girls, walked out to his car and drove off into the night.

CHAPTER TWO

Given the fact that World War II had been over almost three years and no matter how busy everyone's life in America had become, a Sunday night at Barney's By the Sea had remained the same as it had for the last fifteen years. A slow dinner crowd with a noise level so low you could still hear the ocean waves crashing on the beach below.

One waitress, Betty Russeau, casually worked the floor.

Betty had been and still was, a very close personal friend of mine for the past twelve years. She was the girl with a heart of gold, a smile that could melt you in an instant, and an ass that could drive any man totally senseless.

Betty and I first met at a diner she worked called Barlow's, in Westwood. It was around the corner from my apartment, and sparks fired up with us right from the get go. · One late night, we found ourselves alone in my apartment. It was raining rather heavily and I simply offered her a safe and dry place to step out of the storm and towel herself off.

She readily agreed.

I cracked open a bottle of wine, poured two glasses, and after sharing a few slow sips, leaned over and kissed her. Momentarily stunned at first, she quickly kissed me back. Suddenly we found ourselves entangled in each other's arms, legs, and everything else we could possibly share, including all of our hopes, dreams, desires, and most of all, our friendship.

Over the years Betty and I had somehow forged that kind of special relationship between a man and a woman that we casually referred to as close friends. It worked for us, and we both knew we could always count on each other, no matter what.

Barney Hubbs, owner of Barney's By the Sea, was a balding, slightly overweight, eye-patched man in his late fifties, working the quiet bar by himself, just as he had every Sunday night for the last fifteen years. Barney was always busy, cleaning glasses with his special bright blue bar towel, keeping a sharp eye on the front door, or occasionally strolling up to that little service window at the very end of the bar, where every food order that had been placed, somehow, someway, always magically appeared. The small window was also where Barney could keep his one good eye on his alcoholic cook. Jake Farnswell was the only Australian man I ever knew, and the only man that could be totally shit-faced on straight Scotch with a beer back and still manage to put out thirty food orders out without missing a beat or making a mistake.

Nobody knew how the two men met or how Barney lost that eye, and no one ever asked. Having known Barney since we were kids, running around the streets of the San Fernando Valley, I had always known the answers to both, but never said a word to anyone. I went to Barney's grand opening, got Betty a job waitressing there, and decided to set up a sort of home away from home where certain clients with discreet tastes could always feel more comfortable. Telling sad stories to me with a drink or two in hand always greased the vocal chords, especially for the nervous types. Barney always felt having a private eye doing business in one of his little back booths gave the place a certain air of mystery.

Barney and Jake had worked together since the day the place opened, and the way the two men constantly barked at each other you would have thought they were brothers. They weren't, but all the regular patrons loved every bickering moment.

It was nearing ten p.m. and a few patrons were coming in to grab a late dinner. A couple of lonely male singles perched quietly at the bar, sipping cold beer, and staring at any female that walked into the place, hoping she would start up a conversation or miraculously be on the prowl and become a score for the evening.

Tonight's pickings were two choices and two choices only.

Slim and none.

Back in booth number eight, tight against the comer wall in the dark, near the pay phone and the juke box, sitting all alone and feeling very tired, sat Yours Truly, Patrick Miles Atwater, the private dick to noted business people, the crooked and the straight, movie stars, the famous and the not-so-famous, the very rich, the very not-so-rich, and just about anyone else who needed help when there was no one else to turn to or nowhere else to go.

Like poor Mrs. Clifford and her two teenaged girls.

Just shy of my fortieth birthday and an ex-Marine, ex-police officer, and at times even an ex-human being, I had luckily built a strong reputation over the last few years as being a stand up kind of guy, a dick with integrity, a dick with a clear sense of what was right and what was wrong, and my clients knew with private dick Patrick Miles Atwater, their troubles would remain private. Whether push came to shove, they would always get a fair shake from me.

I was sipping my usual Sunday night double Johnny Walker Black on the rocks when Barney gave me the quick nod and Betty arrived with a fresh one. My third of the night.

"This must have been a long week for you, Miles," she said. "I haven't seen you since last Tuesday and now you look like ten pounds of shit in a five pound bag."

Another thing about Betty, she always told me the truth.

Betty also had earned her right to be the only one to call me by my middle name. She loved me and we both knew it, just like we both knew living together as a couple would never have worked, no matter how hard we both tried.

And back in the day we did try, but quickly and painfully realized it just wasn't in our nature or our immediate future.

Things just kept getting in the way.

Things like the great Depression, the war in Europe, my choice of profession, the slew of broken characters filing into my small office door looking for help, and me, always putting those people first above everything else, which was my nature no matter whose heart got hurt in the process.

Through thick and thin, Betty and I had remained friends. Betty had become my rock, my closest friend, and the only female other than my late mother that I would trust with my .38 or my life.

We both knew that in Betty's heart she had secretly hoped we could have somehow worked out all those little details that keep people away from each other. But Betty accepted me, I accepted her, and we both accepted what was. Betty kept herself available but also at a distance. It was the only way our friendship really worked, and neither of us wanted to change that.

Close friends.

"Is everything all right with you?" she asked.

"It will be," I answered, and she gave me that sexy tender smile of hers, brushing my hand ever so slightly as she grabbed my empty glass and slowly walked away.

It had been a long week and I did look like shit. I felt like shit.

My last pay check, small as it was, had involved that no good father of the two teenaged girls of whom he thought nothing of beating and raping, or abusing his wife whenever the sick mood struck him until finally she came to her senses and found me in the phone book. My appearance at her door quickly put an end to her troubles.

After that short and sweet discussion I had with the giant maggot, I freely admit I did incur more bodily injury than usual, and the knuckles of my left hand were still noticeably aching. The beating he took from me was well overdue, and I had convinced myself it was also a deserved pain.

Asshole.

Afterwards, I had to explain to my Los Angeles police department contact, Captain Sherwood, a soon-to-retire Chief of Detectives, how this no good son of a bitch must have accidentally fallen down as I was attempting to hold him, waiting for the police to arrive.

Which explained his two blackened eyes, swollen cheeks and lips, and shattered nose.

Sherwood assured me that he realized these types of falls do occur at times and can become quite painful. Sherwood told Stanley to be more careful in the future.

Another Patrick Miles Atwater case opened and closed. Quickly and to the point.

As I sat in my back booth at Barney's I had no clue about what my next case might be. Turned out to be a case like no other I had ever encountered. A case I called The Woman in the Yellow Dress.

I sipped my Scotch and watched as she stepped through Barney's front door. I didn't know it then, but her name was Rachel Stone Barbieri. She was tall, beautiful, and rich. When I say tall and beautiful she was clearly that, but saying the word rich was a wealth I could never have imagined. I learned that Rachel was heir apparent to a family fortune that had been around since the early 1800's with an estimated worth around seven hundred million.

Her great-grandfather made a fortune manufacturing and selling steel parts for just about every piece of machinery ever invented over the last hundred years, and now the Stone family was highly invested in the manufacture of weapons and ammunition, hotel construction, and real estate world-wide.

World War II alone almost doubled their entire worth.

Like some bomb in the night sky bursting through my ice and glass, her image instantly ignited the entire room.

Slowly, I lowered my drink and focused on her.

Everyone in the entire bar also saw her. Even Betty took notice. It was almost as if time stood still when she stepped into the place with her questioning look, cream colored skin, and those long shapely legs.

Barney suddenly dropped his blue towel and stopped cleaning glasses.

He blinked his one good eye several times and then stood there like some statue, as if struck by lightning, suddenly growing a long limp tongue that fell slowly out of his gaping mouth and rolled down onto his chin.

She carried a small black purse with tiny yellow sparkles and wore a very short, tight, bright, matching yellow dress with matching shoes. Her shining auburn hair flowed down onto her shoulders like soft manicured clouds. Everything about this woman was perfectly put into place from her head right down to her toes.

Even from my booth in the back I could see a humongous diamond ring resting on her finger, three carats easily, and I sensed in that instant, that this lovely little creature, this belladonna from God knows where, was going to become bad news for me.

Very bad news.

Rachel Stone Barbieri was all too perfect, as if playing a role. Not really looking for help like the rest of my clients.

That was my forte, spotting the real from the not-so-real. This woman had the unreal written all over her.

My suspicious mind and all of my thoughts of this vision in yellow clanged like the opening bell of some prize fight when she looked around the room a bit too quickly but walked directly to my table without skipping a beat or asking anyone for directions.

She approached and boldly held out one of my business cards.

"Are you Patrick Atwater?"

I pretended not to be interested. She looked at the card.

"Patrick Miles Atwater?"

Her voice is a bit too strained as if practiced, and although she carried the persona of someone clearly in trouble and in need of help, I could tell there was something very different about the entire delivery.

Something odd. Something off. Something askew.

She obviously needed someone to listen to her story, whatever it was, and then possibly provide a strong shoulder for her to cry on.

She didn't strike me as the crying type. Not in that outfit.

She wanted someone to make this trouble, whatever it was, disappear. Make it all go away. And she came running to me.

She knew the drill and the game. And she played it out perfectly.

She smelled like fresh-cut flowers with just the slightest hint of vanilla. It was the scent of vanilla that told me immediately; I was going to be in big trouble with this one.

Deep trouble.

I felt her coming at me like the wind of some deadly hurricane. And what made it all the worse was although I knew it, I didn't really care.

I welcomed her with a slight smile.

Something just wasn't quite right about this one, and I could smell it on her plain as day, in spite of the freshly-cut flower scent, and that slight hint of vanilla.

This was the job. What I did for a living. My chosen profession. Helping poor lost souls who don't know where to turn or who to talk to when everything around them starts looking like some deep dark endless hole that they just can't get out of by themselves. Even though nine out of ten were always completely responsible for their own misfortunes.

She pretended to be clearly in need of someone, that was for sure, and that someone was going to be me, the guy with the sore knuckles, the cold Scotch, and the answers to all her troubles.

A con was written all over her and I have to admit I was feeling eager to get this case started. If she was going to try and put something over on someone, if that was her game, and given all the private dicks running around this town, I was glad she picked me.

Damn that hint of vanilla. I was ready for her. All I needed was that small first tell.

Damn the torpedoes. Full steam ahead.

"X" marks the spot at Barney's By The Sea and whatever was going on with this sexy firecracker all wrapped up in yellow, had somehow, some way, allowed one of my business cards to drop into her hands and she found me, here at my back booth. I could see she was already thinking from the moment she entered that she had me.

She clearly thought I was going to be caught up in her sad little story.

Hook. Line. And sinker.

I quickly decided to play this one out. Go all the way.

"I'm Atwater. Take a seat," I said, and gave her the quick once over.

She didn't mind my stare at all. She enjoyed it, and slid in across from me.

Betty arrived with that tender smile of hers to take the mysterious lady's order. "Can I buy you a drink?" I asked.

"Sparkling wine," she said quickly and started looking through her tiny black purse with the little yellow sparkles.

Sparkling wine. The true desperate ones, always beautiful, always hiding something they don't want to tell you, always begin their sordid little tale with a chilled glass of sparkling wine.

With a quick knowing wink, Betty turned and walked back to the bar.

"How can I help you?" I lied.

"It's my husband."

It usually was.

I thought it was even a good opening line. She had the proper look and the right amount of emotion upon delivery.

She was good. She was very good.

"I suspect he's having an affair," she announced and sat silently as Betty brought over the wine.

Betty quickly walked away without a word or a look. I stared down at her small purse as she slowly sipped her wine.

"An affair?" I repeated.

She nodded slightly and took another quick sip.

What kind of man with a wife like this goes out and begins an affair? My razor sharp mind figured that if what she said was even half true, then her husband was clearly blind, stupid, queer, or all three wrapped up into the makings of one giant fool.

I guessed immediately that her beginning story was bogus, but let the thought go and played out the initial scene with her.

She tried her best to not get caught trying to play me with her story and I did my part as best I could, pretending to believe her every word.

"How long has this affair been going on," I asked.

"I'm not really sure. I just found out this morning and I've been beside myself all day wondering what it is I should do."

Of course you were.

"How long have you two been married?" I asked.

This time without the smile.

"Six years," she said, and tried to look embarrassed and slightly hurt. She took another sip of wine. She was working this story as best she could.

"What are you going to do if it is true?" I asked.

"Right now? I don't know."

With that little revelation she managed a quick sigh and a small tear welled up ever so slightly in her left eye. She quickly dabbed it away with her ring finger and took in a deep breath as if to calm herself.

She was good but I was better. I had seen this routine too many times over the years.

"So you want me to get you proof. Is that it? Is that why you're here?"

"Yes," she lied. "I have to know. I have to be certain."

"Work like this isn't cheap"

"I can pay your price. Whatever it is?"

I was certain she could but I stayed with my usual price.

"I get a hundred dollars a day plus expenses."

"Will you take a check?" she asked.

"Yes. I'll need at least four days in advance."

"I'll give you ten."

"Done."

She quickly grabbed her checkbook and a small gold pen from her bag and began writing the check.

"I'll need your husband's name and address, the place where he works, and any other pertinent information you might have for me."

"Of course," she said. "I trust you will be discreet?"

"Absolutely," I lied again.

An ever-so-small grin passed over her face as she handed me the check. I could see in her eyes that she had convinced herself her act here was nearly complete.

She thought she had fooled me with her husband story. I was hers to do with now as she pleased. Everything in her plan was now perfectly put into place. All she needed to do was give me the check, a little more information, a few more polite words here at the table, and she would be out the door and on her way.

Mission accomplished.

Her plan, whatever it really was, would be in action with me, the gumshoe with the big fat check, the booth in the back, stuck right in the middle.

She thought she had me where she wanted me, and was paying very good money for that privilege. That was her angle. The rich always think money first, above everything else.

In her mind, the plan she concocted was now good to go.

At least that was what she thought, and I let her think it that way.

I looked down at the name on the check, Rachel Stone Barbieri, 524 Maple Drive, Beverly Hills, California.

Her own account.

Impressive.

Now I knew for certain she was lying. This was the heir-apparent to the Jonas Stone family fortune. She could have an entire Senate sub-committee looking into her husband's dalliances if she so desired. Why was she coming to me? At Barney's By the Sea?

It didn't add up to me.

Rachel reached into her purse again and took out her husband's business card, handing it over to me.

"My husband's name is Enzo Barbieri. He owns a financial investment group over on Wilshire," she told me. "He's been very successful the past few years. He just bought himself a new powder blue Mercedes. I think that the kind of money he is making nowadays has somehow all gone to his head."

Nowadays? A slight slip on her part but I let that go too.

Her statement was weak and she suddenly sensed for the first time I might catch her in this little extra lie about Enzo Barbieri, financial maven, but I quickly let her off the hook with another question.

"How did you get hold of one of my cards?" I asked.

"A friend," she said a bit too quickly, and took another sip of her wine to try to mask her mistake.

There it was.

That little tell I was waiting for.

The real key to this cock-and-bull story she was innocently yet wickedly trying to enroll me in.

Somewhere down this road I knew I would be meeting this so-called friend of hers face-to-face and he, or she, was possibly the real reason a woman like Rachel Stone Barbieri walks in to a Barney's By the Sea writing thousand dollar checks.

A friend she says. Of course it was.

Or maybe not?

I had to know for certain.

"I'm sorry but I'm going to have to know this friend's name."

She looked at me and I could sense her hesitation.

"Is that really necessary?"

"Yes."

"All right. His name is Quentin Thayer."

"Quentin Thayer, the movie star?"

"Yes. He said you helped him once. He said you were a good detective. A good. Private. Detective."

I did know Quentin.

Some young chippie and her two half-brained photographer boyfriends had tried to shake Quentin down with some trumped-up photos for a fast hundred thousand dollar payoff.

I straightened them all out in a timely manner, got the pictures and all the negatives, and Quentin was delighted with my work and the outcome.

I had to admit her being a friend of Quentin's tossed a slight monkey wrench into my thought patterns on this one, but I wasn't completely throwing in the towel and buying her story.

Not yet anyway.

"Does Quentin know about your problem? Your suspicions?"

"No. I told Quentin I wanted to find someone that could look into a personal matter for me. Someone that could be trusted and that could also be discreet. He gave me your card and told me I could come here to find you."

I wondered if and what Quentin really knew about her wealthy husband supposedly doing the bump and shake with some pretty little thing.

I let her story hang in the air for a few moments. Then I let her off the hook a second time with an assuring nod and a quick pat on her hand.

"I'll take care of this and find out what you need to know."

"Thank you," she said.

I put her check in my pocket. We exchanged phony smiles, and I pretended to be all business.

"Do you know who the other party is?" I asked.

She let out a sigh of relief thinking she had dodged another bullet, and looked me in the eye for the first time.

"All I know is that she is blonde, young, and her first name is Shirley or Sheri something."

Another tell and clearly too much information for such a short amount of time. First, she's suspicious and now she's giving me names. Whether she was a friend of Quentin or not, my gut instincts on this one came roaring back.

"Does she work in your husband's office?" I asked.

"I don't know."

She knew. This one knew a lot more than she was saying. A whole lot more.

"I'll need a number where I can reach you without your husband knowing."

"Of course," she said.

Rachel quickly took her check writing pen again and scribbled down her phone number on a cocktail napkin.

"It's my private line," she said.

I took the napkin, looked at it, and smiled at her again.

"Would you like another glass of wine," I asked.

"No thank you," she said. "I should be going."

"I'll be in touch."

"Thank you."

She looked at me for a brief moment, grabbed up her sparkly little purse and walked out the door.

Once again the entire little bar by the beach seemed to stop in time as Rachel Stone Barbieri clutched her small yellow-sparkled purse and briskly walked out.

I slowly sipped my Scotch and looked at the scribbled phone number on the cocktail napkin.

Barney yelled out to Jake.

"Where are my two steaks, Jacko?"

"If they were up your bloody ass you'd know where they were! Wouldn't you?" Jake shouted back. "And how many times do I have to tell you don't call me Jacko! The name is Jake!"

Barney and Jake continued their banter as I decided to head home and call it a night.

I left Betty a ten spot on the table and quietly slipped out the back door.

On the ride home I figured that everything Rachel had told me was a lie except for the part about knowing Quentin.

She couldn't fake that. She knew it was the only part of her story I could easily verify.

Everything else she said was all muddled and askew but for a thousand bucks I was willing to jump in with both feet, take a look at this Enzo and his little company on Wilshire, and hopefully get to the bottom of it before it all went bad or blew up in my face.

The war had taught me to keep my head down and always know when your enemy was making a mistake. She had already made a few with me and I knew deep down I had to be very careful around this one. The fact that my movie star friend happened to be a part of her story gnawed at me a little.

I didn't like the feeling. Not one bit.

After our initial first meeting and the work that I did for him, Quentin and I had become friends. He gave me his private number and we shared a few beers together every now and then.

Now I had a sinking feeling that Quentin Thayer might also be a major player in this little scenario being told to me by the wealthy woman in the yellow dress.

Quentin Thayer was a smart man. A good actor.

Quentin also had a huge reputation with the ladies. Huge was an understatement. If Quentin knew Rachel like she said I couldn't imagine him not trying to bed this one down immediately if not sooner, married or not. When it came to women or movie cameras, Quentin Thayer was always at the head of both of those lines.

Every woman in America wanted to be with Quentin Thayer and fantasized ending up with him. He was handsome, rich, a successful major movie star for the past nineteen years, extremely single, and his name was always linked to every actress he had ever worked with. Wherever Quentin was, you could bet your life there was a beautiful woman somewhere close by.

Always there. Always beautiful.

Before I took a look at Enzo I knew I should first check in with Quentin and listen to his take on who or what this Rachel Stone Barbieri was really all about. For all I knew she could be working me, and my good friend, and her husband Enzo.

Women like Rachel always had an angle, and it always involved a minimum of two or more men through the process.

That much I was sure of.

I made a quick note in my little fact pad to call Paramount Studios the very first thing in the morning.

CHAPTER THREE

The Beverly Hills Hotel was the meeting place for everyone and anyone trying to make it in Hollywood, whether you were an actor, a writer, a deal maker, producer, or maybe just some upscale hooker looking to make a fast buck.

Everyone came to the Beverly sooner or later.

As the black limo pulled into the long drive and up to the front entrance, Freddie, the hotel Bell Captain, instantly thought "hooker" when he caught his first glance of the fabulously dressed, beautiful brunette coming his way.

She was outfitted all in chocolate brown with a large brimmed matching hat, and she was driven by a uniformed driver wearing a matching cap. The limo itself was brand new with a shine so bright that Freddie had to shield his eyes slightly as he opened the rear door to let her out.

"Good evening, Miss. Welcome to the Beverly Hills Hotel. I'm Freddie," he said.

"I'm Danielle," she quickly responded.

The first thing Freddie noticed was her long shapely legs. She placed a folded twenty into his hands, asking if her driver could wait in the driveway until she returned. Freddie instantly agreed, waved the driver to the opposite side, and watched her as she seemed to almost float inside and stand alone at the elevators like some tall chocolate angel.

"Somebody paid major bucks for that one," Freddie thought as he opened the door to the next Beverly arrival.

Freddie took one more quick glance back at the elevators and could feel his heart skip a beat as Danielle smiled back at him. The elevator doors finally opened and Danielle stepped inside.

Freddie tried to think if there was a certain high roller staying at the hotel that would merit the presence of this brown vision of beauty to casually stop in and say hello, but no one came to mind.

Once in the elevator, Danielle took a key from her little brown purse, placed the key in the slot next to the Penthouse button, turned it, and pressed the button. The elevator began to rise.

Danielle checked herself from head to toe as she gazed closely into the sparkling full length mirror at the rear of the elevator.

A bell suddenly rang, the elevator stopped, and the doors opened.

Soft music by Mozart played as Danielle stepped from the elevator into a large one bedroom suite with a full view of the valley and the city of Los Angeles off in the distance below.

A heavy set man about sixty, Ernest Hollowell, sat quietly on the small couch in the center of the suite, wearing a black silk robe, nursing a bourbon on ice, and looking through three very large, dark green accounting ledgers.

Danielle casually removed her hat, placed it on a nearby chair, and walked up to Ernest. She tried to get his attention by raising one leg onto the coffee table, giving Ernest a complete view of everything she had underneath her dress, but Ernest kept his head in the ledgers, staring hard at the numbers in front of him.

"Good evening," she said.

"Good evening," Ernest replied without looking up from his work or giving her any attention.

Danielle put her leg back down on the floor and sighed.

"Hello. I'm Danielle."

Ernest still was not looking at her. The thought that this man may be gay quickly crossed her mind.

"Hello, Danielle."

"Enzo sent me. He told me to treat you well and give you anything you liked."

"He did, eh?"

"Yes. He did. You are the accountant? Ernest Hollowell?"

"I'm Hollowell. You can call me Ernie."

"All right. Ernie. You look very busy. Should I come back a little later?"

"No. You can stay. I'm almost done. Make yourself a drink over at the bar. I only have a few more entries to go through here."

"All right," she said and took a deep breath and ran her hands down the sides of her dress.

Ernie finally looked up at Danielle and was immediately stunned by her beauty. He was impressed to such a degree he suddenly became speechless as he took her all in with his roving eyes.

Danielle broke the awkward silence.

"Over there?" she pointed.

"Yes. Make us those drinks and then I will be all yours."

"Great," she replied.

Danielle smiled and stared down at Ernie and his half-filled glass.

"Jesus Christ. You are one beautiful woman," he blurted.

"Thank you, Ernie. Can I freshen that up for you?"

Ernie suddenly remembered he had a drink and quickly gulped it down and handed the empty glass to Danielle.

"Please?" he asked.

Obviously hypnotized, Ernie caught himself gawking at how strikingly beautiful she was. He shook his head and tried to look back down and focus on the books, but his brain and the swelling between his legs distracted him completely from his work.

Danielle took Ernie's glass and slowly walked to the bar.

Ernie watched her walk and found himself slowly licking his lips.

"You're drinking bourbon. Right Ernie?"

"Right. Straight with a little ice."

"Coming right up."

Ernie took a deep breath and attempted to get back into the ledgers and his work but his mind and body were still clearly focused elsewhere.

With her back to Ernie, Danielle stood at the bar and opened the top of her large black onyx ring, pouring a small amount of liquid into Ernie's drink. She closed her ring, poured herself a short shot of bourbon, turned, and casually walked with the glasses back to the sofa.

Danielle extended the doctored drink to Ernie.

"Cheers, Ernie. To our little evening together?"

Ernie took the glass and raised it up to her.

"To our little evening. Together. Cheers."

Ernie quickly gulped down most of his drink.

"Where's the bathroom?" she asked. "I want to get out of these clothes if that's okay with you?"

"That's a fine idea. Through that door and to the left," Ernie replied.

Ernie took another huge gulp and watched Danielle walk slowly to the bedroom doorway.

Suddenly, Ernie noticed his throat starting to close and began choking uncontrollably.

"What the hell? You bitch!" Ernie screamed.

"Ernie? That's no way to speak to a lady," she said and looked at him with a half-smile and slight tilt of her head.

"What the hell did you give me?" Ernie managed to choke out.

Danielle calmly and casually stepped in front of Ernie.

"Bourbon. Straight. With a little ice. Just as you asked. And maybe just a small little kick of something-something."

Ernie stood up and faced her but could not stop choking.

"Breathe through your nose, Ernie. Take deep breaths. I'm told it's a lot less painful if you breathe in deeply through your nose. Go on. You can do it."

"A lot less. What?" he struggled to say.

Ernie's eyes widened as he took a few short nervous breaths through his nose and reached up to his throat still gasping for air.

"Don't struggle, Ernie. It will all be over in a few more seconds. Trust me," she added, kissing her finger and pressing it to his lips.

Ernie's body suddenly stiffened, his eyes rolled back, and he fell face down onto the floor.

Dead.

Danielle stared down at Ernie's body and drank her bourbon down.

"See," she said.

She moved quickly, taking the two glasses, cleaning them thoroughly at the bar sink and then placing them both back on the display, just as if she were one of the Beverly Hills house maids. She grabbed a hotel napkin, wiped away any fingerprints she may have left, grabbed another glass with the napkin and placed some ice into it.

Danielle used the napkin a second time and poured some fresh Bourbon over the ice. She took the new glass over to the body, placed Ernie's dead hand onto the glass and let it all fall down onto the carpeted floor.

Danielle stepped over Ernie's body and sat down in front of the ledgers. Holding a pencil upside down with the napkin, she used the eraser to quickly turn the pages.

"Come on," she said. "Where are you?"

Danielle found a red file underneath one of the large green ledgers that read Stone Realty. She picked up the file and put it in her purse.

She looked down at Ernie one last time.

"Good night, Ernie. Sweet dreams."

Danielle got up, put on her hat, and casually stepped into the elevator. The doors closed.

Ernie lay dead on the floor next to the fallen glass, with his eyes wide open.

The elevator slowly descended and again Danielle checked her hat and lipstick in the mirrored wall.

The same bell rang again, the elevator stopped, the doors opened, and Danielle quickly walked across the floor and out the front entrance.

She walked to the waiting limo and just as she reached the limo door, Freddie was at her side, smiling and opening the door for her.

"Allow me, Danielle."

Freddie gave her his biggest smile and she quickly responded in kind.

"Thank you, Freddie. You are so sweet."

As she slid into the limo she handed Freddie another folded twenty. Freddie took one last fast glance at those beautiful legs, stuffed the bill in his pocket and closed the door.

Freddie stood up straight and watched the black limo slowly drive away, still wondering which hotel guest it was that had the privilege of her company.

Again no one came to mind.

The limo moved along Sunset Boulevard, heading east at a casual pace. "How did it go?" the driver asked.

"Short and sweet. That liquid is quite effective."

"And the file? The red file? Do you have it?"

"Of course."

"No problems?"

"A piece of cake."

"Leave the outfit and the file on the seat."

"I really like this hat. I like it a lot," she said.

"Leave it. I'll buy you another one."

"Do you promise?" she playfully asked.

The driver looked at her through the rear view mirror and smiled.

"I promise."

Danielle removed the hat and fake brunette wig and shook out her long blonde hair. She quickly removed her complete outfit and her bra, and placed them on the seat next to the file.

The limo suddenly came to a red light and stopped.

Danielle put the hat back on her head and sat naked, striking a pose and holding the red file over one breast while staring into the rearview mirror of the limo.

"How do I look?" she asked.

"Beautiful," the driver said. "Your other clothes are laid out for you. Please? Put them on."

"You can be such a party pooper," she pouted.

As the light changed, both Danielle and the limo driver noticed a man sitting behind the wheel of a black two door Ford coupe in the lane beside them, staring and smiling over at Danielle.

The driver in the Ford also took a quick glimpse at the limo driver as the light turned green and it slowly pulled ahead. Another car behind the Ford suddenly blew his horn, and the coupe made a quick left hand turn heading out to the valley.

Danielle and the limo driver thought for sure they had committed the perfect murder, retrieved an important revealing red ledger they desperately needed, and gotten away cleanly from the Beverly Hills Hotel without any repercussions.

Those were their initial thoughts as the limo driver dropped a now newly-dressed Danielle at her Hollywood apartment and drove away into the warm California night.

But they were wrong.

Dead wrong.

The theft and the murder all went perfectly as planned except for one small detail. A simple twist of fate that one never imagined would or could have made a difference.

The man in the black Ford coupe was Patrick Miles Atwater, heading out to the valley to see a troubled woman named Grace Clifford.

Patrick and Grace's brother, Cliff, had been in the same unit all through the war. They both fought tirelessly and fiercely under George S. Patton for two hundred eighty one days straight, from the bloodied beaches at Normandy until reaching a little town in Germany called Pilsen, where Hitler and his Nazi war machine were finally stopped with the help of the Russian Red Army and an armistice was declared at long last.

Patrick and Cliff had seen more than their share of action, became very good friends, and decided to celebrate the end of the war over a bottle of cold champagne they found completely by accident in a burned out basement. Patrick lifted his glass, made a toast to the end of their fighting, and then watched in horror as Cliff's head suddenly exploded from a bullet fired by a thirteen year old German sniper hidden in a church steeple and completely unaware that the war had finally ended.

Patrick's grief was overwhelming by the loss of his friend, and decided on his way back to the States to do everything and anything he could to help Cliff's sister and her family.

His death also gave Patrick a stronger set of eyes to never miss a detail no matter how large or small, or where he might be.

The black limo, the pretty woman passenger, the man at the wheel and the warm California night were no exceptions.

Not to Patrick Miles Atwater.

CHAPTER FOUR

After my meeting with Rachel I thought I would head home, maybe have one last night cap, and hopefully get a meeting with Quentin sometime in the morning.

As I drove out of the parking lot at Barney's, I noticed a big Dodge start up its engine and turn on the headlights as I pulled away, but didn't give it much thought initially.

Just another Joe like myself heading home, I thought.

But after leaving the coast road and heading into Westwood, I could tell the big Dodge was staying close behind, even though it was a good seven or eight cars back.

The little man at the wheel was well-skilled in the art of tailing without being detected, maintaining the proper unassuming distance. The average person would have never known he was there.

But I was a different breed.

Maybe it was my military training or something they taught me at the police academy all those years ago when I walked a beat, but I have always had a sixth sense about certain things, especially concerning someone I didn't know breathing down my back, whether they were several feet away or a few car lengths back.

I drove into Westwood, parked my Ford coupe on the street right in front of the Sultan Arms apartments, and waited.

I didn't have to wait long.

A few moments passed, and the big Dodge with the little man at the wheel came down the hill slowly, driving past and pretending he was heading somewhere else even though we both knew better.

The Dodge came to the corner and made a quick right turn.

I thought about jumping out of the coupe and running swiftly to the corner to see if the Dodge had parked somewhere nearby, but I knew I would be seeing more of him over the next few days so I decided to remain in the car.

Whoever the little man was working for had their reasons for him to keep eyes on me, and I would pick and choose my own time to find out who and what he was all about.

I locked up the coupe and headed to my apartment.

The newspaper in front of my apartment door ran a huge headline on the death of the great bambino, baseball's legendary Sultan of Swat, the great Babe Ruth. He had finally succumbed to throat cancer.

I had been to New York only five times over the years, working some high profile divorce cases, but it was always during the winter months. I know I would have gone to see him play if I had been there in July or August. I liked baseball and for some odd reason was always a Yankee fan. The Sultan Arms Apartments and the Sultan of Swat were about the only connections I would have to the greatest baseball player ever to play the game.

I picked up the paper and went inside.

My apartment was a small one bedroom and I did my best to keep it neat, beginning back in those days when Betty and I couldn't keep our hands off each other. She always had a thing for cleanliness and it somehow rubbed off on me over the years.

I took off my jacket and tie, grabbed a cold beer from the fridge, and sat in my easy chair. My knuckles still ached and the cool of the beer bottle seemed to ease the pain some as I pressed the back of my hand against the glass. I took out my little note book pad, grabbed my pen, and jotted down some notes from the day's activity.

Monday. Studio, bank, and man with the Dodge.

The next morning I awoke still sitting in my chair. The beer bottle was empty, sitting on the small coffee table next to my note pad, and the last thing I could remember was having some old thoughts of Betty and myself back in the day.

She now was living with Barney's cook, Jake, at her apartment in Venice and the two seemed to be making a real go of it. She had told him everything about our history and he understood that everyone had a past. He never once made my friendship with her an issue, and if our past did bother him he never let on to either one of us. I liked Jake and was very happy that he and Betty were happy too.

From the time Jake moved in with Betty, my good friends arrangement immediately ended, but our friendship remained strong. I was glad to call Betty my best friend and Jake respected that too about her and me. They both got a kick at all the different types that came knocking on my door and Jake was always asking her if I needed any help.

Betty always told him no, even though she knew in her heart Jake would keep asking.

I made my call to the studio and got an eleven-thirty meeting set up with Quentin. I knew I could easily retire selling his private phone number to every woman I met over the next five years. Not one of them would say no; every woman would gladly pay whatever the price, and Quentin himself would savor the thought of having them all lined up to bed on a daily basis because, that was Quentin's life.

Quentin started out as a stunt man doing B-picture westerns at RKO when he was in his early twenties. He had the right looks and physique to match. A young female agent named Sherrie Mann, just starting out at the William Morris Agency, met Quentin at a wrap party barbecue at Gene Autry's house. After spending the following three weeks sleeping with him, she signed him on as her first and only client, and immediately got him a seven year contract with Paramount.

In his first film, Quentin played the legendary William Tell, the man who saved his life by shooting an apple off his son's head with a cross bow.

Women went insane.

It seemed as if every woman in the entire country suddenly lined up at every theater showing and either screamed, cried, or fainted dead away whenever Quentin came onto the screen. It was a mania that had only occurred once before in pictures that I could recall, and that was when Rudolph Valentino rode across a desert in a silent film called The Sheik.

Valentino died a short three years later but the Quentin Thayer mania had lasted over nineteen years and was still going exceptionally strong when he and I first met.

A trio of con artists ran a scam on Quentin, trying to extort a hundred thousand dollars and ruin his reputation and career by threatening to expose some very risqué photos of Quentin and a beautiful young girl they were claiming was only fifteen.

Quentin invited me onto the set of his most famous picture to date, Lafitte, and it was also the one film of the many he had made over the years that brought the most money at the box office, a whopping million and a half, and a figure unheard of at the time. Quentin of course played the title role character, Jean Lafitte, the pirate of New Orleans who helped Andrew Jackson win the War of 1812 against the British. Quentin ran around the set without a shirt for most of that picture, and women went absolutely wild. A new heartthrob had arrived and women could not get enough of Quentin Thayer.

The poster on that film alone sold over one hundred thousand copies.

Quentin and I hit it off from the start and he hired me that day, paid me three times my normal fee, in cash, and in six days I had broken the case.

I discovered that the so-called naked fifteen year old sucking Quentin's nine inch cock in the four black and white photographs was actually a twenty-eight-year-old hooker from Fresno, California, and part of the con trio.

Their little scam immediately fell apart.

I managed to retrieve every negative they had unsuccessfully hidden away, and made a lifetime friend of the number one male actor working in Hollywood today, Quentin Thayer.

If my own mother was still alive and knew that he and I were friends, she would be asking me for Quentin's private number. And she would have paid whatever the price.

I quickly showered, suited up for the day, wearing one of the ties Quentin sends me every Christmas, his little way of showing his appreciation for the work I did for him, and headed out the door to my coupe.

I casually checked the area as I walked to my car and sure enough, up on the hill, behind a blue Ford, I noticed the big Dodge with the little man at the wheel patiently waiting for me to make an appearance.

It was a little before nine but there he was.

Quietly waiting.

I got in the coupe, headed to the bank, and knew at some point today, the little mystery man and I were going to have a serious talk.

Clear the air.

Having deposited Rachel Stone Barbieri's check in my dwindling Bank of America account and putting a few bucks in my pocket for traveling money, I headed over to Paramount Studios for my meeting with Quentin.

As I drove onto the lot and passed the security guard's check-in at the gate, I looked back in the rearview mirror and eyed the big Dodge settling in across the street, awaiting my return.

I parked the coupe, and as I walked past W.C. Fields and a small man he called Charlie, I heard them arguing over some missed payment his wife never received.

I quickly arrived at production studio number eighteen, noticed the warning light was green, opened the door, and went inside.

The set was cold and dark and suddenly a loud bell rang out. Everyone immediately stopped moving around.

I quietly edged towards the small well-lit set and there was Quentin, working his magic in front of a large camera and crew, playing a hard-nosed police detective in a film called Black Sunday, and acting an interrogation scene with a gorgeous brunette.

"Look, Nola. Let me spell this out for you," he said. "We have the gun. We have your fingerprints on the gun."

Another camera moved in silently, slowly pointing directly at the brunette playing Nola. She raised her head and stared up into Quentin's face.

"I don't care what you got," she answered in a tired whisper. "I didn't do it.""What was that, Nola? What did you say? Speak up?"

"I said I didn't do it!" she screamed.

Quentin and Nola's acting was so believable and so perfect and I found myself falling right into the phony storyline, with every word coming out of their mouths as if it were real.

"I understand how these things go," Quentin said as he got in closer to her.

"You do?" she whispered.

"Sure. He came home late. Again. You were there. Still awake. You argued. He struck you. Again. Only this time he hit you really hard. This time it was different. So you got the gun and you shot him. You shot him four times! You shot him until you were sure he was dead! Didn't you?"

Nola and I both jumped as Quentin pressed her hard and yelled into her face.

"I didn't shoot him," she said. "Why won't you believe me?"

Quentin suddenly changed his whole approach, sat down close to her, and lowered his voice.

The second big camera moved in another few inches.

"I want to believe you, Nola. I really want to. Make me believe you. Tell me something so I can go back to the DA and get him to drop these charges! What really happened last night? If you didn't pull the trigger? Who did? Who are you protecting?"

Suddenly Quentin wiped his lower lip with his pointing finger. And I realized he was imitating me.

I did the finger thing to the bottom lip; I did it a lot.

It was a habit I had developed around the age of ten, according to my late mother and I found myself grinning uncontrollably knowing the number one actor on the planet, the man every guy wanted to be like and every woman wanted in their beds, was stealing a small part of Yours Truly and putting it into a movie scene to be captured on film for all time.

As I stood watching and relishing that thought, the director, a silly looking man sporting a gray scarf and brown tam, turned to his assistant, Wendell, yelled "Cut", a bell rang, staging lights shut off, house lights came on, and everyone on the set began moving around.

"Ten minutes, everyone," shouted Wendell.

A young female assistant popped out of nowhere, running past me to hand Quentin a small handkerchief, and he wiped the sweat from the top of his brow.

He looked over, saw me and smiled, whispered something into the assistant's ear and she quickly ran off.

"Patrick, my man," he bellowed opening his arms and giving me a huge welcoming hug that almost lifted me off the floor.

"Hello, Quentin," I said. "You make it all look so easy."

"We're all actors under the skin," he replied. "Can I get you something?"

"No. I'm good. Thanks."

"So what did you need to see me about? Did you get onto the lot all right?"

"I did. Yes. Thank you."

The young assistant hurriedly returned and handed Quentin a large black coffee.

"Thank you, doll," he said and took a small sip.

I thought I would cut to the chase and watch his reaction.

"What can you tell me about your neighbor? Rachel Stone Barbieri?" I asked.

If Quentin had anything to do with Rachel's so-called problem with her husband or was part of some bigger mess that I would soon discover, he never let on to it. He answered all my questions quite calmly and truthfully as far as I could tell.

"Other than she is my extremely wealthy, absolutely beautiful, and unfortunately for me, married neighbor, not much," he answered.

"Are you two friends?" I asked.

"Neighbors, yes. Friends? No. Not really."

"She told me you're her friend, Quentin. Her very good friend."

He could tell I was pressing him a little and he instantly shook it off and mirrored his response to my question.

"Patrick? I'm a movie star. Everybody I know or meet wants me to be their very good friend. They all want to tell everyone that Quentin Thayer is a close and personal friend. It comes with the territory. Right?"

Something in his voice told me he was dancing around my question instead of answering directly. He took another sip of his coffee and leaned in closer.

"If you want to know if I'm fucking her? You know me. If I was? I would tell you. But I'm not. Would I like to fuck her? Who wouldn't? Why she's married to a guy like Enzo Barbieri? I couldn't say. Love is fucking blind. Right?"

Another smile and another sip.

"She came to you?" Quentin asked.

"She did. Last night. Told me you gave her my card and told her where I would be."

"True. I did. Barney's By the Sea. Right?"

"Right."

'"Rachel said she had some personal thing all very hush-hush and asked if I knew someone that could act in a discreet manner. I figured whatever it was had something to do with her Italian hubby. I thought of you right away and gave her one of those cards you left me."

"What can you tell me about the husband?"

"You know me. I don't judge anyone. Live and let live. That's my motto. I've been to their home three times I think over the last few years and seeing those two together is like watching some brother and sister act. Not two people married and in love. You know who her father was? Right?"

I did, but I pretended the information was vague in my mind. I ran my pointing finger across my bottom lip and Quentin pretended not to notice.

"Jonas Stone. No?" I replied.

"That's him. Killed in a plane crash two years back. Him and the mother. Rachel is their only child and inherited everything. Something like seven or eight hundred million. She went off to Europe somewhere to grieve and came back married to Enzo. Go figure. Is he trying to shake her down for some of that family cash or what?"

"You know the drill, Quentin. I don't discuss details about my clients."

"So you're hired? You're on her payroll?"

"Until I sort this all out, I am. Yes. Can I get back to you if I need to?"

"Of course. I miss having you around. You did me a real solid back when, Patrick. Let's get together over a few beers soon and I'll tell you how many actresses are really good in the sack and which ones aren't worth a damn. What do you say?"

Quentin tossed out that winning smile again and took a big gulp of his coffee.

"I'll be in touch," I said, and started backing out.

"Make sure to call me," he said.

"I will."

A makeup girl stepped in and checked over Quentin's look as he waved goodbye to me, and everyone on the set started gearing up. I waved back and stepped outside.

I no sooner shut the studio door and the red light overhead began to blink, signaling no entrance, and I knew shooting of Black Sunday had resumed.

I walked slowly to my car trying to put my finger on exactly what Quentin's play might be in all this Rachel Stone Barbieri business. Maybe he was fucking her and he didn't want to tell me, or tell anyone for that matter.

As I got in the coupe and headed for the gate I put Quentin's conversation aside to concentrate solely on two things.

I would go speak with Enzo Barbieri, he being my first order of business, and then somehow, some way, I would have a little chat which was becoming way overdue with the little man in the Dodge.

As I drove off the lot, turning right and heading out west towards Wilshire, I could see the big Dodge with the little man at the wheel in my rear-view mirror making his turn to follow me down the boulevard.

CHAPTER FIVE

The camera bulb flashed down at the dead body of Ernest Hollowell as the young police photographer, Butch Lockwood, snapped his fifteenth shot of the body from another angle

The call came in as a suspicious death, and Butch wanted to know every detail about the case, but had learned the hard way not to question detectives while they were working their case.

"Make sure you get some shots of the bedroom too, Butch," said Detective Munoz, the lead investigator on the case.

"Yes, sir," answered Butch.

"And no questions this time. Right?"

"Right," said Butch.

"How's the eye?" asked Detective Munoz.

"Much better," replied Butch.

Butch quickly popped in another bulb, walked silently into the bedroom and began taking more photographs.

Detective Munoz had been a cop for sixteen years and was one of the first ever Mexican Americans to make the detective squad.

He was partnered up with Detective Blaine after Blaine's partner had been shot and killed during what they thought was going to be a routine drug bust.

It wasn't.

Both detectives took their Detective shields very seriously, and began making a name for themselves among the squad as two men who never looked at any case as routine, especially Detective Blaine. In spite of their different backgrounds, they got along exceptionally well.

Nicknamed Holmes and Watson by the other detectives, neither ever knew who was supposed to be which, nor did they care.

The first time young Butch worked with them was on a case of a young girl found beaten and strangled in her own bedroom and Butch couldn't stop talking. He shot his pictures but kept asking question after question until Detective Blaine knocked him on his ass and told him politely to stop talking.

"It's a delicate process," Detective Munoz explained as he helped Butch to his feet. "Any talking becomes distracting to the task at hand."

"Communication received," said Butch and never spoke again on a case unless spoken to.

Hollowell had been dead for almost twelve hours, and both Detective Munoz and Detective Blaine wanted to close this one quickly and quietly.

Dead bodies are not good for hotel business unless that body was a famous female movie star found in the nude or some well-known political figure caught with his pants down and lipstick on his Johnson.

Detective Munoz looked at his partner sitting on the couch and could tell by his face he was mentally contemplating several scenarios as to how poor Hollowell met his demise.

Detective Blaine sat and thought a few moments, shook his head, and sighed deeply.

"What are you thinking, partner? Open and shut?" Detective Munoz asked, although already knowing the answer.

This one wasn't going to be open and shut, not by a long shot.

Detective Blaine looked up at his partner. Detective Munoz had seen that look and heard that familiar sigh many times before on numerous past cases. They had been partners with LAPD for over ten years and were a good team. An honest team. And both men had the uncanny ability to sniff out the truth when a suspicious death like this masquerades as something it's not.

"Come on. Give. What do you see?" he asked again.

"I see three things. What we have here, partner, on the surface is an open and shut case," replied Detective Blaine. "Our number cruncher was sitting here, hard at work, having himself a quick belt when he suddenly has some type of seizure or maybe his heart gave out. And? Then? He and his drink wind up there on the floor."

"I can see that and I agree. Now give me the explanation for why you are about to say the word but."

Detective Blaine nods yes and both men smile.

"But. I have to ask myself? Why did this guy, a working stiff accountant, suddenly rate a penthouse suite here at the Beverly just to go over some ledgers? It's not tax time. That's my number one."

"Good point, partner. He must have been looking for something very special? Yes?"

"I would say so. It had to be something very specific because he was being treated much too well for the process. We should check with the desk and see how long he had this room rented."

"Definitely," said Detective Munoz and jotted a note down on his pad. "What's your number two?"

"Number two. I looked through every one of these files. These are all numbered files. And? They are all numbered in order. But right here?"

Using his pen, Detective Blaine holds up a corner of one of the ledgers.

"File number 318 is missing. Two uniforms are searching for it, but I think whoever killed Hollowell? Also took the file."

"Killed Hollowell?" questioned Detective Munoz. "Definitely killed is your number three?"

"Most certainly," answered Detective Blaine. "It wasn't any heart attack. Somebody killed this guy."

"And we know this how?"

"There is a smell of almonds coming from his opened mouth. Bend your ass down there and take a whiff. I did."

"Seriously? You're asking me to smell a dead man's mouth?"

"Just do it."

Detective Munoz knelt down and sniffed at Hollowell's dead opened mouth.

"You're right. It smells like almonds to me too," Detective Munoz said, standing back up. "Cyanide? Right?"

"Right."

"But not suicide?"

"No. If this was a suicide he would have finished his drink. He would have also left a note somewhere. And when he bought it, his glass would have some residue of the poison in it.".

"The glass is clean?" asked Detective Munoz.

"Yes. Pure cyanide burns. People ingest it by mixing it with something. Makes it go down easier. Hence there should be some trace of it on his glass. But there is not even a slight hint of it there. My gut tells me cyanide is what killed him. I'm sure of it."

"Shit."

"Shit is right. Somebody gave Hollowell the cyanide. Then they cleaned everything up. Took file number 318. And then staged what we see here. Do we know who Hollowell worked for?"

Detective Munoz flipped through his note pages and looked back at Detective Blaine.

"Enzo Barbieri. Stone Realty," Munoz replied.

"Double shit," said Detective Blaine.

"Double?" asked Munoz.

"You're kidding me, right?" said Detective Blaine. "Stone Realty. Come on, partner. You're going to tell me you don't know the late, great Jonas Stone, multi millionaire with more money and secrets around the globe? Died in a plane crash?"

Detective Munoz suddenly made the mental connection, feeling like he had just stepped on a land mine.

"Double shit," said Munoz. "Barbieri is married to Stone's daughter. Rachel."

"Double shit is right," said Detective Blaine. "The Stone family has more money than God."

"Maybe they can shed some light on all of this?" asked Munoz.

"Fat chance they would but I'll bet my badge on it that one of them can."

"Damn it. Big money cases are just one big pain in the ass. Do we really want to jump into all this?" asked Detective Munoz.

"If we jump into this? If we do what we are paid to do? We are talking huge amounts of money running around this one, partner. And you are right about this, it's going to make our job a hell of a lot tougher. A hell of a lot crazier. And a hell of a lot more dangerous."

Detective Munoz stared at Hollowell and sighed heavily.

"I'm feeling frustrated already."

"Me too," added Detective Blaine.

Detective Munoz took another deep breath and Detective Blaine loosened his tie.

"There's another beast that will attach itself to this too," said Detective Munoz.

"You mean the press?"

"They will definitely start running alongside us, watching our every move and turn: Running really close like a pack of hungry wolves chasing down their wounded prey. Then the department will start putting their eyes on us. And then, depending on what we find in this deep pile of god knows what? The Feds won't be far behind and may just pull this case right out from under us. You know how these things can go. They always do. Do you still want in?"

Detective Blaine looked at Hollowell.

"Yes I do. And I don't care. Fuck it. Fuck them all. Somebody killed this poor bastard and I say let's find the son of a bitch or bitches and nail them to the wall. Each and every one of them."

Detective Munoz smiled broadly.

"I'm with you and you know I got your back but we're talking hundreds of millions of dollars. That kind of money buys a lot of silence. This one will not be easy. Not by a long shot."

"I still don't care."

"If we jump, we go all the way. No matter what."

"No matter what," agreed Detective Blaine.

Detective Munoz closed his note pad and stared back at Detective Blaine.

"Let's jump, partner" said Detective Blaine. "Let's jump deep. Jump head first. And as long as we have each other's backs we'll come out of this all right."

"All right," Detective Munoz replied and both men nodded, smiled and shook hands on their pact.

"Let's go down to the lobby and talk to Freddie. He'll point us in the right direction."

"Good start," said Detective Munoz. "Freddie knows who comes and goes."

"If this guy Hollowell had a visitor then Freddie had eyes on him coming in and going out. That's for certain."

"Nothing gets by Freddie."

"Let's keep our fingers crossed and hope for a break."

The two detectives took one last look at Hollowell's dead body and headed to the elevator.

CHAPTER SIX

The name Enzo Barbieri sounded more like some Italian baker instead of a financial maven, and the thought of this guy not paying any attention whatsoever to a beautiful wife like Rachel Stone and possibly fooling around with some strange blonde woman named Shirley or Sheni completely blew my mind. Nothing about it made any sense.

I was looking forward to meeting this guy to see for myself what he was all about.

I drove into the building's underground parking lot, left the coupe and walked up the few stairs to the main entrance.

I checked the company list, found Stone Realty on the sixth floor and hit the elevator button. As I stood waiting, I could see my little friend in his Dodge parked across the street.

The elevator doors opened and I went inside.

On the sixth floor, I noticed Stone Realty occupied one half of the entire floor. I stepped through the opened double doors and gave the place the quick once over.

A sweet young brunette sat alone at a small single desk with only a black phone in front of her and a large desk calendar with absolutely nothing written on it. She couldn't have been more than eighteen, wore a name tag pinned to her expensive business attire, and had one of those new all black Reynold's Rocket ball point pens tucked into the side of her long black hair.

I tried to use the name to my advantage.

"Hello, Gloria. I'm Patrick Atwater. I'm here to see Mr. Barbieri," I happily announced.

I handed her one of my cards before she could say a word.

She held up the card, read it over, and looked up into my smiling face.

"A private detective? May I ask the nature of this visit? Mr. Atwater?" she responded.

She had not been a corporate gate keeper for long and I could tell she was trying to respond as professionally as possible. I leaned in very close as if we were meeting for the first time at some cocktail party and used a voice no larger than a whisper.

"A movie studio has sent me here," I lied.

"A movie studio?" she asked. "I don't see any appointment here on my calendar,"

I faked disappointment and she seemed to genuinely buy it.

"The studio told me they would call ahead," I lied again. "I only need a few minutes with him. It concerns his neighbor, Quentin Thayer."

I knew I had said the magic words as Gloria's eyes suddenly widened. She quickly licked her lips without even thinking and I knew I was almost in.

"Quentin Thayer, the movie star?" she said, trying to bring back that professional sound in her voice.

She pulled the pen from her hair and playfully ran it around her lips.

"Yes," I said. "Quentin Thayer. The movie star."

"I'll go see if he's available. Please? Take a seat."

"Thank you," I said, and we smiled at each other.

Gloria ran off somewhere down the hall and I took a quick look around. No photos. No paintings. Just the company logo in large gold letters hanging on one wall. Stone Realty Inc. The place was quiet as a tomb and for all I knew it could be a front of some kind for god knows what.

While running some possibilities through my mind, Gloria returned and gestured one hand towards the hallway like some models do when they show off the newest version of a Cadillac or Chevrolet at the automobile shows.

"This way, Mr. Atwater," she said, and led me down the long hallway to Barbieri's office.

His door was open when we arrived and as I stepped in, Gloria quietly closed the door and left us alone.

Enzo Barbieri was what all the movie magazines called a tall, dark and handsome man. He was clearly that and appeared to be about forty or so, very well dressed. He immediately rose from his large oak desk and extended his hand. I did the same and was impressed with his firm handshake.

"Mr. Atwater. Hello. I am Enzo Barbieri. Please? Sit down," he said.

We sat across from each other and I quickly noticed several contracts open on his desk that I assumed he was busily working on. There was a large photo on the wall directly behind him of himself and Rachel's late father, the true money maven, Jonas Stone. The photo showed the two men at some fishing resort, possibly down in the Caribbean somewhere, standing with a large swordfish between them hanging from a large metal scale.

I saw no photos of Rachel anywhere and thought that odd.

"What can I do for you, sir? What's this movie studio thing all about?" he asked.

"First of all," I lied, "I want to thank you for seeing me on such short notice. I'm kind of under the gun here with my present situation."

"Situation," he asked. "What situation is that?"

"The studios have hired me to put a quick profile together on your neighbor."

"A profile? On Quentin Thayer? What kind of profile?"

"Fairly standard actually. The studios have invested a lot of money into Mr. Thayer. They need some assurances to tell the front offices back in New York that their money is being wisely invested. I'm certain a person like yourself can fully appreciate their practicality in the matter. Anything you can tell me would be held strictly confidential."

"I don't know what I can tell you."

"What do you know about him?"

Barbieri took a long deep breath and I could tell he was truly attempting to answer my question honestly. I liked that.

"What do I know of Quentin Thayer? Movie actors are such an odd sort. He runs by my house every morning. He lives alone. He has a pretty housekeeper named Patty. I can tell you that. My wife, Rachel, got her the job there. Patty works for us also. She's very good. She cleans there three days a week. And? He is a big time movie star. No?"

Barbieri smiled graciously and if he was feeling any discomfort I couldn't see it. I thought about pressing him on how Rachel got pretty Patty the job but decided to let that go.

"Any excessive drinking on his part?"

"Drinking? Not that I have ever seen. He has been to the house a few times. Parties and things. Had the usual cocktail or two but I would not say excessive. No."

"What about drugs?"

"Drugs? I don't think so. Quentin is all about health and fitness."

"And what can you tell me about the women in his life?"

"Women? I have seen beautiful women arrive and depart from Quentin's house. Numerous times. And when I say numerous I mean two or three a day sometimes."

"No men?"

"Men? Are you crazy? We are talking about Quentin Thayer, right? He is the poster boy for feminine conquest. The cocks-man of almost two generations. I would bet that Quentin Thayer sees more vaginas in a single month than most successful Beverly Hills gynecologists do in six months."

"So that's a no on any male company?"

"Never saw a one. Ever. Always female. Always stunningly beautiful. Always."

"So? Overall? You would say Mr. Thayer has been a fairly decent hard working neighbor? Yes?"'

"Absolutely. And a very good actor."

Barbieri sat back in his chair and I could tell our conversation was over. He was honest, straight forward in his responses, didn't have one bad thing to say about Quentin, and I was satisfied for the time being with my little intro cover story.

What I couldn't understand was Rachel's concern.

If Enzo was fooling around with some other twist named Shirley I knew I could catch them at it relatively quickly and get the results back to Rachel.

But my mind kept telling me that wasn't going to happen.

This guy Barbieri just didn't fit the pattern or carry the usual tells I had seen many times before with so many other cheating husbands. If Enzo was a guy that fooled around on his wife he would have been hitting on his gate keeper Gloria for one, and I wasn't seeing any of that happening either.

Cheaters lie all the time. To everyone. They also have a certain faraway look in their eyes when you confront them.

Barbieri had none of that going on.

There was something about the man and his office space but I wasn't attributing it to a man that fools around on his wife.

It was something else. Something darker. I just wasn't seeing it.

Not just yet.

As I left the building I had this deep nagging feeling that something very bad was going to go down.

And soon.

I just hoped I would be ready when that something happened.

I opened the front entrance door and two men in suits, one tall white guy and the other a medium built fellow of Spanish descent, walked past me without speaking. I pegged them for detectives right away by the bulges in both of their suit jackets and the abundant lack of brown polish on their scuffed up shoes.

A young boy was on the comer selling newspapers.

"Extra! Extra!" he shouted. "The great Bambino dies of heart failure."

The kid eyed me straight away and ran up waving one of his papers in my face.

"Paper, mister?" he asked.

I felt bad for the kid and tossed him the nickel for the news. As I pretended to read all about the death of baseball's greatest, I saw my little friend sitting in the Dodge across the street.

I walked to my car, headed out on Wilshire again, and noticed the big Dodge following close behind.

I saw a Walgreens up ahead, quickly pulled into the small lot and dashed inside. I thought my little guy in the Dodge would figure I had stopped for a quick bite at the food counter, and would park himself somewhere in the rear of the lot where he could hide in plain sight and still keep his eyes on the coupe.

I walked straight through the place and went directly to the rear door.

I looked out and saw the Dodge parked at the perfect angle for me to do what I knew I had to do.

The little guy behind the wheel wore a decent suit and tie and looked like he had just gotten himself a haircut a day or two before. His eyes were clearly focused on my parked vehicle next to the store when I quietly walked up and hard pressed the cold steel of my .38 into the bare side of his neck.

"You have until I count three to tell me who the hell you are and why the hell you are following me!" I demanded and instantly began counting.

"One. Two."

The little man quickly raised both hands up and started chattering away like a small scared monkey who just discovered he could speak.

"Don't shoot!! My name is Clovis Edwards. I'm a Special Agent with the FBI!"

I pressed the gun in harder.

"Okay. I got who. Now what do you want with me? Same drill pal. One. Two."

"Please? Do not shoot me! Don't. Shoot. Me," he pleaded.

He waved as if he was about to do a sleight of hand magic trick, and slowly and extremely carefully reached into his suit pocket and with only two fingers, took out his federal identification and held it up for me to see.

I read the I.D. and pressed my gun in harder.

"Okay. You're a Special Agent with the FBI. So. Why the hell are you following me?" I repeated.

"The Bureau is looking into Stone Realty. One of the late Jonas Stone's companies. When his daughter Rachel came to see you last night I was ordered to follow you and report all your comings and goings. Do you have a proper license to carry the weapon you're holding against my throat?"

"Yes I do," I replied. "And I can also fire it if I have to."

"I can assure you, Mr. Atwater, that won't be necessary."

"You know my name?"

"I do, sir. Yes."

"How tall are you, sonny?"

"My name isn't sonny. It's Edwards, Special Agent Edwards and I am sufficiently tall enough. And? I graduated third in my class at the academy."

"Third? Impressive for a special agent man of your stature."

I reached in and took out my license and put it in front of Agent Edwards' face.

"I'm only doing this as a courtesy because I suddenly like you, Special Agent Edwards. And? Shooting you today, I think, would be a grave mistake on my part."

"Thank you," he said.

Agent Edwards let out a huge sigh of relief, put his hands down on the steering wheel and I put the .38 back in my shoulder holster.

"Tell me this? Why is the FBI looking into Stone Realty?" Agent Edwards adjusted his tie and looked at me.

"I'm not allowed to divulge that information," he said. "It is privileged."

I looked him straight in the eye and smiled.

"You won't divulge that information because you don't know why. Do you?"

Agent Edwards smiled slightly back at me and I could tell he was finally calming down.

"No," he said. "I don't know why."

"You're all right, Special Agent Edwards. Let's you and me step inside this Walgreens here and have us a cup of Joe."

"You mean coffee? Correct?"

"Yeah," I replied. "Coffee. Correct. Come on. I'm buying."

"I could use a cup of coffee," he said and got out from behind the wheel. "And maybe a donut or two?"

I brushed a small piece of lint off his right shoulder and gave him the once over.

"You're not much taller standing up. Are you?" I asked.

"As I said? I'm tall enough."

Agent Edwards made me smile a second time and we walked inside and sat down in one of the large green booths at the end of the counter.

I ordered two coffees with donuts, and the way Agent Edwards wolfed his down I could tell he hadn't eaten anything all day.

I ordered more donuts and our attractive looking waitress in the plain green uniform flashed Agent Edwards a quick smile, filled our cups a second time, and ran off to get our second order.

Agent Edwards told me he was single and had only been with the Bureau for a little over three months. He had a certain likability. I knew this man could be trusted.

I thought the best approach here was to try and make a friend.

"I have a proposition for you, Edwards," I said.

"That's Special Agent Edwards," he snapped back as he slurped another big gulp of his coffee.

"Excuse me," I apologized. "Special Agent Edwards. Are you interested in having this conversation or not?"

"Possibly. I'm listening," he said. "What's your proposition?"

"Let's you and I partner up. Instead of you chasing me all over town and me having to keep looking over my shoulder every twenty minutes? Let's share information."

"Share intel? You mean quid pro quo?"

"Yeah. Quid pro quo. I like that term. If I learn something about Stone Realty that I think might be of importance to you and to the Bureau, I'll give you that information. If you happen to discover something, say about Mrs. Barbieri or her husband? You share that with me. I'm not one of the bad guys here. I think you know that about me. I'm a straight up private dick, an ex-Marine, and a good American. The FBI can stand down and rest easy over me I can assure you. Now me? Having a federal agent as a go to guy? Meaning you. And you? Having someone like myself, a guy in the street trenches as they say, could be a very beneficial thing for both of us. Wouldn't you agree, Special Agent Edwards?"

Our second order of donuts arrived before he could respond. The girl in the uniform put our bill on the table, smiled again at Agent Edwards, and walked away.

"Well?" I pushed. "What do you say?"

"Possibly," he said and grabbed another donut.

"Could you be a bit more specific? Special Agent Edwards? Please?"

"Sharing any intel is always good as long as the two people responding can trust each other to always tell the truth."

"Well said."

"Thank you."

"Is that what they taught you at the Academy?"

"Among other things. Yes. I know I can be trusted, Mr. Atwater. The question here is, can you?"

"Yes. I can. No trust? No deal."

"All right. I still would have to get the okay from my superiors."

"Fair enough," I said and picked up the check. "You talk to your superiors at the Bureau and in the meantime? I promise to tell you where I went, who I spoke to, and anything else of importance the next time we meet. Scout's honor. Okay?"

Special Agent Edwards grinned.

"Okay."

We shook hands and Agent Edwards finished off the last donut and his last few gulps of coffee.

"Here's a quick bit of intel coming from a street-wise fellah like myself and going directly to you," I added. "Something I am positive they didn't teach you at the academy."

"What's that?" he asked.

"That pretty little waitress of ours in green and white? She likes you?"

Agent Edwards looked over at the girl delivering a hamburger to a gray haired man at the counter. She casually looked our way and smiled back broadly.

I grinned for the third time.

"See?" I said. "If I were you? Before you walk out of here? Show her your FBI badge and get her name and phone number. I would but she ain't grinning over at me. She's got you clearly in her sights."

"You think so?" he asked.

"Definitely. Listen. Come out to Barney's tonight around nine and I will give you a full report on the day. My word to you. Agreed?"

"Agreed. I'll be there," he said. "Nine o'clock."

"Good."

I paid the check, gave the girl in green and white a hefty tip, and smiled to myself as I noticed she and Agent Edwards starting some sort of dialogue. I went out the front door, heading to the coupe.

I remembered Rachel telling me her husband had purchased a brand new powder blue Mercedes and I noticed his fancy rig parked at the Stone Realty underground parking area with the name Enzo Barbieri painted on the wall above it in large black letters. I thought I would drive back there and check with my own eyes where the man in charge of such a huge family fortune went after the business of the day was finished.

The hunted was about to become the hunter.

Or so I thought.

CHAPTER SEVEN

Detectives Munoz and Blaine sat at their desks going over everything they had on the life and death of Ernest Hollowell.

They didn't have much.

Hollowell was a single man, originally from London, twice divorced, with no living heirs. He worked several accounts constantly, all top notch companies, and his work was always impeccably accurate and well above-board.

Stone Realty had been at the top of his working list ever since Jonas Stone first hired him when Rachel was only three years old.

To Rachel he was Uncle Ernie.

Hollowell was well paid for his efforts, stayed in touch by phone with Jonas discussing investment opportunities or simply providing updates on the family accounts, and whenever there was a company party he was always seated at the family table. He drank but never heavily, didn't gamble, chase the ladies or play the ponies, and for all intents and purposes seemed to be well liked by everyone.

He owned a small house up on Mulholland and didn't appear to have an enemy in the world.

The man was a saint. A dead saint.

Hollowell had checked into the Beverly for a two night stay and brought along all the company ledgers himself. He requested the penthouse suite and paid cash for both days.

Detective Munoz and Detective Blaine had spoken to every company account manager Hollowell handled, including their interview with Barbieri the same day Patrick Atwater came to see him, but no one admitted to giving permission for him to stay at a Beverly penthouse suite, or asking him to scrutinize the ledgers there.

As far as anyone could tell, Hollowell was doing everything on his own dime and his own time on the night he was killed.

The red ledger supposedly missing from the numbered group wasn't really missing at all. It was found exactly where Barbieri said he always kept it, in his locked oak desk drawer, and he was the only one with the key. According to Barbieri, Hollowell always came to the office to do the books and never once removed them from the Stone Realty office.

Barbieri was adamant that he was not the one that put Hollowell up at the Beverly. The fact that his accountant was there at all was a mystery to him and to the two detectives.

Detectives Munoz and Blaine had their own numbers man look the red ledger over and could not find any discrepancies, nor any fingerprints other than those of Hollowell, Barbieri, and the late Jonas Stone.

Ernest Hollowell's untimely death was exactly as it appeared and it had become a mystery.

Why was he at the Beverly? Who wanted him dead? And why?

Simple questions.

But the answers weren't there. Not yet.

The one thing Detectives Munoz and Blaine did discover was the substance that actually killed him.

A young morgue intern, Arlo, an annoying gum chewing nineteen year old, brought the two detectives the answer in the toxicology report from the county morgue, confirming what Detective Blaine had deduced when they first looked over the body.

There was that detectable odor of almonds wafting from Hollowell's opened dead mouth.

Death by cyanide poisoning.

Now another question arose.

Who the hell would have access to cyanide? It's not like anyone could just order some up like a Chinese food delivery.

Detectives Munoz and Blaine asked Rachel Stone Barbieri to come in to talk with them about Hollowell, and what she may know about her husband's locked red file.

Rachel walked into the squad room wearing a dark green business suit and matching hat. At first glance, everyone thought it was the actress Joan Crawford.

"Are you Detective Blaine and Detective Munoz?" she asked as she stepped up to their desks.

Both men instantly stood up and acted as if some European monarch's daughter had suddenly arrived from abroad.

"I'm Detective Munoz."

"And I'm Detective Blaine."

"Hello," she said.

Rachel shook their hands and was quickly ushered to a private area to be questioned.

"Would you like a cup of coffee, Mrs. Barbieri?" asked Detective Munoz.

"No, thank you," she calmly replied.

"Thank you for coming in to see us so promptly."

"Always willing to assist the LAPD," she replied and shifted in her seat somewhat, causing the hem of her dress to slide up ever so slightly above her knee.

The two detectives pretended not to notice.

"What did you want to ask me?" she said.

Detective Munoz chimed right in.

"As you are well aware, Mrs. Barbieri, we are investigating into the death of one Ernest Hollowell."

"Yes." she replied and took a deep breath accompanied by a forced smile.

"What can you tell us about Ernest Hollowell? The man?" asked Detective Blaine.

Rachel appeared saddened at hearing Hollowell's name and quickly retrieved a light green handkerchief from her baby alligator purse, wiping a small tear from her left eye. She took another deep breath, smiled, and looked at the blank wall as if she was looking at Hollowell himself and describing what she saw and felt.

"Ernie was like family to me," she sighed. "I've known him since I was just a small child. He was always a very nice, sweet, intelligent, and friendly man. A genius when it came to numbers."

"He was your father's company accountant, yes?" asked Detective Munoz.

"Yes. Our only accountant, actually. For years. Ernie handled my father's family finances also. Such a terrible thing. Do you know why he was even at the Beverly? The hotel itself hasn't given you any clues to how this could have happened to such a kind sweet man?"

"No," replied a surprised Detective Blaine.

They had asked her in to get information and now she was asking all the questions.

At first Detective Munoz thought that odd but let it go as she bent over and gently rubbed her right calf.

Both men locked their eyes on her long shapely legs.

"These heels. They sometimes give me leg cramps," she said. "Sorry. You were saying?"

Detective Munoz and Detective Blaine both sat up straight and glanced at each other. They were thinking the same thought:

Was she trying to get us off point with a little light flirtation?

Detective Munoz looked straight at her.

"What do you know about a red ledger?" he asked. "A red ledger numbered three eighteen?"

"A red ledger?" she repeated and shook her head. "Nothing. Does it have something to do with Ernie's death?"

"We're not sure. Not as yet," said Detective Blaine.

"I see," she added. "If this red ledger you speak of is business related, you would definitely have to ask my husband about that. I'm not privy to our family's business practices. Not since my marriage. Daddy always handled all that and after his unfortunate accident, my husband Enzo assumed those duties. He is much more capable in that arena than I could ever be. I'm sorry I can't be more helpful."

She leaned down again and this time rubbed her left leg. Detective Blaine glanced over at Detective Munoz and both men shook their heads slightly.

"If I knew anything that would be helpful to your investigation I would tell you. But when it comes to business and accounts it's the men in my family that handle all those things. And how Uncle Ernie died or why he was at that hotel? I have no idea, detectives. No idea whatsoever."

A long silence filled the room. She could feel their eyes staring at her.

"If there isn't anything else?" she asked.

"Thank you, Mrs. Barbieri," said Detective Munoz. "If we have any more questions we will definitely be in touch."

"All right, gentlemen," she said.

"I'll get a uniformed policeman to walk you out to your car," said Detective Blaine.

"Thank you. I would appreciate that," she said.

Rachel and the two detectives rose at the same time and walked out. Detective Blaine gestured to a uniformed policeman, Officer Davis, who graciously escorted Rachel out of the building.

Detectives Munoz and Blaine watched her walk away. So did the rest of the squad including Michelle, the copy girl.

"What do you think?" asked Detective Blaine.

"Hard to say," Detective Munoz answered. "She's either playing us for saps or she's just like the rest of the spoiled offspring we've had in here. Rich and clueless."

"Rich, clueless, and beautiful," added Detective Blaine. "Extremely beautiful."

"Yeah," agreed Detective Munoz. "That too."

"So what's our next move, partner?" asked Detective Blaine. "It seems all of our main players don't know a damn thing."

"And you're surprised?"

"Not in the least. The rich never know anything."

"I know one thing," said Detective Munoz. "One of them is lying. All we have to do is figure out which one it is."

"Simple," Detective Blaine added.

"Yeah. Simple," repeated Detective Munoz.

CHAPTER EIGHT

I sat in the coupe just off the street with a clear view of the Stone Realty building and the underground parking entrance. The sun had just gone down, traffic was slow on Wilshire, and my Ford coupe blended in nicely with the rest of the parked cars sprinkled along the manicured sidewalks. The darkness of the early evening added to the illusion and I was quite satisfied Barbieri would not notice me or the coupe.

Most of the work I did entailed long hours of sitting and a lot of watching.

And also a lot of thinking.

My initial thoughts told me the lot of them were plotting together, each one trying to gain some kind of control of the family funds. Situations like these are always nine times out often about the money, plain and simple, and the Stone family had boat loads of cash and then some. Money like that can make people, rich or poor, do just about anything and this case wasn't going to be much different. I knew I had to stay focused and wait until one of them made a mistake.

One mistake would make all the pieces fall into place.

The idea of Enzo Barbieri fooling around on his wealthy and stunningly beautiful wife did not add up in my mind. It just made no sense to me whatsoever. Chasing down big money made all the sense in the world.

Big money always trumped great sex.

I stopped myself from trying to figure out what Rachel Stone Barbieri and the famous Quentin Thayer actually had in common in this little scenario, and decided to just let it all play out and see where the cards finally fell.

I didn't have to wait long.

I sat there hidden in plain sight for a little over an hour and a half when Barbieri's brand new powder blue Mercedes finally came rolling out onto the street heading west. I started up the coupe and began following from a good distance.

I stayed back about five or six car lengths and made sure to stay behind several vehicles at every red light. We drove west for about twenty minutes until the Mercedes pulled into the driveway of a small beach house sitting up on a hill along with about fifteen other beach type homes. Barbieri parked his car next to a cream colored Chevrolet.

I chose to park near a small clump of trees about a quarter of a mile back. As I shut off my engine, I saw Barbieri in his expensive gray suit walk quickly to the front door and ring the bell.

A tall, beautiful blonde woman no more than thirty, wearing a pearl white sun dress, opened the front door and greeted Barbieri with a big kiss and a hug and they went inside, closing the door behind them.

Was this the Sheri or Shirley, Rachel spoke of? Were her suspicions actually true? Was Barbieri really cheating on his gorgeous wife with some little blonde bimbo living here at the beach?

I couldn't believe the thoughts racing through my mind at that very moment but knew my eyes didn't lie.

There he was, standing in the dark, hugging and passionately kissing the strange blonde that Rachel had described to me. And that kiss they were sharing was clearly a lover's kiss, not some simple peck on the cheek hello and how are you doing today that a man might receive from his mother or his sister.

I decided to try to get a closer look.

I got out of the coupe and made my way to the back of the house. Luckily for me there was another small clump of trees and some large rocks sitting just above the deck, giving me a clear view of the entire back area overlooking the ocean below, and with enough cover and darkness for me not to be seen. I leaned against one large rock and by stretching my neck somewhat, could peek down to the wooden deck.

A light shined out onto the deck from the two French doors at the rear of the house. I could hear muffled laughter and some big band music playing.

I looked down at the ocean below and up at the full moon above. The music became louder when the two French doors opened suddenly as Barbieri, still wearing his suit jacket and tie, stepped out onto the moonlit deck holding a glass of what appeared to be red wine, walked casually to the railing, sipped from the glass and looked out at the ocean waves breaking onto the sand.

I stretched my neck higher to see the blonde coming out from the house, quickly heading for Barbieri as if she was just beginning a double time march. By the time I realized that she was gripping a large knife in her left hand, she had raised that arm and plunged the entire blade deep into his back.

I froze, but my eyes kept taking in the details.

Barbieri instantly dropped the wine glass and it crashed onto the deck, scattering into several pieces. His entire body suddenly stiffened. He turned and began walking awkwardly and stiff legged back towards the house, both arms flailing behind him as he tried to reach the knife handle.

The blonde backed up slowly into the house and Barbieri followed her, still struggling and looking like the Frankenstein monster learning to walk for the first time.

Without thinking, I pulled my .38 and ran down to the railing. I made it in a couple minutes and quickly jumped onto the wooden deck.

I took a few deep breaths, stepped up to the opened French doors and entered the house cautiously.

Big band music blared from the radio sitting against the wall and the drums had taken over and were pounding out some solo tom-tom rhythm. I ignored the music, kept my gun pointed out in front of me, and as I slowly moved forward I kept trying to figure out what the hell it was I had just witnessed and what I was now walking into.

I kept taking in the details as I stepped forward.

The living room was nicely furnished. One small lamp was lit and sat on a dark wood end table next to the couch. Nothing real expensive caught my eye, and the two cheap looking paintings of some Dutch women from another time and place staring back at me from the dark of the room on the opposite walls told me straight away that this was one of those so-called high-end beach rentals.

Whoever this blonde was, clearly didn't own the place.

No one was in the room and I saw no signs of any fights or arguments.

The music intensified.

A single bottle of wine stood open next to the pulled cork and a metal corkscrew. Alongside was another wine glass, similar to the one I had seen in Barbieri's hand just before he was stabbed, holding a small amount of liquid and with a deep red lipstick stain across the top edge of the glass. It all sat on a small coffee table in front of the small couch. I took a fast peek out the front window, thinking they both might have somehow made it out the front door, but there wasn't any blood trail on the floor and the front door had the gold chain still locked in place high above the door knob.

I turned and walked quickly down the dark short hallway, feeling my heart beginning to pound in my chest. I took a quick deep breath, poked my gun and my head into the hallway bathroom and then into what appeared to be the guest bedroom. They were both empty.

I took another deep breath and moved down the hallway to the master bedroom. Again I poked my head and gun into the room and saw Barbieri lying face down on the bedroom floor with the large black handled knife still stuck firmly in his back.

I knelt down next to his body to check if he was still breathing and suddenly realized I hadn't checked behind the bathtub curtain. I slowly turned to check the doorway but the blonde was already standing next to me with a syringe in her hand, which she instantly stuck into my left shoulder close to my neck.

I turned my head slowly and faced her, but before I could make out any of her facial features in the poorly lit room, or even get a shot off, both of my hands suddenly went numb, my head and vision became clouded, and I began to black out from whatever the substance was in the syringe.

The last thing I heard was the music fading off in the distance and my gun hitting the bedroom floor as it fell from my paralyzed hand.

I mentally cursed myself for not being more cautious and silently hoped this wasn't going to be the end of me as I fell helplessly onto the bedroom floor and felt my body smack right up next to Barbieri's.

All the lights went out and I faded into a vast sea of darkness. I could still feel my heart pounding heavily in my chest and realized I was still breathing and then total unconsciousness washed over me and I was out.

My last thought was focused on my own stupidity for not checking the bathroom curtain. I knew better but it was too late.

The game afoot was over.

Over and out.

CHAPTER NINE

Special Agent Edwards sat in his car staring at his watch. He had driven up the coast and was ten minutes early for his first agreed intel meeting with Patrick. He waited until it was exactly nine o'clock before entering Barney's By The Sea.

The place was empty except for Jake sitting alone at the far end of the bar eating a late steak dinner. Business had been slow and quiet tonight and Betty was busy totaling up her last four customers at table three when she noticed Agent Edwards walk in. Barney was washing the last few bar glasses and cleared his throat loudly, his subtle way of alerting Betty that a new customer had just entered.

"I see him, Barney," Betty said as she quickly grabbed a menu, dropped the bill on table three, and walked up to Agent Edwards with a welcoming smile on her face.

"Good evening and welcome to Barney's By The Sea. Are you here for dinner or cocktails, sir?" she asked.

"Neither," replied Agent Edwards. "I am here to meet Patrick Atwater."

"What time was your meeting?" asked Betty, always watching out for Patrick's back.

"He told me nine o'clock."

"And you are?"

"My name is Edwards."

"Well Mr. Edwards, Mr. Atwater is not here at the moment but if he told you nine o'clock then I am certain is on his way and possibly just running late. Did you want to have a seat at his booth or would you like to wait at the bar?" she asked.

"His booth will do," he replied and quickly looked around the room.

"Follow me," Betty said and led Agent Edwards to Patrick's booth and ushered him to a seat with his back to the front door.

Agent Edwards slid into the booth and Betty saw holster and gun under his suit jacket. Betty pretended not to notice and set the menu down on the table.

"Would you care for a cocktail or a cup of coffee?"

"Coffee sounds swell," he said. "Black, please"

"Coffee black coming right up." she replied.

Betty walked to the bar and nodded to Barney to step in closer to her.

"Who's the little fellah?" asked Barney.

"He says his name is Edwards and he's here for a nine o'clock meeting with Patrick. He only wants a coffee, black."

"It's already passed nine," said Barney as he looked at the clock on the wall and poured out a cup of coffee. "That's not the Patrick we know. He's never late for a meeting. Not with a new client. Never."

"If there is a meeting," she added.

"You seem a bit nervous, Betty. What is it?"

"There's something else," added Betty.

Barney leaned in closer.

"What is it?" asked Barney. "Does he have a German accent?"

"No."

"Russian, maybe?"

"No. He's packing a gun. Left side."

Barney stared over at Patrick's booth and whispered to Betty.

"He's too damn short to be law enforcement. Bring him his coffee and Jake and I will check into him after your customers leave."

"Okay," said Betty and took the coffee over to Agent Edwards.

"Here you are, Mr. Edwards, one coffee, black. Can I get you something else? A nice piece of apple pie maybe?" Betty asked and out of the corner of her eye caught her customers paying their bill at the bar.

"Nothing, thanks," said Agent Edwards and blew over the edge of his cup before taking a small sip. "Good coffee."

"Thank you," she said.

Betty glanced to her right and saw the four customers smile, wave back at her, and walk out the front door. Betty took a deep breath and looked down at Agent Edwards.

"Would you do me a big favor, please?" Betty asked.

"A favor? What kind of favor?" he asked.

"Would you mind placing both of your hands on the table please?"

"On the table? Can I ask why?"

"Just do it mate," said Jake as he poked Agent Edwards from behind on his left shoulder with the point of a double barreled shotgun.

"All right," said Agent Edwards.

Agent Edwards slowly placed his two hands flat onto the table.

"I'll take that piece you're carrying" said Barney as he reached into Agent Edwards's holster and removed his handgun.

"What's this all about?" asked Agent Edwards.

"We're not used to strangers entering my establishment carrying weapons," said Barney.

"My weapon is a government issued M1911 and I am Special Agent Clovis Edwards with the FBI. Sir."

"I know an M1911 when I see one, shorty but the FBI? That's bullshit," said Barney.

"It's not bullshit. I can assure you."

"You can't be with the FBI. You're three feet tall, for Christ's sakes. No one your size would ever be hired by the FBI."

"As I said, I can assure you, sir, I am the correct height and I have identification to that fact in my inside right hand pocket."

"Do you now?" said Barney.

"Yes. I do. I can show it to you."

"Betty here will fetch it."

Barney nodded to Betty and she reached in and took out Agent Edwards' ID and badge and opened it.

"Holy crap. This guy is the real McCoy, Barney. He is Special Agent Clovis Edwards," said Betty and held the ID up for Barney and Jake to see. "Just like he says."

Jake and Barney stretched their necks and looked at the ID.

"Looks real to me, Barney," said Jake.

"It is," said Barney.

"Nice likeness," said Jake. "Makes him look taller."

"Sorry mate," apologized Barney as Jake moved the shotgun and Barney placed the M1911 on the table.

"We didn't know you from Adam and Patrick Atwater is never late for any of his new client meetings."

"Never?" asked Agent Edwards as he put his gun back into its holster and Betty handed back the badge and ID.

"Never," repeated Betty. "I saw your gun when you sat down and didn't know what to make of it."

"Better safe than sorry," said Agent Edwards. "I'm not a client. Mr. Atwater and I are sharing information on a case. Has Patrick called here? Saying he'd be late?"

"He did not, sir. No. And no hard feelings about Jake and me pointing that shotgun at you?" asked Barney.

"We're good."

"My apologies also for my words about your stature" added Barney.

"No problem. My height seems to be the topic of discussion today. Patrick is a lucky man to have you all watching his back."

"And we do, mate. And we do," said Barney.

"And now we'll watch yours, too," Jake added with a grin.

Jake and Barney smiled at Agent Edwards and walked back to the bar.

"May I sit down?" asked Betty.

"Please," said Agent Edwards.

Betty slid in across from Agent Edwards and straightened the napkin holder.

"Something is clearly wrong," she said. "If Patrick told you nine o'clock and couldn't make it here on time he would have called us."

"You're sure about that?" he asked.

"Dead sure," said Betty. "Patrick Atwater is a stand-up guy. He's also a man who keeps his word and his integrity. Always. I know him. If Patrick tells you he will meet you at nine and he doesn't show? Then I know something is not right."

"Maybe he's having car problems?"

"No matter, he would still call. Something's happened. Something bad. I know it. Something has happened to him and it's not good."

"All right, let's give him another twenty minutes or so and if he doesn't show I'll make a few calls and we'll try to locate him. How does that sound?"

"That sounds good."

Agent Edwards took another sip of his coffee and smiled at Betty.

"Sounds to me like you and Patrick have known each other for some time," he said.

"We have some history," she replied. "Ancient history."

"Before the war?" he asked.

Betty smiled broadly.

"Yes," she said.

"Good friends?" he asked.

"Very good friends," said Betty. "How do you know Patrick?"

"We just met each other today. By accident."

Betty stared at Agent Edwards.

"It wasn't by accident. You're both working the same cases."

"Something like that."

"Can I get you more coffee?" she asked.

"Please," he said.

Betty got up and walked to the bar.

Agent Edwards glanced down at his watch and noticed it was almost nine-thirty. If Patrick was in trouble Agent Edwards wondered where he might be and just how much trouble he might be in. Agent Edwards pondered what his next move should be and how he might assist his new-found friend.

Betty poured more coffee and stared anxiously at the clock on the wall.

CHAPTER TEN

I didn't know it at the time, but several hours had passed before I suddenly heard myself breathing and I slowly opened my eyes.

I was still lying on the bedroom floor. I sat up and rolled my neck and my forehead felt like it was about to explode into a million pieces. I took several deep breaths and the pain in my head went straight behind my eyes and rushed down my spine, and for a moment thought I was going to black out again.

Barbieri's body was not in the room but I saw my gun lying on the floor next to my right foot. I picked it up, got myself to a standing position, and looked down at my watch.

My watch read five thirty.

I had missed my promised meeting with Agent Edwards and knew it was going to take some fast talking on my end if I was ever going to set myself straight with him again.

I rolled my neck slowly a second time, took a few more deep breaths, and headed slowly back to the patio entrance.

I noticed that the wine bottle and all the other extras were gone from the coffee table, and someone had shut off the light in the lamp.

The French doors to the patio were wide open and I had to shade my eyes from the early morning sun just coming up as I stepped out onto the patio. I could see that all the pieces of the broken wine glass had been neatly swept up and any traces of the spilled wine had been washed away.

As I became aware of the ocean waves crashing below me, the smell of salt air blowing into my face and nostrils, the intense pain in my head, neck, and back began to slowly subside and I felt the eerie presence of someone close by.

I turned my attention back to the rear of the house and I saw him.

Enzo Barbieri, eyes wide opened, sat dead in a large wicker chair, still wearing his expensive gray suit and jacket. His pants zipper was down and his long erect penis jutted out from between his legs like some broken skin-colored flashlight.

I looked up to his face and I saw a bullet hole placed squarely in the center of his forehead. A large blood spatter and several broken pieces of his brain and skull plastered the entire back of the chair, most of the wall behind it, and with several smaller blood stains on the bubbled glass bathroom window nearby.

"Son of a bitch," uncontrollably rolled out of my throat.

I grabbed Barbieri by the shoulders, pulled his body forward slightly so I could see his back and I stared at where I had seen the knife go in. But there wasn't any knife, or even any sign of a stab wound at all.

I gently placed the body back against the chair and looked it over entirely from head to toe. It was obvious Barbieri was having his Johnson serviced, most likely by the blonde who met him at the door, but it was highly unlikely she would also be the one putting a bullet in his head at the very same time.

I leaned in and took a closer look at the bullet hole.

It sat dead center just above his eyes and had a slight downward angle. The small dark circle around the bullet hole told me whoever pulled the trigger had placed the gun directly on his forehead moments before the gun was fired. There was no way little blondie could have been on her knees working her pearly whites and then suddenly pull out a handgun say strapped to her inner thigh, reach up, shoot Barbieri, and manage the angle of the bullet hole. It was much too awkward of a shot.

Someone else shot Barbieri.

My conclusion was definite and the bigger question now was who pulled the trigger?

A mild sense of dread washed over me.

I quickly checked my .38 and when I saw one round was missing a huge light suddenly went on inside my head and seemed to shine across the entire patio.

The cards had now clearly been dealt.

The last piece of Rachel Stone Barbieri's puzzle fell into place.

I found myself smiling at what she thought was her ingenious plan to obviously murder her husband, for whatever reason, make it appear he was cheating, and then set me up for the fall.

I was certain the bullet inside Barbieri's head would turn out to be a match to my .38, and that alone would be enough for the LAPD not only to arrest me but to also convict me.

I knew I had to come up with a plan quickly to not only figure this out and save my own ass, but also find the people responsible for Barbieri's murder, whoever they were, and to be held accountable.

If I was going to do that and do it fast, I needed help. But I also needed some time.

As my mind started putting my own puzzle together I heard a car drive up and park in front of the house. 1raced into the living room, looked out the front window, and saw the LA black and white police car parked out front with two uniformed policemen inside.

Someone had called this in, hoping I would still be lying out cold in the back bedroom. I ran out through the French doors, jumped over the rail, and headed up to the rocks and the small clump of trees. I didn't stop running until I reached the Ford coupe.

I fired up the engine and noticed the two policemen had already broken in the door and gone inside the house. As I started to pull away I looked to my right and saw some man walking his dog. We locked eyes for a moment and I could tell he got a very clear look at me and the coupe.

When it rains it pours.

I drove slowly at first trying not to attract any attention until I made the turn at the corner. I floored the gas and raced the old Ford straight back to the coast highway, heading quickly back towards the city.

I ran the LAPD scenario once more through my head.

The man with the dog would definitely give them my description and the make and model of my automobile, and when they speak to Rachel she will calmly confirm it must have been me at the scene. Then they will get a court order, pull my license, grab and test my gun. It will match to the hole in Barbieri's head. Then, I will be arrested for first degree murder.

Most men at a moment like this would turn to panic or despair.

I was a different breed.

The war taught me to stay calm no matter how much hell is being thrown at you.

If you remain calm, stay focused, and hopefully, if the gods shine a little luck on you, and point you in the right direction, then you will see yourself through just about anything. I was betting heavily on the gods' good favor but inside I was feeling like Davy Crockett facing five thousand Mexicans at the Alamo.

Time would tell.

A slight smile came back across my face as I drove down the highway because I knew even though things were not looking all that good for me and before the LAPD would actually apprehend me, I could still get one more crack at whoever it was behind Barbieri's demise, and this time I would be dealing the cards.

All the cards.

This time it would be me in the front seat driving straight to the truth and making damn sure whoever was responsible was going over for this.

It wouldn't be me going down for it and I wasn't going to stop looking until I had all my questions answered.

I figured I needed a day or two at the most to set things in motion. As long as I could stay far away from the LAPD I could make it all happen.

First things first.

I had to ditch the coupe.

I drove into Union Station and it seemed rather quiet, a few people with bags standing at the cab station, four or five baggage handlers filling out tickets, and one crying child being dragged inside by what looked like his grandmother. Several uniformed policemen stood out front and didn't pay me any special attention or give me the eye as I slowly passed them by and drove into the parking lot. I parked the coupe, put the keys under the front floor mat, stepped out of the car, and walked casually away. I knew an APB would be out on me and my vehicle within the next hour or two but as long as I wasn't in it I still had some options open. Hopefully I could get to a phone and start putting things into action.

Betty would be my first call.

CHAPTER ELEVEN

Betty told herself that Patrick would be okay no matter what and as she fell asleep after her long shift at Barney's and her short conversation with Agent Edwards, the sun rose and began shining directly into the room, forcing her eyes open and she realized Jake was slowly exploring her stomach area with long kisses and making small circles with his warm, wet, tongue.

It had been some time since the two of them had a relaxing morning together like this one, and she was definitely not going to let it pass.

She took a deep breath to let Jake know she was awake and then slightly arched her back and opened her legs. Jake felt her response and slid his tongue straight down and slipped it deep inside her.

Betty's climax came quickly and her entire body began to shake as the enormous rush of pleasure waved through her. She gently pressed her hands onto Jake's head and ran her fingers gently through his hair.

Jake continued doing small circles with his tongue, and her second climax seemed to have a slight flowing motion to it.

Jake got up on his knees, smiled down at Betty, and she took him into her hands and guided his erection into her. She wrapped her hands hard against his bottom and after a few short strokes he came inside her like a broken water pipe, accompanied by his usual deep groaning noises she had grown quite accustomed to and also thoroughly enjoyed.

Jake rolled over onto his back and sighed deeply.

"We need to do this more often, darling," he said.

"Absolutely," she replied.

Betty looked over at Jake, smiled broadly, and for some reason remembered another time back in the day when it was Patrick saying those exact words to her.

Or maybe it was her saying those words to him.

Either way, Betty squashed the memory and thought about how much she loved Jake and how happy and safe she felt with them living and working together.

But her memories kept floating back, and she realized Patrick would always hold a very special place in her heart that would never change.

Never ever.

The phone suddenly rang and Betty and Jake instantly looked at each other. They knew it wasn't Barney calling. Not this early. A phone call at this hour could only be one person, and they both knew it.

It had to be Patrick Miles Atwater and he definitely was in some sort of trouble and clearly needed their help. It was the only time Patrick ever called.

Jake stared at Betty.

"Well go on, love. Answer the phone." he said.

"It's him. I know it," said Betty.

"We both know it. Go!" added Jake.

She got out of bed and walked naked to the phone. Jake watched her walk away and a boyish grin formed across his face.

"If he needs me, love, I can be out of here in ten minutes max," he said and looked at his pants hanging over the chair.

Jake really liked Patrick and always wanted to get involved doing anything that pertained to one of his cases, but Patrick had never asked for his help.

Not even once.

Patrick had called several times since he and Betty got together. They were always late night calls or early morning ones but Patrick always asked for Betty and Betty never said no, no matter what it was. Patrick had always told Jake that if he ever needed some strong back up, or an extra set of eyes on a client, Jake would be the first person he would call.

But he never did. It was always Betty.

Patrick liked Jake too, and was glad that he and Betty had found each other and making a decent go of it.

Jake sat up in bed, hoping this could be the time Patrick needed his help.

"Five minutes, if it's an absolute emergency," he added.

"I'll let him know that, honey," she replied and picked up the phone. "What's happened?"

Jake leaned in closer hoping to catch what it was Patrick was explaining to Betty, but he knew he'd have to wait to get all the details.

"Okay. I got it."

Betty hung up the phone, looked at the wall clock, and turned to Jake.

"Patrick needs to borrow the Hudson for a few days."

"A few days? What's happened to his car?"

"I don't know. He didn't say."

Betty gave no more information, walked quickly to the bathroom, turned on the shower and got in.

Jake jumped up from the bed and practically ran into the bathroom.

"Do you want me to follow you in my car?" he asked.

Betty yelled to him over the sound of the shower water running.

"That won't be necessary. I have to bring him back here."

"Here? Is he all right? He's not hurt, is he?" Jake asked.

Betty shut off the water and pulled the shower curtain back. Jake reached over and handed her a clean towel and she began drying herself off.

"He's not hurt, honey. He just needs my car and you and I will have to ride into work together for a few days in your vehicle. That's all."

Jake looked over Betty's naked body and wiped a small droplet of water from her right shoulder.

"You didn't wash your hair."

"No time," she replied.

"He doesn't need any muscle or back up?"

Betty knew Jake had to ask and his question made her smile. She kissed his cheek and stepped out of the tub.

"Not this time, baby. Just the car."

Betty felt his disappointment as she walked back to the bedroom. She quickly threw on her bra and panties and climbed into a pair of slacks and a sweater.

"We'll be back before you know it, I promise to fill you in if he gives me any more details. Okay?"'

"Sure. Okay. I understand completely, love. Where are you picking him up?"

"Tail of the Pup."

"Oh Christ. Tail of the Pup?"

"Relax. It's not going to be like the last time."

"How do you know for sure?"

"For one thing it's daytime, not the middle of the night, and Patrick would never intentionally put me or you for that matter, in harm's way," she assured him.

"I know that love, but the last time you and Patrick met there some bloody wanker did shoot off his side view mirror."

"Patrick didn't know that was coming and he still protected me, handled that asshole without using his gun, and this time is not anything like that so please don't be worried."

"I'm not worried. I'm jealous."

"Jealous?" she asked.

"Yes," he said. "I'm jealous that you and Patrick keep having all this great fun mixing it up with all those clandestine characters he deals with and leaving me here waiting by the bloody phone."

"I'm sure your time will come eventually."

"I'm hoping so, love. Bring us back a few chili dogs, eh? I love those things."

"I can. I guess."

Jake smiled.

"Thank you. Do you have money?"

"I have my tips from last night still in my purse."

"Be careful, love," he said.

"I will," she said.

Betty stepped into her shoes, and kissed Jake deeply.

"I love you. I have to go."

"I love you, too."

"I will call you if I have to."

"I'll be here. Waiting."

"Just stay by the phone."

You know I will."

Betty smiled one last smile at Jake, grabbed up her keys, and went out the door. Jake heard the big green Hudson's engine starting up, and as it drove away from the house, he sighed heavily and walked slowly back to the bathroom and turned on the shower.

Betty headed straight for the Tail of the Pup and tried not to worry about Patrick and what that woman in the yellow dress had gotten him into but every time she told herself everything would be okay her thoughts kept running horrific scenarios and none of them had Patrick in a good or safe place. Every time Patrick had called her, something was clearly not going well. If he also had to ditch his car meant the situation was beginning to take a bad turn. Betty resolved herself to the fact that at best Patrick wasn't hurt or wounded.

Not yet anyway.

A little over forty-five minutes had passed when Betty and Patrick entered the house together. Jake sat on the sofa drinking a large cup of black coffee.

"You know where the phone is," Betty said and Patrick quickly nodded his hello to Jake as he walked over to the phone, picked it up and dialed.

Betty sat down next to Jake and handed him a bag with four chili dogs. Jake opened one up; began eating and Betty sipped at his cup of coffee.

"Is everything all right?" Jake asked.

"Yes," she said. "Everything is fine."

"Do you want one of these?"

"Maybe later."

Patrick started talking to someone on the other end of the phone but Jake and Betty were clearly out of earshot.

"Does he need my brass knucks again? I can go get them."

"No. He just needs the car. Like I said."

Jake and Betty sat in silence as Patrick continued his phone conversation. Betty took another sip of Jake's coffee.

"If it is bad? You can tell me."

"I know that," she said.

"So?" he asked. "Is it bad?"

"It's not good," she replied.

"Not good?" he repeated.

"It's that good-looking dame from the other night. The one with the long legs and all dressed in yellow."

"That bird was a real looker."

"Someone killed her husband."

"Bloody hell! Someone? Not Patrick?"

"No. Not Patrick."

Jake shook his head as he took another bite of his chili dog and slowly processed the information. He leaned in closer to Betty and they stared at Patrick still on the phone.

"If anyone asks? He wasn't here. Right?" Jake asked, already knowing the answer.

"That's right."

"And we haven't seen him?"

"That's the drill," she said. "For now."

"I know the drill, love. Who is he talking to?"

"That little guy that came into Barney's last night."

"The Fed in the little suit and tie?"

"Yes."

Patrick hung up the phone and walked over to Betty and Jake.

"Sorry about all this, guys. I can't stay. I have to go."

"We understand, mate," said Jake.

"Be careful, Miles," Betty said.

"I'll get through all this," he said. "Thanks for the car."

"You can count on us for anything, Patrick," Jake added in. "Anything."

"Thanks, Jake."

Patrick smiled at Jake and hurried out the door. Betty looked at Jake.

"This isn't upsetting you. Is it?" she asked.

"Upsetting me? Are you kidding? I love this stuff! Patrick's a good bloke. It will all work out. I'm sure of it. Are you okay?"

Betty took a deep breath and shook her head.

"I think so. Yes. I'm okay."

Jake smiled and took another bite of his chili dog. ·

"These are really good," he added.

Betty smiled at Jake and sipped his coffee.

"So tell me everything and don't leave out a word. How bad is it and what's our next move?"

CHAPTER TWELVE

The coroner's vehicle had been parked at the beach house next to three police black and whites, two unmarked detective cars, a forensics truck, and two press vehicles for about two hours. The man with the dog, several neighbors, and four newspaper people were huddled to one side of the street trying to see what had happened and hopefully get a full report from whomever was in charge.

But no one was stepping forward with any information. Three tight-lipped uniformed policemen stood outside the house keeping everyone far back from the scene.

Agent Edwards maneuvered his Dodge up the street and parked between two police cars just as the coroner and his three assistants wheeled out the covered body of Enzo Barbieri, placed it in their vehicle, and slowly drove through the neck-stretching crowd as they headed back to town.

Agent Edwards flashed his Federal identification at the first police officer about to tell him where he could or couldn't park, and proceeded to walk inside.

Forensic people were everywhere, going over every inch of the house, and the young police photographer, Butch, was busily snapping pictures from every possible angle.

"Detectives Munoz and Blaine?" Agent Edwards asked and flashed his ID once again.

"Down the hall," said Butch, clicking his camera and snapping a quick shot of Agent Edwards standing at the front door entrance.

The flash bulb blinded Edwards slightly for a second, and once his eyes cleared he headed down the hallway.

Detectives Munoz and Blaine had been called in on this as a courtesy from the Malibu police department, as it was most likely connected to the other homicide they were presently investigating.

Both men were looking at the bedroom floor when Agent Edwards stepped into the room.

"Gentlemen," he began. "I'm Special Agent Edwards with the FBI. You are Detective Munoz and Detective Blaine?"

"We are. What can we do for you?" asked Detective Munoz.

"Malibu police are stepping down and giving this to you?"

"They are. Yes," said Detective Blaine.

"I have some information that is pertinent to this case and possibly to your other homicide over at the Beverly."

Detective Munoz and Detective Blaine looked at each other with surprise.

"The FBI seems to be well informed," said Detective Munoz. "You have something that will shine a light on this?"

"I do," replied Agent Edwards. "But I need a favor from you both."

"A favor," asked Detective Blaine.

"Yes."

"We're not granting any favors to anyone until we hear what you have to say," said Detective Munoz.

"Fair enough," agreed Agent Edwards. "The FBI has had Barbieri under our radar for several months and I have been working in tandem with a private eye named Patrick Miles Atwater."

"In tandem?" asked Detective Blaine.

"That's correct," said Agent Edwards

"Why is the FBI looking into Barbieri?"

"I'm not at liberty to answer that Detective. Not yet. Do you two know Patrick Atwater?"

Detective Munoz and Detective Blaine shook their heads no simultaneously.

"We do not. No." answered Detective Blaine.

"As a Special Agent of the FBI, I want you both to know I am personally vouching for Mr. Atwater."

"Vouching?" questioned Detective Munoz. "What's Atwater got to do with all this?"

"And why does he need vouching from the FBI?" Detective Blaine added.

"Atwater was tailing Barbieri. He followed him here, and he saw the man stabbed out on this deck."

"Stabbed?" asked Detective Munoz.

"That's correct," said Agent Edwards.

"But Barbieri wasn't stabbed," said Detective Blaine. "He was shot in the forehead with a .38. Nobody was stabbed. Not here, Agent Edwards."

"Atwater and I know that now. We also know that when you check the bullet in Barbieri's head it is most likely going to match to Atwater's gun."

"Atwater carries a .38?" said Detective Blaine.

"He does. Yes. But he's being set up. He had nothing to do with this killing."

"Set up? By who?" asked Detective Blaine.

"We don't know as yet, Detectives, but hopefully with all of us working together?"

"In tandem?" asked Detective Blaine.

"Yes. Together we will get to the person or persons responsible and get this entire mess worked out. Would you two walk with me for a moment?" Agent Edwards asked.

Detective Munoz and Detective Blaine threw questioned looks at each other but followed Agent Edwards out to the back deck.

Agent Edwards crouched down and looked closely at a section of the deck. Detective Munoz and Detective Blaine watched and wondered.

"You want to tell us what this is all about? What the hell are you looking for?" asked Detective Munoz.

Agent Edwards stood up and looked up at the rocks and the trees at the side of the house.

"I want you to listen to me, Detectives. Listen to me carefully. Please?"

"We're listening," said Detective Munoz. "You have our undivided attention. Right partner?"

"Absolutely," added Detective Blaine.

Agent Edwards pointed up to the rocks above.

"Atwater followed Barbieri here and was up there. Watching. He saw Barbieri come out onto this deck with a glass of wine in his hand and stood here. Looking out at the ocean. A blonde woman walked out from the house, with a knife, and stabbed Barbieri in the back. He dropped the glass and it shattered. Barbieri staggered back into the house trying to get to the knife."

"Hold on," interrupted Detective Munoz. "Barbieri wasn't stabbed and we found no broken glass out here anywhere. I'm looking at the deck right now and I'm not seeing any wine stain."

Detective Munoz leaned down and smelled the wooden deck.

"No whiff of any alcohol, either. Are you sure about this private dick Atwater?" asked Detective Munoz.

"Yes. Quite sure."

"Then tell us this," asked Detective Blaine. "How does a guy with a knife stuck in his back, magically wind up with a bullet hole in his head, no sign of any knife wound whatsoever, and his cock hanging out of his expensive gray suit. Is he some relative of Houdini or what?"

"For the moment, that is the big mystery, gentlemen, and that is why I am here requesting a favor. A favor as a professional courtesy. To the FBI."

"A courtesy?"

"Yes."

"For you and this Atwater?" asked Detective Blaine.

"Again. Yes."

"We are still listening," Detective Munoz replied.

"I want to take up this portion of wood deck. If there is no trace of wine or broken glass underneath, as Mr. Atwater explained to me in detail that there very well should be, I will pick him up myself and deliver him to you both personally."

"And if there is a wine trace or some broken glass?" asked Detective Blaine.

"If there is, and only if there is, Detectives, Atwater is asking you both to leave him alone. Give him two days to play this all out and he'll come in on his own."

"With the gun?" asked Detective Munoz.

"With the gun. Yes." answered Agent Edwards.

"Sounds to me like this guy Atwater needs two days to get himself into the wind," said Detective Blaine.

"If that is true, Detective Blaine, the FBI will find Mr. Atwater and bring him to you on a silver platter. My word on it," said Agent Edwards.

Detective Munoz looked down at the deck, sighed heavily and looked over at the police officer standing by the back door.

"Officer?" asked Detective Munoz.

"Yes sir," replied the officer.

"Go out to the forensics vehicle and bring us back a hammer and a small nail puller."

"Yes, sir," the officer replied again.

"You're not really buying this story?" asked Detective Blaine. "Are you?"

"Right now? No. I am not. But? As a courtesy? To the FBI? And for right now? At this moment? Let's see what's here," answered Detective Munoz.

"Okay, but for the record? I have my doubts about this guy Atwater," said Detective Blaine and stared out at the ocean.

"Duly noted partner," said Detective Munoz.

Detective Munoz sighed again, looked over at Agent Edwards, and the police officer ran into the house.

"Thank you," said Agent Edwards.

"You're welcome," replied Detective Munoz.

A few silent moments passed. The officer returned, handing the hammer and the nail puller to Detective Munoz.

"Give it here," said Detective Blaine and got down on one knee.

He took the hammer and the nail puller and began opening up a small area of the deck. Detective Blaine pulled up two boards and looked closer.

"Well? What do we have?" asked Detective Munoz.

Detective Blaine reached down and picked up two small shards of glass, placing them in the palm of his hand to show Agent Edwards and Detective Munoz.

"Looks like a broken wine glass to me," said Detective Blaine. "Look how thin it is. This piece even has a small trace of color right there."

Detective Munoz leaned down, smelled the glass, and looked over at Agent Edwards.

"Tell Atwater he has his two days. But you listen to me. If he is playing us? And playing you? He will sorely regret it. And I do mean sorely. Two days and he comes in with the gun and everything he has on this whole fiasco. Everything. Agreed?"

"Agreed. And thank you," said Agent Edwards. "Thank you both, Detectives."Agent Edwards nodded to the two detectives and walked out. Detective Blaine stood up and both watched Agent Edwards walk away.

"Do you think we're being played here, partner?" asked Detective Blaine.

"Two more days isn't going to make a bit of difference. Not to us. Not with this," replied Detective Munoz. "Let's utilize the next two days and look into this Patrick Miles Atwater. Find out what kind of a private dick he really is. And this little guy, Special Agent Edwards of the FBI."

"He is a little short to be a Special Agent, don't you think?" asked Detective Blaine.

"I don't know. How tall is Hoover?"

"I think they're both about the same height."

Both men smiled.

"This Agent and Atwater are far more out in front of this thing then we are right now. Let's see what they can do and what they can tell us."

"Agreed," said Detective Blaine. "I think we can work with that."

Detective Blaine carefully placed the two pieces of broken glass into a small paper envelope.

"God help them both if they're running some kind of game on us," said Detective Munoz. "Even Hoover and the entire FBI won't be able to help them."

Detective Munoz took the envelope, and walked away.

Detective Blaine smiled again and followed Detective Munoz into the house.

CHAPTER THIRTEEN

I drove Betty's Hudson up the long drive to the Beverly, hoping Agent Edwards had convinced the police to give me the two days I had asked for. I told Edwards where I would be and to call me straight away with any news.

Good or bad.

I figured running around in the Hudson, no matter what the news was, would still give me the time I needed. I was sure Rachel and whomever else she had in her comer were busy planning their next move to either have me arrested for Barbieri's murder or simply do away with me and make it look like I did the deed and disappeared.

I wasn't about to let either scenario occur. Not on my watch.

I pulled into the entrance, stopped the Hudson, and a surprised looking Freddy opened the door.

"Got yourself a new car, Patrick?" he asked.

I stepped out and quickly handed Freddy a fifty dollar bill.

"It's resting down at the train station, Freddy. You got anything for me?"

Freddy kissed the fifty and quickly stuffed it into his pocket.

"It must be important," he said.

"It is."

"Have you been reading the newspapers?"

"No," I said.

Freddy grabbed one of the numerous copies of the LA Times evening edition sitting by the entrance doorway and stuck it into my hand.

"Page six," Freddy said.

I quickly leafed through the pages. There, near the bottom of the page next to the Lucky Strike cigarette ad was the headline, Man Found Dead at the Beverly Hills Hotel LAPD investigating.

The article didn't identify the dead man but did request anyone with any information to call the LAPD and ask for Detective Munoz.

"Did you call this in?" I asked.

"Of course I did. The hotel would never let something like a possible homicide get out to the papers. Bad for business."

"Is that what this is, Freddy? A possible homicide?" I asked.

"I think so. The two detectives in charge pressed me pretty hard on this one. Munoz and Blaine."

"What did you tell them?"

"Patrick? You know me. I gave them nothing. I have a reputation to uphold here. I can't do this job and talk to cops. There's a certain code at stake."

"You gave them the usual. Saw nothing. Heard nothing. Know nothing."

"That's my tune."

"So what do you have for me?"

Freddy smiled, looked around, and leaned in closer.

"The dead guy is an accountant. Worked for Stone Realty."

"Stone Realty?" I repeated.

"That's what I said. Here's the real kicker to this as I see it. The guy checks in for two days but doesn't take a regular room. He takes the Penthouse Suite. And? The first night he's here I also get a limo come in with the usual uniformed driver, only this rig has some hot looking brunette dressed all in chocolate brown. Head to toe including this matching wide brimmed hat and a very large matching purse. One of them shoulder kind."

My brain suddenly flashed the sight of the hat and the girl but I couldn't quite place it.

Freddy noticed my sudden lapse in concentration and touched my shoulder.

"You okay?" he asked.

"I'm good. Go on," I said. "Continue."

"The broad hands me a twenty, asks if the limo could wait in the driveway and she heads straight to the elevators."

"She took the one that leads to the penthouse?"

"Yes, she did. At this point, I'm trying to run down in my mind who she could possibly be seeing. Errol Flynn isn't in town and this ain't no election year. Then I think about the guy up in the Penthouse but before I can make any sense of it she's back in two shakes, quickly handing me another twenty and a big phony sexy smile, and her and the limo drive off."

"Do you think she killed him?"

"If she did she didn't fuck him to death. Not that fast."

"Did you get a name?"

"She said her name was Dorothy. No. Danielle. That was it. Danielle."

"Danielle? Are you sure?"

"Yes. You don't think she was stupid enough to give me her real name. Do you?""Stranger things have happened. What color was the limo?"

"Black. Long and black."

Again my brain flashed the girl, the wide brimmed hat, and now the long black limo joined the momentary jog of my memory.

"If you think of anything else, call me?"

"Don't I always?"

"Thanks, Freddy."

"I'll keep you posted. I got to go. Duty calls."

Freddy smiled and quickly ran over to another car pulling up to the front. I put the newspaper back on the pile and went inside.

The Polo Lounge was world famous. Every movie star wanting to be seen could usually be found there at any given time. Everyone from kings and queens to your average Joe was always welcome, as long as you knew the rules. They were simple and precise. No photographs. No autographs. No bar tabs. Everyone at the Polo behaved themselves like ladies and gentlemen and when they didn't, they were banned for life.

I spent a lot of time at the Polo and Bobby the bartender knew me by name, knew what I drank, and was like my guy Freddy on the outside. Bobby could always give me the inside scoop if I had a question about anyone coming or going, or if they happened to be spending the night and who they might be spending it with.

I never knew his last name, and never asked.

When I walked through the red padded door the place was pretty quiet, just a few couples spread out in booths or at the bar nursing their expensive cocktails and sharing polite conversation. I placed a ten dollar bill down on the bar, nodded a quick hello to Bobby. He set a Johnny Walker rocks and my change at the end of the bar and went back to pouring a martini for a guy sitting alone on one of the plush bar stools who looked a lot like Alan Ladd in a blue suit and tie but I couldn't say for sure.

I made a beeline for the phone booth back near the rest rooms, closed the folding door but left it slightly open to kill the light above my head. I dropped my nickel and made my phone call without being seen.

I dialed the number for Agent Edwards, who picked up on the very first ring.

"This is Edwards," he said.

"You sound much taller over the phone," I joked.

He laughed.

"How did we make out?" I asked.

"You were right. Broken glass and some red wine trace right where you said."

"Are they going to back off? Give me two days?"

"As a courtesy to me and the FBI. Yes."

"Good. They think I might be playing the lot of you, though. Right?"

"Yes. They do."

"They're LA detectives. They think like LA detectives."

"They just can't figure any of this out. They're frustrated."

"I told you us working together would be mutually beneficial. Thanks for stepping up for me. I owe you one."

"How are things going on your end?" he asked. "Are you making any progress? Will two days be enough?"

"I can't say for certain. Not yet."

I suddenly heard voices coming from the rest room area and as I instinctively turned to look, I saw Quentin Thayer walking casually arm in arm with a strikingly beautiful blonde woman.

"Son of a bitch," I said.

"What is it?" asked Agent Edwards.

"Hold on. I'm watching a familiar face walking to the bar."

"Who?"

"Quentin Thayer."

"Is he alone?"

"Quentin is never alone. Not when it comes to beautiful women."

I watched Quentin shake a few more hands as he and the blonde made their way back to the bar.

"I think we just caught ourselves a break, my friend," I said.

"What do you mean?" Agent Edwards asked.

"Not sure yet. Stay by your phone and I'll call you the moment I have something."

I hung up the phone and watched as Quentin and the blonde beauty slowly walked out. I walked swiftly to the bar and chugged down my drink.

"Thanks, Bobby," I said and leaving the remainder of my change on the bar, stepped through the red padded door once again and headed out.

I stood in the lobby and saw Quentin deeply kissing the blonde as they waited for their car.

My head suddenly felt like a hand grenade went off when I saw Freddy pull up in a cream colored Chevrolet. It was the same car I had seen at the beach house, parked in the driveway next to the powder blue Mercedes.

Quentin tipped Freddy and he and the blonde got in the Chevy and drove away.

I knew I had to move quickly. The gods had suddenly given me something solid and I wasn't going to let it drive off into the night. I ran out to the driveway as fast as my legs would take me.

"Are the keys in the Hudson, Freddy?" I asked and stuffed a five dollar tip in his hand.

"Under the mat," he said.

I jumped in the Hudson, quickly found the keys, started up the engine, and headed down the long drive.

The gods were still with me as I caught the cream colored Chevy waiting at a red light at the bottom of the hill with another vehicle right behind them. The blonde was snuggled up tightly next to Quentin. I watched through the small windshield of the Hudson and could tell the blonde was going down on Quentin as they waited for the light to change.

The car between us sounded their horn as the light flashed from red to green.

Another grenade suddenly blew across my brain as I remembered the night I too was stopped at a red light next to a certain long black limo with a beautiful topless brunette sitting in the back wearing a wide brimmed chocolate hat and a male uniformed chauffeur in the driver's seat.

"Could it be," I thought. "Could I really have been given such a simple break to put two and two together and have it actually add up to four? Could the blonde in the cream colored Chevy somehow and in some bizarre way be the same brunette I had seen that night in the limo and was she also the one that stuck me and put me out for several hours back at the beach house...?"

The more I tried to add things up and put them together, the more questions kept running through my mind.

Was Quentin now a new target or was he an intricate player in this entire thing too?

What was the motive here?

Why was the accountant killed?

If I was being made the fall guy for Barbieri's murder, then Rachel had to be the one orchestrating everything. She was the only link I could see so far looping all of this together like a tight knit sweater.

The Chevy turned right, the car between us turned immediately left, and I now had a clear view of Quentin and the resurfacing blonde in their cream colored Chevy, figuring they must be heading to Quentin's palatial home in the Bel Air Estates.

I was still sorting questions and adding up numbers in my head when it occurred to me just how Rachel Stone Barbieri, the woman in the yellow dress, might fit into this equation.

I was confident the answer would come, and knew that when it did, I had better be ready or this whole affair could come crashing down on my head.

Hard and fast.

Quentin pulled up to the Estates guard station at the gate and quickly passed the Chevy through. I took a deep breath, slowly pulled up to the gate and rolled my window down.

I frantically searched my brain to come up with some believable story as to why I had to be in Bel Air on this particular night but again, the gods came to my immediate rescue.

"Mr. Atwater? Good evening, sir. You got a new car?" asked the guard at the gate.

As luck would have it, he was the same guard I had seen and spoken to several times when I had worked the case for Quentin. I recognized his face straight away but for the life of me could not remember his name.

"I did," I blurted out blindly.

"Working with Quentin again? Keeping a private eye out for him?" he asked grinning broadly.

I smiled and laughed slightly pretending to enjoy his little joke.

"As a matter of fact? I am," I lied and then added a little intrigue to the entire situation.

"I'll be watching his house tonight. Give the other shift guys the heads up and let me know if any of you happen to see a big brown Dodge come by with a little guy behind the wheel. Dark suit. Dark hair. Okay?"

The guard got so excited with the prospect of being included as an intricate part of my private eye work I thought he was going to wet himself.

"Will do, Mr. Atwater. Will do," he exclaimed, taking down the info on a pad near his desk and waving me through.

"We'll keep an eye out," he said as I drove the Hudson past him.

I knew exactly where Quentin's house was and quietly parked beneath some trees where I had a bird's eye view of his place and the next door neighbor's.

The Barbieri house was completely dark, and only one light shined from the downstairs over at Quentin's. Then that light went out, and a few seconds later a light from an upstairs room, which I remembered being Quentin's bedroom, suddenly came on.

A few moments passed and Quentin's house went dark.

I sat there in the Hudson and stared at the cream colored Chevy sitting in Quentin's driveway, my mind wandering back to the night when I sat at that red light next to the long black limo.

I saw the brunette clearly in my mind, her full naked breasts swaying nicely as her arms and hands played with the wide brimmed hat and her eyes stared forward at the uniformed driver wearing the chauffeur's hat.

Another hand grenade exploded across my eyes, causing me to sit up suddenly in the dark and accidently hitting the car horn.

For a brief second, a small partial half of an instant, I also clearly recognized the face of the man behind the wheel.

The face belonged to Quentin Thayer.

The picture of the driver had been stuck in a small spot in my brain and now that picture had become completely clear to me. I was certain it was Quentin behind that wheel because the memory told me that there, in the brief light of that evening, and in that tiny mid second, Quentin Thayer did something that put it all into clarity.

Quentin Thayer did my signature move.

As he looked over at me he slowly wiped his lower lip with his right forefinger, probably in a failed attempt to hide his face, but that one instant frame suddenly seemed to me like some huge still life movie poster photo with the famous Quentin Thayer playing the small role of some rich topless brunette's limo driver.

"Son of a bitch," I muttered.

The sound of the car horn must have spooked the neighbors because suddenly all kinds of lights began coming on down the block, including those in Quentin's driveway.

I started up the Hudson and drove off into the night.

More questions raced through my mind. The motive had to be money but Quentin and Rachel had money. Lots of money.

Their play was quite involved which told me their objective must be something very big and equally involved and for whatever reasons, Enzo Barbieri was in their way. And the fact that I was still up and running told me now I was in their way too.

The thought made me instinctively reach and check that my .38 was still in its proper place. It was and I had a sneaking suspicion I would be using it in the very near future.

CHAPTER FOURTEEN

Special Agent Edwards sat in his small apartment drinking a cold beer, staring hard at all the information he had pieced together on Stone Realty, Enzo Barbieri, his beautiful wife Rachel, and the unfortunate accountant, Ernest Hollowell, found dead at the Beverly Hills Hotel.

Edwards had been extremely precise in his digging, sticking only to articles that could be factually verified. Once he had gotten the go ahead from the front office to take a hard look at Stone Realty and the people working behind those closed doors, especially Enzo Barbieri, he knew he was clearly onto something very big.

At first glance, Stone Realty appeared to be exactly what they declared to the world they were: A company dedicated to the rebuilding of Europe after years of horrific war, and establishing America as the number one power in the world.

The Fascists and the Nazis were gone and the so-called Democratic way of life was now to become the new norm.

Or so it seemed.

All pieces of the Stone Realty puzzle were up there on the board, but the picture didn't make sense until the unfortunate plane crash that killed Jonas Stone. Then Enzo Barbieri stepped into the driver's seat, taking over complete control of the business and the families' finances.

Agent Edwards had tons of information on Enzo Barbieri as well as the wheeling and dealings done by Rachel's father, Jonas Stone, over his forty-five year career working with the elite rich and power-hungry wealthy of Europe and the United States.

It appeared that the defeat of Adolf Hitler and his Nazi regime finally gave the United States the number one position and number one say in how the spoils of war were to be divided up between the allied forces that pulled together to end World War II.

Jonas Stone knew this all too well, and was one of the chief orchestrators among that wealthy inner circle defining how the world would operate for the next hundred years or more.

Russia and China were not to be trusted, and the powers that be knew it would take at least fifty or sixty years for these extremely poor backward countries to either catch up to the new fast-paced world economy or suffer their own destruction from within.

Stone Realty pretended to be a company hell-bent on rebuilding Europe and creating housing in America for returning soldiers looking to start living the good life. The reality was that Jonas Stone, together with several other extremely wealthy individuals, were dividing up the planet, controlling the world's wealth and its economy; creating a strong world-wide military force and a secret intelligence network to constantly monitor anyone or any faction deemed a threat to their new world order, instantly crushing that opposition without the world knowing the reasons.

Special Agent Edwards looked into the major corporate holdings around the world. About twenty or so names kept rising to the top of the list, with Stone Realty being the one constant name connected monetarily with each and every one he looked at.

"Could it be coincidence?" questioned Agent Edwards.

He thought not.

As he stared at his board he could see how countries were disappearing and corporate holdings were becoming the new power structure. It was if an invisible veil of corporate greed and power had wrapped the world up and was now theirs to totally control.

In the midst of all this rebuilding, Jonas Stone made a fatal mistake. Jonas became disagreeable to the group. He lost vision. Every new order of business had to fatten the pockets of Stone Realty first, or he would simply vote against anything that wasn't in his best interests or the interests of Stone Realty.

Jonas Stone simply became too greedy, demanding too much power and control to oversee this new order.

It appeared to Agent Edwards that Enzo Barbieri, a handsome man from an extremely wealthy Italian family, was deliberately but cautiously sent by the powers that be to step into this American family, wine and dine Jonas' beautiful daughter, Rachel, win her heart and marry her. Once Jonas was out of the picture, Enzo would take over the reins at Stone Realty, maintaining the status quo and the delicate balance to keep the new planet order running as they all saw fit.

Barbieri met Rachel at his uncle's estate in Milan during one of the bi-yearly meetings the group held. He was so overwhelmingly charming that sparks between them occurred almost immediately, and the two lovers were married that following summer.

It was clearly the wedding of the year, costing several hundred thousand dollars, attended by people of extreme wealth and power flying in from all around the world, with many well-known actors, actresses, producers and directors from Hollywood; including the famous womanizer, Quentin Thayer.

It was likely at the wedding that Barbieri and Quentin became acquainted, which possibly led to the two becoming neighbors at their affluent Bel Air Estates. Agent Edwards wasn't completely sure of the validity of this thought, but scrutinizing the photos of Quentin kissing the new bride, shaking Barbieri's hand, and sharing a drink with Jonas Stone convinced him to believe it was entirely probable.

Agent Edwards was checking into one more fact concerning Quentin Thayer and the late Jonas Stone, and was patiently waiting for a phone call to provide the necessary verification he needed.

Once the call came in, he was looking forward to sharing that little tidbit and everything else placed up on his board with Patrick.

He knew that Patrick was a straight shooter, a good man, and a man that could be trusted to share any information he had gathered. They both were looking for the same thing.

They wanted to reveal the truth.

Both men were formulating their own theories on how and why a top notch accountant had mysteriously died in a fancy hotel, while the new owner of one of the richest companies in the world was found in a small beach house with a bullet in his forehead, his cock waving in the ocean air, and the construction of an elaborate scheme to make it look like Patrick Miles Atwater was the man responsible.

Agent Edwards hadn't shared his theory with Patrick yet, but he believed that when Jonas Stone and his wife were tragically killed in a plane crash and Barbieri neatly stepped in to take over control of Stone Realty, the powers that be realized they might have made a mistake and now had a slight flaw in their ingenious little plan.

That flaw was Rachel Stone Barbieri.

Like father. Like daughter.

Rachel was the epitome of the beautiful spoiled brat. She knew her family was very wealthy, but was always kept in the dark about the actual numbers associated with her family's fortune, numbers that were enormously huge and growing larger on a day-to-day basis.

When Rachel's father suddenly died, Barbieri's attitude towards Rachel had clearly changed, just as she had told Patrick. Barbieri became more secretive, more unavailable, and seemed to be working more hours a week than he had ever worked while Jonas was alive.

So Agent Edwards surmised that Rachel secretly enrolled Ernest Hollowell, the trusted family accountant, to look into the business practices now controlled by her Italian husband and to report that information back to her. When she finally saw the real numbers associated with Stone Realty, the full extent of the true worth and world-wide holdings, she was flabbergasted by its immensity. She decided to step in and take some action of her own.

This fortune was family money. Her family. Her heritage.

Her blood.

Her family fortune was not going to be handed over to some rich Italian wearing expensive suits, pretending to be something he clearly was not, thinking he could now control her and a fortune of such magnitude simply through marriage.

Rachel was not going to let that kind of money slip away from her.

Not ever.

Whether she knew Stone Realty was also a large part of an inner circle of powers that be in the new world order didn't figure into her thinking, nor did it matter to her.

Rachel Stone Barbieri didn't want to become a queen and rule the world. She wanted to live like the queen that she considered herself.

And if Enzo Barbieri was planning to prevent that, she could not let that happen.

Agent Edwards nodded his head at the rationale of this scenario and swigged down the last few gulps of his beer. He knew Patrick would most likely agree with his theory. They were becoming a good working team at discovering the truth.

Agent Edwards grabbed another cold beer, popped the top with a bottle opener, glanced over at the phone, and waited for it to ring.

A loud knock sounded at his front door and by the sound Agent Edwards could tell that it was definitely what people called the policeman's knock.

Three raps in succession with all three as strong and loud as the first.

Agent Edwards opened the door and found Detective Blaine standing there still wearing his hat, coffee stained tie and wrinkled suit, holding up two paper containers of suds from the Gold Cup Bar from across the street.

"I come bearing gifts," he said. "May I?"

"Come on in," Agent Edwards said and closed the door as the detective stepped inside.

"I assumed as an officer of the law you drank beer."

"I do."

Agent Edwards raised his bottle and nodded yes. Detective Blaine put one container in the small fridge and opened the other, touching it to Agent Edwards' bottle.

"Skoal," he said, taking a big gulp and wiping the foam from his top lip.

Detective Blaine let out a huge burp from somewhere deep down in his throat and smiled.

"Damn, that's cold. And good. I wanted to stop by and have a little sit down with you."

"A sit down," the agent repeated.

"Yeah," he continued. "My partner and I just finished speaking with Rachel Barbieri. Questioned her about her dead husband."

"And?" Agent Edwards asked. "Was she cleared?"

"No. We spoke to her for over three hours. And? We got nothing out of her except that she loved her husband and thinks your new friend Atwater is good for this."

"You know that's not true. Right?" Agent Edwards asked and took a good long swig of his beer.

"We know. It's all too pat. We see that. We also thought if we worked together with you and Atwater, we could wrap this up before we have to start dealing with high-priced lawyers explaining to us why their client is unavailable."

Detective Blaine looked at Agent Edwards' work on the board.

"Jesus Christ. You got everything up there except for the kitchen sink. All that there, Special Agent Edwards, is extensive and impressive. When you do your homework, you really do your homework."

"Thank you," said Agent Edwards. "I like to be thorough."

"This is beyond thorough. Do you want to give me the run-down?"

"I can, being we will be working together. Have a seat."

Detective Blaine grabbed a kitchen chair, straddled it like he was riding a horse, tipped back his hat and took another swig of beer as Agent Edwards began outlining his theory.

"This? Detective Blaine? Is all about money. Big time family money."

"It always is. Ain't it?" said the smiling detective. "Lots of money and some beautiful broad wanting to get her hands on it no matter what it takes or who gets in her way."

"Yes," agreed Agent Edwards and continued explaining his theory.

CHAPTER FIFTEEN

I parked the big Hudson in its usual spot across the street from the Sultan Arms. I knew Rachel would have some new plan prepared now that she was aware I was still running around town with my .38 intact.

I gave the street a quick look and went inside.

It felt good to be in familiar surroundings. I no sooner threw Betty's car keys down and loosened my tie when a light-handed knock tapped at the door. Briefly, I considered it was Agent Edwards standing outside in the hall, waiting to tell me he had wrapped up this whole grab bag, nailed the players cold, and was now coming by to celebrate with a bottle of Johnny Walker Scotch or some ice cold champagne.

But I knew better.

This was it.

It was show time and I knew I had to be ready and focused.

By now the new plan had been put into place. I was about to become the number one star in this second attempt to position me where they wanted. I took a deep breath and opened the door, prepared for whatever was about to come my way.

There she stood.

Rachel Stone Barbieri.

In the flesh.

"Hello, Mr. Atwater. May I come in?" she asked.

Her hair and makeup were perfectly placed with just the right accents to give off a subtle sexy glow from the single light fixture above her head. She quickly turned to the left and looked down the hallway as if someone was following her. I could tell she was trying to push for a fast entry, so I opened the door wider and let her step inside.

"Come in," I said and quickly shut the door.

As she walked past me, I caught that slight hint of vanilla that seemed to follow her wherever she went.

She wasted no time and began her hustle straight away.

"Enzo is dead, Mr. Atwater. He was murdered at some beach house. I've been at the police station answering all kinds of questions."

I did my best to play out my part.

"They don't suspect you, do they?" I asked.

"No. They think you killed him."

"Me?" I answered with a damn good surprised expression and even threw in my signature move indicating deep thought and concern by running my fore finger across my lip. "That's rich but the joke is on them. I didn't do it."

She pretended right back, softening her tone as if she had just found a wounded puppy.

"I know you didn't do it," she said and lightly touched my shoulder. "I hired you to watch my husband, not to kill him. If I thought for a moment you did this, I wouldn't have come here. I didn't want to go back to my house or to some hotel. I didn't want to be alone either. Whoever killed Enzo might want me dead, too. I'm frightened, Mr. Atwater. Very frightened."

She was good.

She was very good.

She sighed heavily and stepped in a little closer to me. I gently grabbed her with two hands and looked into her face.

"Don't worry," I said. "You're safe here."

"I know I am," she said. "But you're not. The police are going to come here and arrest you."

"Arrest me?" I said pretending to show concern. "We should go. But where?"

She pretended to give my statement some thought.

"I have a cabin up in Big Bear. We could go there. You can stay until we figure this all out. But we have to leave. We have to leave now."

So there it was.

A quick trip to Big Bear was the new play and the overly concerned Rachel Stone Barbieri was going to deliver me up like some fatted cow going to slaughter.

I decided not to make it easy for her and see how far she was willing to go to turn her little scheme around to her favor.

"Look," I said. "I want to be straight with you. I didn't kill your husband. Whoever did kill him went to a lot of trouble to make it look like I did. If the police are going to arrest me I'm not worried as long as you are safe. I may need a good expensive lawyer to prove myself out of all this, but if anything happened to you in the process I could never forgive myself."

She looked at me intently, appearing to listen to every word, but I could see she was just pretending; waiting for her moment to turn it all around again.

"Let's go up to the cabin. You and I. Now. And together we can figure this out. Please? I'm so scared."

She began to shake slightly and suddenly pulled me in with a warm hug, practically pressing every inch of her entire body into mine.

Then she slowly looked up into my face, and with this half-pleading smile across her lips, she kissed me.

I kissed her back and let her decide when we should finally stop. She was clearly pulling out all the stops.

A few moments passed before she lifted her face from mine and whispered like we would be in mortal danger if we spoke in normal voices.

"Please?" she pleaded. "Let's go. Now."

She gave an outstanding Oscar-winning performance and I was thoroughly enjoying myself, knowing full well what this woman and her cohorts were capable of if I gave them an opportunity.

I had to play it all out before some other poor sap got himself murdered, but I also knew going up that mountain with her was exactly what had to happen if I was to find the truth of why Enzo Barbieri and his hard-working accountant had met their untimely deaths. From this point on, I was the main player in their game and they were not going to let me fall by the way side.

Not a second time.

In my head, I began devising a plan when my phone suddenly rang.

"Don't answer it," she pleaded. "It might be the police or the people that killed my husband."

I reached out and gently touched her cheek. She responded by pressing her hand into mine.

"It's all right," I said. "I'm expecting a call."

"You are?" she asked, and I could detect a slight hint of worry in her eyes.

"Yes," I said.

I stepped back, gave her my best reassuring grin, and picked up the phone.

"This is Atwater," I said.

"This is Edwards. I'm here at my place with Detective Blaine and I've got two things you need to hear."

"I'm listening," I said.

"Your actor friend, Quentin Thayer is originally from Wales, not Brooklyn like his publicist wants everyone to believe. Twenty years ago, before he came to America and became a famous movie star, he did a two-year stretch in England for embezzlement while working for Jonas Stone. Stone was the one that got him out of jail and into the United States. I just got a confirmation on the phone and dialed you right away."

"Interesting."

"Detective Blaine tells me Rachel Stone says you're the one good for her husband's murder. She also said she thinks you have a major hard-on for her. He's not buying it. If she shows up watch your back."

"Too late for that," I said, hoping Agent Edwards would pick up the hint.

He did.

"She's already there?" he asked.

"Yes," I said.

"You need to get away from her."

"Not yet," I said.

Standing there listening to Agent Edwards' words, I finally put all the pieces of the Stone Realty jigsaw puzzle into place. Quentin and Rachel were in this up to their eyeballs right alongside their little blonde friend, whoever she was, and what I had to do was to get them to spill it all out.

At the same moment, I knew Agent Edwards would wonder what I was talking about but I had to keep playing along, letting

Rachel think she was still in total control of me and what they had planned for me.

"What?" I suddenly asked frantically. "When?"

"What are you talking about?" asked a confused Agent Edwards.

"Are you certain?" I asked.

Now totally perplexed, Agent Edwards answered.

"Certain about what? Quentin Thayer or Rachel Stone?" he asked.

"Thanks for the heads up," I said and quickly hung up the phone.

"What is it?" Rachel asked.

"I have a friend down at the police precinct," I lied. "You were right. The police are on their way here to arrest me for the murder of your husband. We do need to get out of here. Fast."

"We'll take my car," she said.

I nodded in agreement and we went out the door.

CHAPTER SIXTEEN

Agent Edwards hung up the phone and stared for a few moments at the cast of characters up on his board. Detective Blaine broke the momentary silence.

"What is it?" he asked. "You and this Atwater have something?"

"Rachel Stone Barbieri is at his apartment."

"Right now?" he asked.

"Yes."

"That's not good."

"He didn't come right out and say it but when I mentioned he should watch his back if she showed up, he and said it was too late for that. We should get over there right away."

"And do what? Arrest her for being rich and beautiful?"

"Of course not. But I just think I, I mean we? Should be watching his back. That's all."

"No need to do that. Atwater is a big boy. He knows what he's doing and he can handle himself. And besides, just for your information? We already have eyes on him."

Agent Edwards was surprised but still concerned for Patrick's safety.

"Eyes? Whose eyes?" he asked.

"Look? Thanks to you and the FBI, we agreed to give Atwater two days, but that didn't mean we wouldn't watch his every move in the process. Manny and I have our police photographer, Butch, staking out his place. If anything gets odd or crazy he'll call in the cavalry."

"Has Butch ever done any surveillance? There is a certain art to it."

"The kid is green as hell but he's not stupid. He knows the drills. He's been dying to do some actual police work instead of taking pictures of dead people every other day. We thought this could be a good start for him."

"A good start? Is he reliable?" asked Agent Edwards.

"Very reliable. And very conscientious," answered Detective Blaine. "He'll do fine. Let's go grab a bite to eat. I'll have my partner Manny meet us at Atwater's in say, half an hour, and we'll check it out. Sound like a plan you can live with?"

Agent Edwards relaxed somewhat and suddenly realized how hungry he had become.

"Okay. There's a good diner over on Third."

"Perfect."

"My treat," offered Detective Blaine.

Agent Edwards grabbed his car keys.

"I'll drive," he said as they walked out.

Outside, heading to the big Dodge, a black two-door Chevy pulled up and out jumped Butch the photographer.

"What the hell are you doing here?" asked Detective Blaine.

"I'm reporting in," replied Butch.

"Reporting in?" asked Detective Blaine. "Haven't you heard of a telephone?"

"I knew you were here but I didn't have the phone number. I was thinking on the drive over someone should invent those wrist type walkie-talkies like Dick Tracy uses. It would really speed up communications. Don't you think?"

Detective Blaine couldn't believe his ears. He sighed heavily and looked over at Agent Edwards.

"One day doing actual police work and he thinks he's Dick Tracy. What's going on at Atwater's?"

"He left with some woman in a brand new lemon-colored Buick," answered Butch.

"A lemon-colored Buick?" repeated Detective Blaine. "You didn't think to follow them? Find out where they were going?"

"I was going to, but Detective Munoz told me to keep an eye on Atwater's apartment."

"So you came here?" asked Detective Blaine.

"To report in, sir. Tell you what I observed. Detective."

Agent Edwards stepped into the conversation with a question.

"Did you get the license number on the Buick?"

Butch quickly reached in his top shirt pocket and took out a small pad.

"I did, sir. Yes," he answered and read from the small page.

"California plate. Had proper 48 tags. Reading Six, Victor, Eight, One, Two, Four. Sir."

Detective Blaine took the small sheet of paper, glanced at it quickly, stuffed it into his pocket and looked at Agent Edwards.

"Let's get over to the precinct and put out an all vehicle alert and maybe we'll get lucky."

"What are the odds?" asked Agent Edwards.

"They're not the best," said Detective Blaine. "But for now it's a shot we have to take. The car could be anywhere and off into any direction."

Agent Edwards nodded his agreement and headed to his car.

"What do you want me to do now, sir," asked Butch.

Detective Blaine reached in his pocket, took out a ten dollar bill, and handed it to Butch.

"Meet us back at the precinct but stop and get three turkey sandwiches, three fries with lots of catsup, and three large coffees. Black. Get something for yourself too if you'd like."

"Thanks sir. Sorry for screwing up."

"You didn't screw up. You followed orders. You did okay, Butch. You did okay."

"I did?"

"Absolutely. You got the license number. That was good work. Go get the chow and I'll talk to the big bosses upstairs and look into that wrist watch communicator thing and see what we can come up with." answered Detective Blaine.

Butch smiled broadly.

"Really?" he asked.

"Fuck no. But it is a good idea, kid. Get a move on."

"Yes sir!"

Agent Edwards started up the Dodge, Detective Blaine went to his car, and Butch stuffed the ten spot in his pocket; and ran over to his vehicle.

Agent Edwards hoped the lemon-colored Buick would be found quickly before Patrick found himself up against it all with no back-up.

Two murders.

Agent Edwards did not want to hear about a third. He knew they were playing a very dangerous game with very dangerous people and Patrick was clearly heading into harm's way.

CHAPTER SEVENTEEN

The drive up the mountain went relatively quickly.

Rachel did most of the talking. She told me again how she and Enzo first met and what a true European gentleman he was.

At first.

Enzo always wore the best, bought the best, and only dated wealthy, beautiful women. He seemed quite taken by Rachel when they first set eyes on each other and although Enzo's family was extremely well off compared to us blue-collar working stiffs, his old European money was not anywhere near the numbers that the Stone family carried. Having a few million in the bank compared to several hundred million around the world is like comparing fresh-picked apples to old boxed oranges, only in Enzo's case the oranges had all turned bad. Marrying into the Stone dynasty was a major step up for him and also for his family's seemingly paltry coffers.

Rachel began using a certain strained tone into her voice as she went on and on about how Enzo had completely changed once he was handed the reins to the family fortune, and no matter what she said or tried to do, he remained distant and aloof towards her. According to her, his attitude became so unbearable it forced her to come to me for help.

Rachel also said her dear departed father, Jonas, had stepped on a lot of people's toes putting the family fortunes into high gear with his worldwide real estate holdings, numerous business interests, and major government contracts. The Stone family were definitely wealthy world-class players, and she tried to steer me to thinking that possibly her father's plane crash was not an accident, and that Enzo and Hollowell's murders were most likely connected by unknown persons trying to destroy, undermine, or take over what Jonas Stone had worked so hard to create for so many years.

Then she said something really interesting.

"People with that kind of money and power can get away with just about anything they choose," she said.

I pretended to be listening but I was really hearing her open confession as to how the rich and privileged live out their lives. They think of themselves as an entitled people.

Almost in a royal sense.

Above reproach.

How dare anyone get in their way. These people had power and money and could do whatever it was they decided. And if anyone, rich or poor, got in their way, they were simply removed from the equation.

Remove them through whatever means necessary, and remove them quickly if that was the last ditch option to solve their dilemma.

I was not about to allow her or anyone working alongside her to place me in that position. I was not about to be removed from anyone's equation and a large part of me was looking forward to getting up to that cabin and bringing everything to a head.

She smiled slightly again as we passed a road sign reading "Big Bear 13 miles." I smiled back and casually checked the side view mirror to see if anyone might be following us.

"There's a little mom and pop market at the top of the hill," she said. "I'll run in and get some supplies for a few days."

"Great," I said and noticed the full moon peeking over the mountain top. "Do you need some cash?"

"No. Your money is no good in this car, Mr. Atwater."

"Call me Patrick. Please?" I asked.

She glanced at me and smiled and I could tell by the look in her eyes through the moonlight she thought she had won me over for sure.

"Patrick," she said and reached out and touched my knee. "I'm glad we are doing this."

"Me too," I lied and touched her hand firmly.

She held my hand, squeezing it tightly for a brief moment and then grabbed the steering wheel with both hands.

"I'm definitely going to need a good lawyer," I said. "No matter how I turn this around in my head, I am going to need some strong legal assistance. Somebody sharp. The police are not going to go easy on me. That's for certain."

"Don't worry. We'll get you whatever you require. My word on that," she replied.

I did my best to show concern and mild relief at her heartwarming offer of coming to my much needed rescue.

"Thank you," I said.

We rode in silence for the next few minutes until the car reached the top of the hill and I could see the bright red letters of the Hilltop Market sign.

Hilltop Market was a small building and there were no other cars in the lot as Rachel drove in and parked under the single street light.

"I won't be long," she said, quickly jumping out of the car and striding into the market.

I watched her brisk walk to the front entrance and could tell she clearly did not want me inside the market.

My curiosity got to me and I quietly got out of the car and approached the large glass front window to look inside.

The store was small with only two short rows of food choices. There were no shopping carts, just small hand held baskets so anyone staying a few days could stock up on the necessary odds and ends. Wine and beer were offered from a tall glass cooler which also held several bottles of champagne. This might have been a mom and pop place, but the clientele were clearly the rich and famous set and "roughing it" on this part of the hill was not my definition.

An older couple stood behind the counter next to the cash register and I assumed they were the owners. I looked down the aisle and saw a phone booth at the rear of the store. My eyes caught Rachel walking straight to the back to the telephone, and she sat down and quickly closed the folding door.

Obviously, Rachel was alerting her team. She was letting them know she had me where they needed me.

I decided to take every precaution and do everything she was about to ask me to do. I quietly stepped back, unseen by mom and pop, and went back to the car to wait.

I knew I had to stay sharp. This was not a time to lose focus. I took a deep breath and tried to remain calm.

About ten minutes went by before Rachel came out of the store carrying two brown shopping bags, one with a long loaf of freshly-baked bread sticking out the top. I jumped out and took one of the bags.

"Get everything we need?" I asked.

"We're good. For a few days at least," she replied.

We set the bags in the back seat, she started up the car, and we headed into town. The hilltop town consisted of one stop light and two main streets converging, lined with several high-end clothing shops, a small hotel called Bigsbys, two local bars, an ice cream shop, a steak house called Sally's, and one Texaco gas station, that sat about a block and a half down the street from the traffic light.

Rachel made a left turn and headed up a winding two-lane road edged with numerous fir and pine trees on both sides. We came to a dirt driveway near a light blue mail box with large black letters that read SB. I assumed it stood for Stone Barbieri and wondered why they didn't have the actual names written out for the world to see. Rachel turned into the driveway and followed a single dirt road for about two minutes until we came into a large clearing of manicured lawn, a circular drive with a small fountain at the center, and a two-story A framed house made of blond wood, stone, and large panes of glass.

I had to admit, her so called "cabin" was impressive.

"Nice little place," I said.

"Wait 'til you see the view," she answered and parked the car close to the fountain.

I grabbed both bags while Rachel unlocked the front door with a large gold key she took from her pocket and we went inside.

"Stay where you are and I'll turn on the electric," she said and opened a small door that went down three steps.

I tried to adjust my eyes to the darkness when suddenly I heard a loud click and the small lamp in the living room came on.

A wooden staircase on the right led to two upstairs bedrooms next to each other and divided by a large bathroom that I assumed could be accessed from either side. The downstairs area was spaciously open with a floor-to-ceiling stone fireplace. Three dark green love seats sitting on a Persian rug formed a large U in the room, and in the rear was a small kitchen off to one side, boxed in by a compact counter with three barstools.

The entire back half of the house was all wood and glass and I found myself drawn to it right away, as if some wooded forestry force had suddenly compelled me to stand and look outside.

The view was spectacular, to say the least.

Standing there you could see the entire west end of the valley in all its greenery, and looking out beyond the tree line you could see the faraway lights of Los Angeles.

"You were right about this view," I said.

"It was the view and also the feeling of privacy that made me buy this place the first time I saw it. I thought Enzo and I could come here, unwind, maybe do some skiing in the winter."

Her words and voice both trailed off and she stared silently out the window.

. "We never did."

Rachel turned to me, took both bags, smiled, and went into the kitchen.

"Are you hungry?" she asked as she began to empty the two bags and put things away.

"I'm not hungry, but I could use a drink," I said.

"The bar is under the stairs. Here. You'll need this."

Rachel slid a small bag of ice onto the counter and smiled.

I smiled back and loosened my tie.

"You have thought of everything."

"I'll have a Scotch. Neat," she said.

I walked to the bar, grabbed two glasses, and poured the Scotch.

I turned with a glass in each hand and was surprised to suddenly see her standing directly in front of me. She stared up into my eyes, slowly stepped forward, ran her hands down my arms, grabbed my wrists gently, and with very little effort softly pushed my hands back against the small ledge on the wall and kissed me.

My instant thought was to keep reminding myself no matter what, this was all part of the act, part of the plan, and her attempt with this seduction process was just that.

A con.

A play.

A means to her end. And to mine if I didn't stay sharp.

Her body pressed deeply into mine and I quickly let go of the two glasses set on the shelf and kissed her back.

She instantly responded to me, and our hands began exploring each other's bodies as we pressed together under the stairs.

"Such a long time since I've been with a man," she whispered. "Am I being too forward?"

She was playing her part extremely well and even though my mind was not buying one thing she said to me, my body responded.

"Not at all," I said and kissed her again. "I understand completely."

She pulled back for a moment, touched my cheek with her hand and looked into my face.

"Let me show you the upstairs," she said.

She smiled slightly and I could tell she thought what she had working with me was clearly getting the job done and keeping her future plans for me intact.

"Bring our drinks."

I grabbed the drinks and followed her up the stairs.

I didn't get a sense that there might be someone else in the house or possibly waiting for us in the master bedroom. I was quite certain we were still alone. I kept playing the obedient lover with one eye on her and the other watching for anything out of the ordinary or the unexpected.

I followed Rachel into the master bedroom.

The room was a good size and had a double bed with a brass headboard sitting against a floor-to-ceiling mirrored wall, giving anyone a total view of any space in the room.

Rachel turned on one small lamp, walked over and stood in front of me, and with her eyes locked on mine, took her drink from my hand, drank every bit straight down, and reached up and kissed me again.

"Do you like the room?" she asked.

I pretended to notice.

"I do. Yes," I replied and slowly sipped my Scotch while trying to listen for any activity that might be playing inside or out besides the one right in front of me.

"The mirrored wall was my idea," she said.

"Nice touch."

Rachel smiled, pulled off her sweater, unhooked her bra and let it fall to the floor, and as I stood gazing at her full breasts, she unbuttoned her slacks and slowly pulled the side zipper down.

"I need a hand getting these off," she said and laid down on the bed.

I quickly swallowed the remainder of my Scotch, got down on my knees in front of her and slid her slacks down past her ankles, tossing them onto the floor next to the bra.

"Panties, too," she said, sighing as she rolled her head and neck slightly.

The strong scent of the vanilla cream she wore rushed through my head and nostrils as I grabbed her damp silk panties, and pulled them off and flung them onto the floor. Her vagina was very warm and wet to the touch and it was also completely shaved which took me by surprise.

"I've shown you mine. Now you show me yours," she whispered.

I tried my best to hide my real thoughts knowing full well the kind of game she was playing with me, but her seduction was first rate and my body was quick to respond.

I stood up, stepped out of my shoes and trousers and pulled off my shirt in record time but as I reached for my boxer shorts, she quickly sat up onto the edge of the bed and stopped me with her hands.

"Wait. Let me do that," she said.

She could see through the fabric that I was hard as a rock and as she slowly slid my boxers to the floor my Johnson popped up and out and almost poked her in her eye. She laughed, took hold of me with one hand, placed her other hand on a cheek of my ass, and took my erection deep into her mouth.

She was going all out on this one.

Nothing left to chance.

I listened to her breathing and making several humming noises as she slowly took her time with me. Then she stopped, looked up at me, sat back on the bed, and spread her legs out slightly.

I slowly knelt down onto the bed directly in front of her and she gently took hold of my erection and put me inside of her.

"Go very slowly," she said and closed her eyes and placed her hands flat on the bed.

I made love to her exactly as she requested and after about ten minutes of us slowly and silently moving together, she began making a slight moaning sound.

"Oh. Faster now. Please?" she whispered as she reached her mouth up to my right ear.

I could sense she was about to climax and began thrusting inside her, moving faster and harder as we responded to each other.

"Oh. Yes," she said. "Oh god yes. Yes! Yes!"

Suddenly her entire body seemed to constrict and shake as her orgasm shuddered throughout her body and ignited her senses.

"Yes!" she screamed and grabbed both cheeks of my ass, pulling me deeper inside her as my own orgasm suddenly shot out of me like molten lava, making her entire body shake once again, sensing I had come right along with her.

I slowly rolled over and laid next to her, both of us still breathing heavily and trying our best to regain some composure.

We laughed playfully and looked at each other.

"That was wonderful," she said. "Most men don't like to be told what to do when they're making love."

"I've always tried to be a good listener," I replied.

"You are," she said. "You, Patrick Atwater are very good listener, and a very good lover."

I laid there waiting for her to ask me if we should go a second time and wondering if instead she was going to call in the cavalry to get her plan locked up when suddenly, my brain began to get cloudy and my vision started bouncing around like some piece of film not set in the projector correctly.

I began rapidly blinking my eyes, trying to focus as best I could, and my entire body suddenly started to tingle and became unresponsive no matter what I attempted to do.

"Don't be alarmed. You're not dying. You'll only sleep for a little while until we figure out what to do with you," she said and gently brushed my hair off my forehead with her outstretched hand.

"Son of a bitch," I thought to myself.

She was good.

She was very good.

All this time I was thinking I was one or maybe even two steps ahead of her and instead she was ten steps ahead of me, the police, and anyone else trying to bring her down, and now she had me right where she needed me.

I tried to think how she drugged me and it suddenly became crystal clear.

It was the God damn ice.

Somehow she managed to drug the entire bag. She had her Scotch neat and I was so busy being smart and focused that I fell right in with my hard cock hanging out and my dumb eyes wide open but totally unable to see it coming.

She was damn good.

Diabolically good.

I tried to speak as she lay naked beside me, watching the drug take its effect on my brain and body, but I couldn't utter a sound. As I slowly passed into darkness a second time, I hoped I would be waking up at some point to get one more shot at her.

"This next time I would make it stick," I told myself. "This next time I would stop trying to be so God damn smug and smart and get right to the heart of the matter. If I get a next time."

In my drugged state, I was positive that Rachel Stone Barbieri was responsible for two murders and if I got that second chance

I was hoping for, I swore to myself just before blacking out that I would make her pay.

If I got that chance?

If?

The last thing I remembered was her smiling down at me, slowly stepping off the bed, and getting herself into those silk panties lying on the floor.

The blackness waved through me and I was down and out.

CHAPTER EIGHTEEN

Agent Edwards was beside himself. He and Patrick had worked out a good plan to give them a few days to bring the Stone case to a head and now he was sitting in a Los Angeles police station with the two lead detectives running the investigation, while Patrick and Rachel Stone were nowhere to be found.

Detective Munoz and Detective Blaine began to entertain another theory and thought there might be a slight, unexplained, possibility that Patrick had willingly left his apartment with Rachel Stone, not to get some answers but to get on some private plane headed out to god-knows-where.

The detectives had men checking the train stations, the airports, and all the bus schedules but doing that would take time, and as yet no one was coming forward with any leads.

Agent Edwards assured the detectives that Patrick Miles Atwater was in no way selling himself out for any woman, beautiful or otherwise, or for any amount of money she could promise him. Patrick was all about the truth and solving the case. He abhorred murder of any kind. The detectives immediately dropped their notions and agreed with the FBI man, which only made Agent Edwards more concerned for his co-partner and now, his new friend.

"I think she took him somewhere and I think he went along willingly trying to gain her trust," said Agent Edwards. "Do we have a list of properties owned by Rachel and Enzo Barbieri?"

"Are you serious?" asked Detective Blaine.

"Yes, I'm serious," replied Agent Edwards. "Is that a problem?"

"No problem," answered Detective Blaine. "No problem at all."

Detective Blaine looked at Detective Munoz and nodded.

"Butch?" hollered Detective Munoz.

Butch came running into the large room where the three men had most of the information on the deaths of Enzo and Hollowell.

"Yes, Detective?" asked Butch, sipping on a large cup of black coffee.

"Bring in that list we have of real estate holdings on Stone Realty," asked Detective Munoz.

"Seriously?" asked Butch.

"Yes. Special Agent Edwards here wants to look it over."

A large grin washed across Butch's face.

"Okay," said Butch.

Butch left as quickly as he entered and Agent Edwards could tell he was missing something extremely large in the communication.

"All right, detectives. What am I missing? What is it you're not telling me?" asked Agent Edwards.

"Just give us a few seconds, Agent Edwards," said Detective Munoz. "You'll see exactly what you're missing."

Agent Edwards took another bite of his turkey sandwich and grabbed the last cold French fry lying buried in ketchup in its cardboard take-out tray as Butch entered, huffing and puffing from carrying two large cardboard boxes filled with papers. Butch placed the boxes on- the table and took a deep breath.

"Here they are," he said.

Agent Edwards stepped up and looked into the first box which was stuffed with papers in stacks of four and five pages, each describing every property Stone Realty owned outright.

"You have to be kidding me," he said

"I wish I was. But no," said Detective Munoz. "We are not kidding anyone. There are over six thousand properties here all owned by Stone Realty, and that's just the ones in California."

"If we are going on the notion Atwater and Stone are driving somewhere close by," added Detective Blaine.

"If you want to see the ones from the rest of the country, they are in a special room down the hall," said Detective Blaine.

"Jesus," said Agent Edwards. "A room?"

"A filled room," said Detective Munoz.

"Jesus," Agent Edwards repeated.

The FBI had been looking into Barbieri strictly on a surveillance level to observe his comings and goings. Agent Edwards was their lone man on the job and he knew their real estate holdings were extensive, but this, to him, was mind-blowing.

Agent Edwards looked down at the boxes, sighed heavily, and slowly shook his head.

"We left the global holdings locked up back at Barbieri's office," said Detective Munoz. "We have four of our guys going through them now."

"Not that it will help us locate Atwater," said Detective Blaine.

"This is going to be like finding a needle in a haystack, gentlemen" said Agent Edwards.

"You're absolutely right," said Detective Blaine. "Only we won't be finding any needles. Not tonight. Shy of some miracle occurring? We won't be locating Atwater unless he calls one of us directly."

"That might be our only hope at this juncture," said Agent Edwards. "A phone call would simplify everything but that is highly doubtful, and until if and when that phone call might occur, we need to do something. Agreed?"

Both detectives nodded yes and sighed heavily.

"Agreed," said Detective Munoz.

Agent Edwards started looking through the other box of papers, also stacked in bundles of four and five pages each.

"Are you really going to look through these files? Every one of these?" asked Detective Munoz.

"Not me. Us. All of us," replied Agent Edwards. "That is the plan for the moment. I figure we just might get lucky or maybe even create a miracle in the process."

"A miracle? Is that all we need here?" asked Detective Blaine. "You're not asking for much. Are you?"

"I am asking for the impossible. I know. And if we are going to do this we're definitely going to need more coffee. Lots of coffee," said Agent Edwards as he pulled out a stack of papers and began going through them, one by one.

"Butch?" asked Detective Blaine.

"I got it. Four coffees coming up," replied Butch.

"Better make that eight coffees and grab a sack of donuts too," said Detective Munoz.

"On me this time," said Agent Edwards and gave Butch a ten dollar bill.

Detectives Munoz and Blaine each grabbed a stack of papers and began looking through them as Butch left the room.

About a half-hour later Butch returned with the coffees and donuts and proceeded to assist by taking a stack of properties and leafing through them himself.

Detective Munoz smiled nodded his approval at Butch and took a sip of coffee.

"What am I looking for here?" asked Butch.

"Good question," answered Detective Blaine and all heads turned toward Agent Edwards. "What are we looking for here?"

"Let's look at how many properties are, say, in a sixty-mile radius of Atwater's apartment," said Agent Edwards.

"Sounds like a good start," said Detective Munoz. "Would that include Palm Springs?"

"Yes. Definitely," answered Agent Edwards.

"What about Lake Tahoe," asked Butch.

"Too far, I think," said Agent Edwards and began making a separate pile of properties.

All four men knew they were fighting a losing battle and the longer they had to look through the impossible mountains of paper, the more desperate Agent Edwards started to feel for Patrick's safety and the whereabouts of Patrick and Rachel Stone Barbieri.

Agent Edwards' only hope was that Patrick was okay and that he would be calling before the night was through to tell him he had closed the case and had Rachel and whomever tied up in one tight neat package.

He had no idea of how unreachably far that thought was from the actual truth.

Patrick Atwater was in a bad way and there was nothing Agent Edwards, the FBI, or the LAPD could do to help him. Agent Edwards rubbed his eyes and kept searching through the paperwork.

CHAPTER NINETEEN

As I suddenly came to and opened my eyes, I could only see out of one of them. I was lying face down on a pillow and my right eye stuck out just far enough for me to see through the nearby window and notice the light of the single lamp that Rachel had turned on when we first entered the room.

For a second time, I laid there cursing my own stupidity when I suddenly heard the sound of another vehicle arriving, the engine shutting down, and two car doors quickly opening and closing. I was hoping it was Agent Edwards coming to my embarrassing rescue but I threw that thought aside when I became acutely aware that I still couldn't move any muscles in my body. I could roll my eye and breathe but that was all I could muster for the moment.

It was still dark outside and I figured the dose I got from the ice cubes was nowhere near the amount I took at the beach house. I felt glad I was still alive and tried my best to move, but whatever was still running through my veins definitely had total control over me.

I could hear voices, people talking downstairs, but it all sounded like it was coming from inside some large vat of industrial goop. As hard as I struggled to hear, I couldn't make out a word that was being said.

I tried to concentrate solely on moving my body and began taking slow deep breaths, hoping to stimulate some of my muscles and get me moving, but the damn drug would not let go and kept holding me fast.

The mumbling got louder but became more clear, and I could tell whoever it was down there was finally coming up to check on me. I closed my good eye and did my best to act unconscious.

Given my condition it wasn't much of a stretch.

As I laid there naked under the sheet, the door to the bedroom opened and I recognized the male voice.

"Jesus, Mary, and Joseph, Rachel, is he dead?" he asked. "He looks like he's dead."

That male voice was clearly Quentin Thayer. All doubts about his involvement immediately flew out of my head. The motive for this wasn't quite clear yet, but Quentin was definitely number two on the hit parade and just as I was wondering who the third party might be, Rachel gave the answer.

"No," Rachel answered. "I drugged the ice cubes just like Danielle told me."

Danielle? That was the name given to Freddy at the Beverly the night Hollowell was murdered and the same night I got the glimpse of the attractive brunette in the black limo.

I ran down the scenarios and odds in my head.

Two women named Danielle on the same night. One blonde and the other a brunette.

Not likely.

She did give Freddy her real name and she also had to be the blonde at the beach who stuck me with drugs. My players were all present and accounted for, and finally complete in my mind's eye: All the conspirators were in the same room at the same time, with me at either the mercy or the wrath of Rachel Stone Barbieri, Quentin Thayer, and now their little blonde friend with the syringes and all that chemical knowhow, the sweet and deadly Danielle.

Drugs, sex, and money, the three major motives for just about anyone involved in murder and deception.

I wanted to jump up out of the bed, naked or not wouldn't have mattered a pinch to me, and tell all three of them that they were going down for the murders of Enzo Barbieri and the accountant Hollowell, that all their planning and plotting was for naught, but I still couldn't move a damn muscle. I laid there like some Greek statute, naked as a jay bird, surrendering to the fact that all I could do was listen and pretend I couldn't hear a thing.

What I heard was not sitting well with me at all.

"Check his eyes, Danielle," said Rachel.

The blonde stepped over to the bed, pulled my right eyelid up with her thumb and looked closely at my face.

"He's still under," she said and lifted up the sheet that was covering me. "Nice ass for a soon to be dead man. How was he in the sack?"

I couldn't believe my ears. I was going to be their next victim and the two women stood there casually discussing my lovemaking techniques. I wanted to stand up and face them both but then I heard a small crack in their little threesome nutshell.

"You fucked him?" Quentin quickly and angrily interrupted.

"Of course I fucked him," Rachel answered. "I had to get his attention. This guy is smart. He's no dummy."

I noticed I was breathing faster as anger raced through my veins, and tried to slow myself down.

"Dummy or not, I still want to know, how was he?" Danielle asked again.

It became obvious that sex, drugs, and large amounts of money were what these three were all about and if a little extra murder had to be thrown into the mix, then so be it.

"I'll put it this way, Danielle," Rachel said. "When he's gone? I'll miss him."

"You'll miss him?" asked Quentin.

"That's what I said," she replied. "Stop sounding like some wounded puppy. It's annoying, Quentin."

"I'll get the stuff and we'll get this over and done with," Danielle said and tossed the sheet over part of my shoulder.

"The sooner the better," Rachel responded.

Rachel glanced at Quentin, still staring at the bed.

"What's wrong with you, Quentin? You look like your fucking dog just died. My little exercise here with Mr. Atwater got your panties in a bunch? Is that what's put that stupid look on your face, darling?"

"You didn't have to fuck him," Quentin said.

"Yes I did and nobody is ever going to tell me who I fuck or who I choose not to fuck. You got that, Quentin?" she asked.

"I got that," he said. "I just don't like it and I don't like the thought of anyone fucking you except me."

"And Danielle," she added.

"And Danielle," he repeated.

"I can't believe you. Fucking him upsets you but killing him doesn't bother you one bit," she said.

"I'm not the one doing the actual killing," he said.

"You are such an actor, Quentin, so dramatic. Get over your bleeding heart routine right now and come on down stairs. We still have a lot of work to do"

Their voices slowly drifted away and I sensed they had all gone back downstairs.

For whatever reasons, Quentin had become extremely jealous and upset, and the way Rachel responded to him told me what she really was underneath that phony poor-little- rich girl act she had laid out for me and the LAPD detectives.

Talk about actors. Quentin was one of the best in the business but he had nothing over Rachel Stone Barbieri when it came to pretending.

I started running scenarios in my head as to what I needed to do and how quickly I needed to do them when suddenly I heard a slight scratching noise and realized some movement had started to come back into my fingers. I scratched eagerly at the pillow case under my head.

I went back to my deep breathing and tried to stay calm. I heard clearly what Danielle had said and figured it was only a matter of time before she was back to put me down for the big sleep.

I was not going to let that happen.

I felt my toes tingling and knew the drug was finally wearing thin. The stinging of a thousand needles being poked into me began to run up and down my legs, passed through my ass and scrotum, ran straight up my spine, down through my arms and up through my head.

I quietly rolled over onto my back, pulled off the bed sheet and slowly sat up. My entire body kept tingling crazily and my eyes were adjusting to the low light in the room. I took another deep breath, rolled my head and neck, and stood up and stretched out my arms. I knew I had to move quickly and quietly. I grabbed up my clothes lying in a heap on the floor, threw them on including my shoes and socks, and as I looked around the room for some kind of weapon I saw my loaded .38 still in the holster and sitting across the room on a dark leather chair.

I took one step towards the gun when suddenly the bedroom door flew open wide and Danielle and I found ourselves staring directly into each other's eyes.

Glancing down, I noticed right away that Danielle was holding a syringe. She suddenly reacted, raising the syringe to stick me, but I quickly grabbed her wrist with both hands and held the long silver needle up and away from me.

She was a strong woman, and I felt how the drug she gave me earlier had weakened my own strength as we stood there stretching and struggling with each other in silence before she called out.

"Quentin? Rachel?" she yelled. "We have a problem up here!"

She reached out with her other hand and punched me hard across the face. I instantly pulled her into me and gave her a quick head butt. The blow stunned her and she dropped to her knees. I leaned back on my right foot and punched her squarely in the face with a hard right and as I let go, she reeled backwards out of the room and fell onto the small landing at the top of the stairs.

I looked down at her and as she rolled over to look up at me, she realized she had fallen onto the syringe which was now sticking out of her right leg. She looked down at Quentin and Rachel standing frozen in the living room and her mouth began moving up and down as if she was trying to say something, but no sound was coming out. Her eyes rolled back in her head, her body stiffened, and she fell back onto the floor, dead.

I quickly grabbed my .38 and stepped out onto the landing.

"Hey, you two," I said. "I'm coming down. Don't either of you move a muscle."

"Sure pal," Quentin said a little too calmly. "Come on down."

I started down the stairs with my gun in front of me and saw Quentin and Rachel standing silently in front of the gray stone fireplace. I walked slowly and carefully down the stairs, keeping my gun pointed at Quentin.

Quentin slowly raised a gun of his own and held it next to Rachel's head.

"Drop your gun, Atwater, or I'll shoot her," he said.

I got to the bottom of the stairs and kept walking to the back of the couch.

"I mean it. I'll kill her," he warned.

I looked at him and laughed.

"No, you won't," I replied.

"I will! Now drop your gun or I'll fire."

"Drop the act, Quentin. I know all three of you are in this together."

"You don't know anything," cried Rachel. "Do what he says! Please?"

"Let me guess. You are afraid he really will pull that trigger? Is that what has you shaking in your two hundred dollar shoes?"

"Yes. Please. Do what he says!"

"Two actors," I said. "Acting like fools."

"I'm not acting here, Patrick. Put your gun on the coffee table right now or I will shoot her."

"Please," she pleaded. "Don't let him kill me!"

"I'll do you both one better," I said as I pointed my gun at Rachel and fired one round that grazed her shoulder. She instantly dropped to the floor.

"Oh my god," Quentin said. "You've killed her!"

I stepped up close to Quentin, placed my gun to the side of his head and swiftly took the gun from his hand.

"Don't kill me! We have money! Lots of money!" Quentin screamed and cowered slightly away from my gun.

"Shut up, Quentin," yelled Rachel. "Shut your fucking trap and get away from me!"

"You're hurt," he said.

"It's just a scratch."

"Both of you! Sit your asses down. Do it! Now," I demanded.

Quentin and Rachel both sat on the small love seat. Rachel looked at her shoulder and pressed some of her sweater fabric on the wound.

"I think I will need a doctor," she said.

"A head doctor, maybe," I said.

"I mean a medical doctor. This is really starting to hurt."

"Good. You'll get a doctor soon enough," I said and handed Rachel my handkerchief. "Here. Press this on your shoulder. It will do better than that piece of sweater you're using."

"Thank you," she said and pressed the handkerchief onto the wound.

"Your little blonde friend upstairs is dead," I said.

"You killed Danielle?" she asked and pressed the handkerchief harder onto her shoulder.

"No. She killed herself. She fell on that pig sticker she was going to put into me. Which one of you shot Enzo?" I asked.

Rachel and Quentin looked at each other but didn't say a word. I fired another shot into the love seat right next to Quentin's left arm.

"Jesus Christ, Atwater!" screamed Quentin.

"Which one?" I said and fired another round a little closer.

"Danielle!" Quentin said. "It was Danielle! She shot Enzo."

"No, she didn't. She was on her knees working his Johnson. She gave you my gun and you stepped up and put that round in his head. Didn't you?"

Quentin looked at me and didn't speak. I cocked the .38 back.

"Answer me! You shot him!"

"Yes. I shot him. I did it."

"I have to admit you three chumps had a fairly decent plan. But murder has a funny way of becoming extremely messy and those damn complications always have a knack of suddenly popping up out of the blue and getting in the way of dopes like the two of you who think you have all the sordid details neatly worked out. The perfect plan. I have to admit, Rachel, you had me almost buying the entire scenario. The sad looks, that yellow dress. Unfortunately for you, Rachel, hiring me was your first mistake. You should have hired some other gumshoe and maybe your plan would have worked. But the gods were on my side right from the get-go."

"The gods? What the hell are you talking about?" asked Rachel.

"I'm talking about the night your boyfriend here and little blondie killed the accountant, Hollowell. A certain bell captain I know over at the Beverly, his name is Freddy, told me he remembered some good-looking woman all dressed in chocolate brown with a wide brimmed matching hat, who arrived in a black limo with a uniformed driver."

"That's a common occurrence at the Beverly," said Quentin. "Lots of limos and drivers ride through there."

"That is true and that's what you figured, I'm sure. But it was you, Quentin. And little dead blondie in that fancy chocolate get-up. And I know that for a fact, a fact that will be in my final report when all this goes into the record books."

"You don't know a damn thing," said Quentin. "He's bluffing us."

"Shut up, Quentin," she said.

"This is no bluff, Quentin. It was the two of you," I repeated. "You and Danielle. I'm certain of it."

"And you are certain of this? How?" asked Quentin.

"Yes. Please enlighten us," Rachel added.

"A little red light told me, sister" I said.

"A little red light?" asked Quentin. "What red light?"

"Shut up, Quentin," Rachel replied.

"I didn't put it all together at first. The night Hollowell was murdered I was on my way to the valley to see a client. I stopped at a red light on Santa Monica. Right next to this long black limousine. I saw little blondie in the back with her top off playing with that wide brimmed chocolate hat of hers. Beside seeing those breasts bouncing around I saw something else."

"Something else?" asked Quentin.

"Yeah. I looked at the driver for a quick second. And I saw you, Quentin. I saw you sitting behind that wheel wearing that little black cap, and just before the light changed and we all drove off our separate ways? I saw it."

"Saw it? Saw what?" asked Quentin.

"You. Doing my signature move."

"Your signature move?"

"Yeah. You know the one. It's the one you used in that movie you're filming. The one where you play the private eye. I saw you do it the day I came on set to see you. Asking you about Rachel."

"And what exactly is your signature move?" he asked.

"You probably did it to try and hide your face but I saw you do it just the same. It goes like this."

I wiped my lip with my forefinger and smiled at Quentin.

"That's a great story, Atwater, but it won't hold up in a court of law," said Quentin. "You want to prove somebody committed a crime you need proof. Facts. And the facts appear to Rachel and me that you and poor dead Danielle up there are the ones that planned out everything."

"Me and Danielle?" I asked.

"Yes," said Quentin. "We can tell stories, too. Who do you think a jury will believe? A down-on-his-luck nickel-and-dime private dick like yourself, trying to scam America's number one movie star and his beautiful grieving neighbor for money?"

"Okay. If that's how you two want to play this, we can go there. But before leaving this room you're going to tell me what this was all about. You're going to tell me everything and I want the truth."

"You want the truth?" asked Rachel.

"Yes," I said. "From both of you."

"There's so much you don't understand," said Quentin. "So much at stake."

"Shut up, Quentin," said Rachel.

Quentin raised his hands and bowed his head.

"Listen to me, Atwater. I'll give you the truth. Here it is. The truth is as easy as ABC, with the accent on the A," said Rachel. "You got that?"

"I'm hearing it. But I'm not getting it."

"Well that's your truth and that's all you're going to get."

"Accent on the A?" I asked.

"That's right. Stop thinking like a private dick and start thinking smart."

"What does that mean?"

"It means you will never know the truth. A two-bit dumb assed gumshoe like yourself will never figure it out. Never."

"And why's that?"

"I'll tell you why. A guy like you doesn't have the kind of money or the amount of resources. For one."

"For what?"

"To find out what this is all about, lover."

"Don't call him that," said Quentin.

"I'll call him whatever I want, Quentin. I didn't do all this to have some hundred dollar a day nobody try to tell me how things are going to work out."

"Is that so," I asked.

"You are in way over your pay scale here, Patrick. I'll tell you what I'll do for you. Give this some thought. Let's put the two murders on Danielle, tell the LAPD how you came in and saved Quentin and me from being killed by her, and I will cap it all off by giving you a million dollars in cash, delivered to you tomorrow morning, and we can all go our separate ways. How does that sound?"

"We put this all on Danielle and you give me a million dollars?"

"That's right. You put it on her and you get a million in cash."

"That's very generous," I said.

"It's more than you deserve, Atwater," she said. "Do we have a deal or not? Yes or no?"

"Sorry, doll. Not going to happen. Not with me. Not today. Not ever."

My answer made her face begin twitching suddenly.

"All right. Five million?" she said.

I smiled at her and shook my head no.

"Like I said. You hired the wrong guy this time, sweetheart. You and Quentin are going over. Murder one. The both of you. No amount of money is going to get you out of this one. Not with me in the middle of it."

"Listen to her, Atwater. Be reasonable," said Quentin.

"Sorry, pal. No deal."

"You men are such assholes," announced Rachel. "Look what you've done, Quentin. You brought us a gumshoe with a fucking heart. A gumshoe with fucking integrity."

"That's right, sister" I said.

"A dead gumshoe," she hissed.

Rachel suddenly pulled a small pistol from the love seat cushion and quickly fired two shots directly at my chest.

Both shots found their marks.

I reeled back and managed to fire off one round from my .38 before my head and back slammed hard against the cold floor.

I looked up at the wood beamed ceiling and saw where my bullet landed. I could hardly get a decent breath into my body and I could smell my own blood running from my chest.

Everything began to get fuzzy.

"Well played, darling," said Quentin.

"No help from you," she said.

"What's our next move?" said Quentin.

"Shut up, Quentin. Please? Just shut up. I need to think."

"Did you kill him? Is he dead?" he asked.

I could see Rachel's ankles walk past me as she looked me over and picked up my gun.

"If he's not, he will be soon enough. He was standing right about here. Wasn't he?" she asked.

"Yes," answered Quentin. "Why are you asking? What are you thinking?"

"I'm thinking about that next move. Just like you asked," she said.

"How are we going to play this now?"

"First of all, Quentin, there is no we. Not now," she said and pointed the gun at Quentin. "Actually not ever."

"What are you saying?"

"I'm sorry, Quentin, but your connection with me and my late father has finally run its course. I'm sorry to have to tell you this but it was always me and Danielle. So? Your services are no longer needed. Nor are they wanted. Once this deal was finally done, Danielle and I would have had everything two girls in love could ever have wanted."

"Two girls in love?" he asked.

"Yes! That woman lying dead up there was everything to me! Everything! And now that she's gone? Everything has changed and so has your part in all of this. Your time with us has to come to a close."

"You and Danielle?" he asked. "In love? Really?"

"Yes. Always were. Right from the beginning. It must sting a man like yourself. Just a little. Huh?"

"You are one lying, evil bitch!"

"When I have to be. Goodbye, Quentin."

Two more shots rang out.

I saw Quentin's body hit the floor and then my .38 plopped down too as Rachel tossed my gun and walked out the front door.

I suddenly noticed I could not catch my breath easily and as I heard a car engine start and a vehicle drive away, everything went black.

CHAPTER TWENTY

Agent Edwards opened his eyes and realized he had fallen asleep face down on the table amongst several piles of papers. He and Detectives Munoz and Blaine and even the young police photographer Butch had spent the entire night looking through every nearby California property owned by Stone Realty in attempts to find Patrick and Rachel, but had gotten absolutely nowhere.

It was a valiant effort but the property lists were so long everyone wondered how Stone Realty could even keep track of such an overwhelming amount of owned real estate.

Agent Edwards took several deep breaths as he struggled to rally himself, and realized he desperately needed a shave and some mouthwash. Detective Munoz entered looking rested, refreshed, and carrying several coffees, a carton of fresh mixed donuts and a small cardboard box.

"Good morning, Edwards," he said.

"Good morning? I'm not too sure of that as yet," answered Agent Edwards.

Detective Munoz stared at Agent Edwards and shook his head.

"What?" Agent Edwards asked.

"You look like a whipped dog and you are beginning to smell a bit gamey."

"Thank you, Detective. I'm sure I do appear that way and now that you mention it, I feel exactly like that same gamey dog this very moment," he replied. "You went home?"

"We all did. You crashed on the table around 4 a.m. and we all voted to go home and get some rest. It's amazing what a hot shower, a close shave, and a good healthy dump can do for a person's well-being. Here. This is for you."

Detective Munoz handed the small cardboard box to Agent Edwards.

"What's this?" Edwards asked.

"I got you a fresh shirt, a new tie, a new tooth brush and some toothpaste. I know you're not leaving here until we find Atwater so I thought you could use it. There's a locker room down the hall. On the left. Go take a shower and become a new person. I'll save you a donut."

"Thanks. I want the chocolate."

"Done."

Agent Edwards took the box, grabbed a coffee and walked out. Detective Munoz picked up a sugar glazed donut and a coffee and began looking through the mound of papers again.

The locker room felt cold and damp and the heavy scent of tile cleaner permeated the entire area. Agent Edwards took another deep breath and gazed at himself in the mirror. He was consumed and concerned for Patrick's safety, but something else was slowly eating at him. He had made his quid pro quo pact with Patrick to share any and all pertinent information openly and honestly concerning Rachel and Enzo Barbieri as things developed, but he had withheld one important piece of information. As he looked into his eyes he felt guilty, and wondered if he had told Patrick, informed him as to what he knew, perhaps Patrick might not be in harm's way as Edwards highly suspected he was.

He decided to take a hot shower and made a mental note to share everything he had held back the moment he and Patrick saw each other again. The thought gave him a new sense of strength and he snagged a fresh towel from a nearby pile and moved to an open shower stall.

The water running down his body felt invigorating but Agent Edwards knew no matter how much water and soap he used, the guilt he felt inside would never wash away until he spoke once again to Patrick.

Refreshed and dressed in the new shirt and tie Detective Munoz so graciously provided, Agent Edwards stepped into the room, grabbed his saved chocolate covered donut, and looked at Detective Munoz who was staring out the window.

"Something interesting out there, Detective?" asked Agent Edwards.

Detective Munoz turned and looked at Agent Edwards. His face had a serious tone.

"What is it?" asked Agent Edwards.

"We just caught a break on Atwater."

"A break? Is it a good break or a bad break? What do we have? Is he all right? Is he alive?"

"He's alive. Barely. I took the call just a few moments a go. Somebody put two .32 shells in his chest."

".32? Jesus Christ. Where is he?" asked Edwards.

"He's up in Big Bear. Some A-frame cabin. I've got an ambulance on the way to him. Butch is getting his camera and Detective Blaine is outside bringing a car around for us as I speak."

"Great! Let's get going."

A huge sigh of relief came over Agent Edwards to know that Patrick, although seriously wounded, was still alive and kicking.

Detective Munoz and Agent Edwards headed quickly for the stairs.

"Do you know some Aussie named Jake? Does all the night time cooking at Barney's By The Sea?" asked Detective Munoz.

"Jake? Yes. I met him once. Has he heard from Patrick? He's the one who made the call?"

"No. His girlfriend Betty called us asking for you. Evidently this guy Jake took it upon himself to play detective and keep an eye on Atwater. We'll get all the gory details once we get up there."

"Gory details?" asked Edwards.

"There's two more bodies up there at that cabin. Both dead. One of them is Quentin Thayer."

"The actor?"

"How many Quentin Thayers do you know?"

"And the other?"

"Female. Identity unknown."

Agent Edwards and Detective Munoz stepped out into the morning sun just as Detective Blaine pulled up in an unmarked four door Ford.

"Let's go," said Detective Blaine. "Where the hell is Butch?"

Detective Blaine no sooner got the question out when Butch came running from the building carrying his camera.

Detective Munoz got in the front passenger side, Butch and Agent Edwards jumped in the back seat, and the big Ford pulled out of the lot and onto the street.

"Did you bring enough film and flash bulbs?" asked Detective Munoz.

"I grabbed a shit load," said Butch.

The ride up to Big Bear took a little over an hour and half. When the big Ford drove up the long dirt road leading to the cabin, the ambulance had already taken Patrick to a local doctor named Belafsky.

There were two local police cars on the scene, a coroner's vehicle, and a heavy set man named Grundy, the mayor of the little mountain community. Grundy was telling the local newspaper reporter, a young man in his early twenties wearing a card in his hat band that read "Press" what he had witnessed once he was called to the scene.

"Looks like a small circus," announced Detective Munoz.

Detective Blaine parked the Ford right behind the lemon colored Buick.

"No sign of the ambulance," said Detective Munoz.

"Probably came and gone," said Detective Blaine.

"We need to take complete control here. The biggest thing to ever hit this community is under-age drinkers or squirrel bites. We don't want this to get out of our hands," said Agent Edwards.

"I agree," said Detective Munoz. "Let's get a lid on this right quick."

Both detectives looked around at Agent Edwards.

"I'll flash my Federal ID and then you two take over everything," said Agent Edwards. "I want to find Patrick, hear what he has to say, and then I'll get back to you as to what I know or have learned."

"Done," said Detective Munoz, and Detective Blaine handed the car keys to Agent Edwards.

"Butch?" asked Agent Edwards. "Start taking pictures of everyone here and everything inside. And I do mean everything. Top to bottom. Inside and out."

"Will do," said Butch and everyone quickly poured out of the Ford.

Agent Edwards held up his badge and walked briskly up to Mayor Grundy.

"Good morning. I am Special Agent Edwards of the FBI. Who's in charge here?"

"At the moment, Agent Edwards, I guess I am. Mayor Bill Grundy."

Mayor Grundy reached out his large right hand and the men shook their hellos.

"I need to inform you, Mayor Grundy, that this situation is now under Federal jurisdiction."

"Situation? There are two dead bodies in that house," said Mayor Grundy.

"The FBI is well aware of that fact, Mr. Mayor, and I am taking over this entire investigation as of right now."

"The FBI is welcome to it, Agent Edwards," said Mayor Grundy.

"Thank you. What's happened here is a result of a previous related investigation and we will have to ask you, your local police, and the local press here, to kindly and respectfully step away until we can assess the entire scene."

"I understand completely and we are all quite happy to comply," answered Mayor Grundy. "The local sheriff is up in Canada at the moment fishing, and some Australian man called in the two local deputies here, and they called me. There are two dead bodies in there, gentlemen. One of them is Quentin Thayer! The actor! This is a family community. Not some place for these Hollywood hot shot types to come up and treat our little hill top like some lurid love nest."

"A love nest?" asked Agent Edwards. "Is that what you think we have here?"

"Yes, sir. It looks to me like it was some kind of love triangle gone badly. And I do mean badly."

"The FBI is well aware of the facts here, Mr. Mayor. Where was the wounded man taken?"

Mayor Grundy and the young reporter were surprised at how much Agent Edwards already knew what had occurred at the cabin, and the sudden jaw-dropping looks on their faces told Agent

Edwards that he and the Detectives would have no problems from the locals as they investigated and assumed control of the scene.

Agent Edwards approached the local reporter and flashed his badge.

"I'm Special Agent Edwards, son. What can you tell me concerning the ambulance that left this scene?"

The young reporter stared down and paged through his notes.

"The ambulance left at eight thirty-two and took the wounded man to Doctor Belafsky's home. He's the local doc here in town. Has a place over on Blue Bird Lane. I'm Danny Richardson. Hilltop Gazette. Sir."

"Nice to meet you," said Agent Edwards and nodded at Richardson. "Do you know where this doctor's house is exactly?"

"I do. Yes. Sir."

"Good. I would like you to ride along with me to that establishment. I want to speak with that wounded individual."

"Yes, sir!" gushed Richardson as he put his pad and pencil in his pocket. "I can do that."

"Excellent," said Agent Edwards. "Did the Australian gentleman ride along also?"

"The Australian? He did. Yes," added Mayor Grundy.

"Who gave him permission?"

"Permission?" asked Mayor Grundy.

"Yes," said Agent Edwards. "Permission to leave the scene. As you said there are two dead people here, Mr. Mayor. Two deaths that need to be explained."

Mayor Grundy became suddenly speechless.

"The Mayor did," said Richardson. "He gave him permission to ride in the ambulance. The Australian said the wounded man was his friend."

"I see. And you believed him?"

"I did. Yes," said Mayor Grundy. "The man seemed quite genuine."

Agent Edwards took a deep, sighed slowly, and looked over at Butch.

"Photographer?" asked Agent Edwards.

"Yes, sir?" said Butch.

"I need a photo of these two gentlemen please? For the official report."

"Yes, sir," said Butch.

Butch stepped up and raised his camera as both men stared with blank expressions and Butch took the shot. Detectives Munoz and Blaine smiled slightly at each other as they listened to Agent Edwards over-acting his authority.

"I'll also need you both to give an official on-scene statement to Detective Blaine and Detective Munoz who are here with me on this investigation and I will also ask that you both please wait here until my associates and I can survey the entire scene properly."

"Of course, Agent Edwards," said Mayor Grundy. "Whatever you require we are more than happy to comply. Sir."

"Thank you," said Agent Edwards.

Detective Blaine took out his note pad, began a dialogue with Mayor Grundy, and Agent Edwards and Detective Munoz walked past the two uniformed deputies standing at the front door and went inside.

The coroner sat at the small breakfast counter smoking a cigarette as Agent Edwards and Detective Munoz entered and introduced themselves.

"Good morning, I am Special Agent Edwards with the FBI and this is one of my associates, Detective Munoz of LAPD. We will be taking over this investigation."

"I'm Allen. Frederick Allen, county coroner."

"What do we have here?" asked Agent Edwards.

"Two deceased individuals," said Allen. "One male. Quentin Thayer. The actor. Shot two times in the chest at close range with what appears to be a .38. The gun is over there on the floor where

I found it. And one deceased blonde female, unknown, up on the landing, dead, and appears to have died from an overdose of some type injected into her leg. I will know more when I get them both on my table. I will be the one doing these autopsies? Is that correct? I am the official coroner on the scene?"

"For the moment, Mr. Allen? The answer is yes unless I hear otherwise from my superiors."

"I know the drill," said Allen and crushed out his cigarette. "I'll be waiting outside if that is okay?"

"That will be fine and thank you," said Agent Edwards.

Butch entered and began shooting pictures of the entire scene.

"No one else is here on the scene?" asked Agent Edwards.

"No one else deceased," said Allen. "The ambulance took the wounded man to Doctor Belafsky's along with an Australian man named Jake who called this all in. Let me know when I can remove the bodies from the scene?"

"I will. We'll need a few more minutes. When you step outside, please give the other detective out there your statement?"

"Sure," said Allen as he walked out.

"Thank you," said Agent Edwards.

Agent Edwards looked over at Quentin lying across the small love seat with his dead eyes wide open and then noticed the large pool of blood on the floor behind the couch near the gun and realized it must be Patrick's blood.

"No Rachel Stone Barbieri," said Agent Edwards. "Let's find out what the late Mr. Thayer drives and put out a call to all cars. Maybe we'll get lucky. Catch her driving to god knows where now."

"Will do," replied Detective Munoz.

"I'll go see what Patrick can tell us and get right back to you. You good here?"

"We got this."

"All right," said Agent Edwards.

Agent Edwards took one last look at Quentin, nodded over at Detective Munoz, and breathed another big sigh.

"You know Barbieri is good for this," asked Agent Edwards.

"That's how I'm seeing it."

Agent Edwards nodded again and walked out.

Agent Edwards found Danny Richardson patiently waiting by the Ford.

"Danny?"

"Yes, sir?"

"Let's go see that Doctor."

"Yes, sir," answered Danny.

Both men got in the Ford with Agent Edwards behind the wheel.

"Which way?" asked Agent Edwards.

Danny pointed straight ahead.

"Down that way and turn right,"

Edwards drove down the long dirt driveway, turned right onto the main road and made his way slowly past the many neighbors gathering on the road, talking amongst themselves about what was going on at the fancy cabin with the two police cars and the coroner's vehicle parked out front.

"Do you investigate this sort of thing a lot," asked Richardson.

Agent Edwards answered the question with a slight nod.

"We're not going to discuss this case any longer. Which way now?" asked Agent Edwards.

"Make the next left," answered Richardson and put his note pad in his pocket.

CHAPTER TWENTY ONE

I opened my eyes, heard some birds jabbering away and wondered if I was dead or alive. I looked around the small room but the only thing I recognized was my suit jacket, my shirt and tie all hanging neatly on two wooden hangers attached to one of the four metal hooks lined up together on the wall by a door, with my shoes and socks sitting atop a wooden chair.

I turned my head slightly and felt this tremendous rush of pressure on my chest and found it extremely difficult to take a deep breath. I looked down and noticed the bandages wrapped around my chest and flashed back to the last time I could remember being awake.

I remembered trying to return fire with my .38 and that Rachel suddenly grabbed a gun hidden in the couch and quickly put two slugs in my chest. I recalled seeing those thin ankles of hers and her last conversation with Quentin just before my own lights went out.

Suddenly Betty's man Jake and some dark haired well-dressed man with a stethoscope around his neck entered the room.

"Hello, Mr. Atwater. I am Doctor Belafsky," he said.

"Hello, Doc."

"You are a very lucky man."

"Lucky?" I asked.

"Lucky to be alive," he added.

"Where the hell am I?" I asked. "And what the hell are you doing here, Jake?"

"I followed you and that woman from your place to that cabin," said Jake. "Betty told me she was bad news and said I should keep an eye on you. So I did."

"She did, huh?"

"That would be a yes, mate."

"You finally got to do some real detective work. How do you like it?" I asked.

"I'm considering early retirement."

"Smart thinking," I said

Doctor Belafsky took hold of my arm and checked my pulse.

"Lucky for you he was nearby and found you when he did. If he hadn't you would have eventually bled out from those wounds in your chest and we would not be here in this room having this or any conversation."

"Is that a fact?" I asked and smiled over at Jake.

"It is," answered the doctor.

"Then I guess I really am a lucky man," I said. "Am I still in Big Bear?"

"Yes. You are at my home, Mr. Atwater. I have a practice in town but because of your condition, the early hour, and the fact that the nearest hospital is over thirty-five miles down the hill, the ambulance brought you straight here."

"Does this mean I'm going to live?" I asked.

"The weapon used was a small caliber and both bullets lodged deeply in your left pectoral muscle perforating an artery ever so slightly. You will be quite stiff in that shoulder for several weeks and you might find breathing slightly uncomfortable but to answer your question? Yes. You should survive this quite nicely. I normally by law have to report all gunshot wounds to the police but being that the FBI is here I have been informed by them that such a report will not be necessary in this particular case."

"The FBI?" I asked.

"That little bloke Edwards is out front and wants to talk to you," said Jake. "The doc here wanted to check on you first before he'd let anyone in to see you. I'll send him in now if that's all right?"

"That will be fine," said Doctor Belafsky. "You're going to need rest, Mr. Atwater, and lots of it. I'll give you something for the pain and some antibiotics to take with you. Your bandages will need to be changed every day and I will show you how to do all that before you leave here."

"There isn't much rest in my line of work, Doc. Lots of bad people out there.""Maybe you should consider changing careers?"

"Not in this lifetime. Maybe in my next one."

"I put one of my cards in your suit jacket pocket. Call me if you have any problems."

"I will, and thank you."

Doctor Belafsky smiled and walked out but before Jake reached the door I stopped him.

"Jake," I said.

He turned and grinned at me.

"Yeah, mate?"

"I want to thank you, too. Thanks for having my back. I thought I had a handle on this one and all I managed to do was make one bad mistake after another."

"You're welcome. Everyone makes mistakes now and again. You're a good man, Patrick, but truth be told, it was Betty who sent me out to keep eyes on you."

"Your woman's got good instincts."

"You just keep doing what you're doing. Betty and I will always have your back."

"Thank you. I'll remember that."

"It was also a bit of fun for me. Up until the gunshots and the two dead bodies. We'll have to do it again sometime. Eh? Under better circumstances of course."

"Sure. Next time. Sounds good."

"Get well, mate."

Jake grinned a little broader, nodded and walked out.

I sat up a little higher and reached for the tall glass of water sitting on the small table by the bed. Taking a sip from the plastic straw, I realized how unsteady I was as my left hand began shaking uncontrollably. I put the glass down and sat back as Agent Edwards stepped into the room.

"You're alive," he said.

"I am. Barely."

Agent Edwards stood and stared at my wrapped-up chest.

"Is the doctor giving you something for the pain?"

"He must have. I'm not feeling any at the moment. He said he'd give me something to take home with me."

"I'll take you down the hill if you think you're up to it."

"I'll need a little help with my shirt."

"Sure."

Agent Edwards helped put on my shirt and as he buttoned me up we sat in silence for a few moments. I put on my socks and stepped into my shoes and noticed Agent Edwards looking out the window.

"What is it?" I asked.

"I'm just happy to see you alive. I'm glad they didn't take you out."

"I did my dumbest to almost make that happen."

"I have to ask you some questions. How it all went down? You know the routine."

"I do," I said. "You need it for that special FBI official report? Right?"

"Yes. Right."

"I'll tell you everything. I am assuming sweet Rachel is in the wind?"

"She is."

"I can't wait until her and I meet again. Help me with the jacket and we'll get out of here."

"In a minute. I need to tell you something. Something I should have said right from the beginning of our little arrangement. When we first met."

"You mean our quid pro quo?"

"Yes."

"Let me guess. You finally called that waitress who was giving you the eye?"

"No. But I will. When this is all done. What I have to tell you is completely different. And off the record."

"All right. I'm listening."

I sat back on the bed and stared up at Agent Edwards.

"Montez Carrillo."

I heard the name clearly but drew a complete blank.

"I never heard of him. Am I supposed to know who that is?" I asked.

"No. I'm not even supposed to tell you or anyone anything about him."

"But you're telling me."

"Yes. Montez Carrillo is from Europe. Madrid, Spain. It's been my real assignment to locate his whereabouts and stop him."

"Your real assignment?"

"Yes."

"Enzo Barbieri was leading you to him."

"He was."

"And what are you stopping Montez Carrillo from doing?"

"I was recruited right out of the academy by J. Edgar himself to first, head up my own personal team, and second, to dismantle this man's entire organization by any means possible. This assignment of mine has top secret status and includes numerous perks."

"Top secret? Face to face with Hoover? No offense, Edwards, but how did you, a green recruit of such moderate stature still very wet behind the ears, get to be the one agent out of how many?"

"Thirty-six," he said.

"Out of thirty-six new recruits, you get picked for this type of assignment?"

"No offense taken. Hoover wanted someone he could totally trust and also someone that no one would easily suspect. I report and answer only to Hoover."

"That is a perk, and impressive. So who the hell is this guy and what are you dismantling?"

"Montez Carrillo is the man in charge of any and all large or small shipments of heroin coming into this country."

"All heroin?"

"Yes. All. He has complete distribution and complete control."

"Heroin? In the good old U.S. of A.?"

"Yes."

"For that kind of control Carrillo must have some powerful friends here in the States. How did this guy manage to become a man of such power and control?"

"For starters? Carrillo was working for years with Jonas Stone."

"Jonas Stone? Holy shit. So this is all about the drug trade."

"That's right. Major drug trade. We are talking large shipments."

"You're telling me Stone built his financial empire with illegal drug money?" I asked.

"Yes. But something happened and they had a falling out."

"And then Jonas accidently falls out of the sky."

"Yes. Carrillo has been operating in Europe since the mid-twenties and now that the war is over he wants to expand his operations into America."

"And Jonas said no?" I asked.

"We don't know for certain but we think that there is a clear power struggle going on around all of this."

"If this is so top secret, why are you telling me all this?" I asked.

"Because my investigation led me to Enzo Barbieri. I found out that he's been Carrillo's man in Italy since the stock market crash."

"Jesus Christ. These are some dangerous people you're dealing with, Special Agent Edwards."

"These people are highly dangerous. My biggest mistake, and yours also, was never having the foresight to even suspect that the wealthy, beautiful, Rachel Stone Barbieri was someone obviously either wanting in on Carrillo's newest enterprise or hell bent on revenge for her father's death and has some devised plan in play."

"You suspect those are her motives in all this?"

"I do. Yes. It's clearly one or the other."

"My gut tells me she wants full control of her family fortune and if she can do that, she wants to control the drug trade too."

"I agree with you. When you begin to connect all the dots it makes sense. Anyone else even remotely connected to Barbieri has been eliminated. She's the last woman standing and now in complete control of Stone Realty and all their global holdings. Her one big mistake was getting you placed right in the middle of it all."

"Lucky me. She's responsible for two murders and she killed Quentin with my gun. That's three people dead because of her. She can't run anything if she's locked up in a federal prison."

"Right now she is on the run and knows she has to be caught before we can stop her. She'll go underground, just like Carrillo, live her life and run her operation with only a few people actually knowing who she is or where she is hiding."

"Do you have any viable leads?"

Agent Edwards looked at me and the biggest grin I had ever seen suddenly grew across his face.

"I have one. A big one," he answered.

"You know where she is?" I asked.

"At this very moment? No. But I do know where Carrillo is going to be in three weeks and I'll bet you a steak dinner at Barney's By The Sea that little miss rich-bitch will be there too."

"You'll get two birds with one stone?"

"If we get lucky."

"We?" I asked.

"We," said Agent Edwards. "I thought you might want to be there when we take them down. Yes?"

"Absolutely," I said and we smiled at each other and shook hands. "Does this put me on your top secret team?"

"If you want in? If you're up for it?"

"I do want in and I am up for it. In spades."

"Then welcome. Detectives Munoz and Blaine are also on board."

"Good men. Do we all get special G men badges? Like the one you carry?"

"Not necessary. For the moment."

"Does Carrillo know we're coming for him?"

"Not as far as I know."

"Then what are we waiting for? Help me the hell up and let's get to work."

"First things first. Tell me about the dead blonde on the landing," he asked.

"Blondie was in this right from the first."

I struggled to my feet and Agent Edwards helped me get vertical.

"I only knew her by her first name. Danielle. She and Rachel had what I would call a unique relationship."

"Unique?" he asked. "You're saying they were lovers?"

"Ladies only, from what I could gather just before Rachel shot Quentin. Men like Quentin and myself were never going to be part of their final plans. Whatever that was supposed to be?"

We walked slowly down the short hallway. The two holes in my chest felt like they were going to pull me inside out with every step but the thought of catching Rachel Stone Barbieri red-handed suddenly made the walk much more tolerable.

"This is going to be fun for me. A lot of fun," I said.

I began coughing and the pain shooting through my chest quickly stopped me in my tracks.

"Are you feeling okay?"

"Not at the moment, Agent Edwards. But trust me. Give me a few days and I will be. I will be."

"Are you sure?" he asked.

"Trust me. I'll be better than ever."

"If you need to rest?"

"I don't need rest. I just need to keep moving until we put Mrs. Barbieri in those federal handcuffs of yours."

"And Montez Carrillo," Agent Edwards added.

"Him too," I said and tried to look like every step I took wasn't more painful than the next.

Agent Edwards smiled, nodded, and opened the front door.

"Let's get to work," said Agent Edwards.

"Roger that," I answered and stepped out into the new day sun.

CHAPTER TWENTY TWO

The car ride down to Key West was long and tiresome, especially for a woman like Rachel Stone Barbieri. She was not at all used to this style of travel but knew if she was to be successful in her endeavors, this type of under-the-radar travel was not only necessary but imperative to her plans.

Rachel slept soundly in the back seat as forty-three year old Luis Vendone, a French citizen living illegally in Florida for the last twelve years, drove his black Buick southward along the two lane highway to their destination, a large house owned by Luis' family and used specifically when certain people or products needed to be moved from one place to another without interference from any outside forces, specifically law enforcement. Luis' family paid large amounts of cash to all the local powers that be to buy the silence necessary for their goods and services to keep moving, and if someone tried to interfere with their business practices or attempted to overtake their power structure in any manner they were quickly dealt with and never seen again.

The locals called Luis' underground operation "escadron de la mort" which is French for death squad.

Luis Vendone ran the entire operation. He was a man without fear and ruled with an iron fist, an enigmatic smile, and also helped the community by donating large sums of money for four schools, a hundred bed hospital, and several parks for the children to play.

Rachel Stone Barbieri was a prize package and Luis was prepared to see her get to where she needed to be without question or interference from anyone.

The Buick turned right and began a long ride up the palm tree-lined road to the main house. Rachel awakened and sat up.

"Are we here?" she asked.

"We are here," he replied and parked the car just past the front entrance.

"Is it safe, Luis? Really safe?"

Her question felt like someone just poked him with a sharp stick but he quickly let the feeling pass and looked back at her. She smiled weakly and looked out the car window at the darkened house. The back seat was dimly lit but he could see the slight fear in her eyes as she stretched her neck to look around. Suddenly Luis wanted to hold her close in his arms and whisper into her ear that all would be well but he knew that would never happen, so no whispering was necessary.

Not this night.

Luis and his crew had every possible scenario covered. Rachel had paid a small fortune for her passage to Florida and it was only the first leg of her journey. Luis would make certain she was not only protected, but that all her plans would magically fall into place just as she had told him so many months earlier. Much was at stake here. Huge profits had been promised for all aligning themselves with Rachel Stone Barbieri.

And all who would not, would simply have to be eliminated.

The new order of the day for her new enterprise.

"You are safe here," he reassured her.

"Are they here?" she asked.

"Yes," he answered. "They are here. They have been waiting for you since breakfast."

"How many?"

"Four this time. One to speak, and three to watch his back. They offered up their weapons to show us good faith."

"Does this spokesperson have a name?" she asked.

"His name is Ponce Delgado. He is a first cousin to your new partner."

"A first cousin," she repeated.

"Yes," he replied.

Rachel stared out the window and laughed.

"My new partner," she said. "I have too many doubts about him. All he wants is my money and my connections."

"I can kill all of these men for you now. Tonight." said Luis. "Or?"

"Or what?" she asked.

"We can go in and hear what Senor Delgado has to say for himself?"

"And if I don't like what I hear?"

"Then I will make them disappear. For you,"

Rachel took a deep breath and looked at Luis.

"How do you want me to play this?"

"I think it would be best if I did all the talking. Your presence and your silence will speak volumes to these men. And it will place a small amount of fear into all of them."

"I like that," she said. "How do I look?"

"You look strong and well rested. You go in first, you sit, I will show you where, and you will be served some hot tea. Just act as if you are the only person in the room. Can you do that?"

"I have been doing that my entire life, Luis."

"Let's go in," said Luis.

Luis and Rachel both smiled, got out of the car, and started up the seven brick and mortar stairs leading to the large double wooden doors. Luis opened one door, nodded to Rachel, and she stepped inside.

The foyer was large and well lit. A wide wooden stairway went up the right side to the second floor bedrooms and a long red carpet ran the length of the walkway leading directly ahead into the kitchen. A large living room on the left contained a long plush sofa and matching loveseat, two dark leather chairs sitting directly in front of an all-white brick fireplace with three logs burning slowly, and further down the opposite end of the room were four dark skinned men sitting at a large black dining room table. All were smoking and drinking coffee and immediately stopped talking as Luis and Rachel entered the living room.

"You may sit here, Mrs. Barbieri," said Luis as he motioned her to one of the leather chairs by the fire and gave her an assuring wink with his right eye.

Rachel nodded, sat down, and as she crossed her legs could feel the men's eyes taking in her presence. Rachel calmly settled back in the chair, took a deep breath and did her best to completely ignore the men in the dining room. A small woman wearing a kitchen apron suddenly entered carrying a single cup of hot tea and placed it on the table next to Rachel's chair.

"Thank you," Rachel said politely.

"Por nada," said the woman and quickly walked away back to the kitchen.

Rachel picked the tea cup from the saucer and took a sip. Luis walked to the dining room table and the man called Ponce stood up to shake hands. The two men stood at the table and spoke for several minutes completely out of her ear shot, until Rachel noticed out of the corner of her eye that Luis was walking over to her.

"This man called Ponce has asked permission to speak with you," Luis announced. "I think you should listen to what he has to say."

"Very well," she replied.

Luis turned and waved Ponce over to the fireplace.

"Mrs. Barbieri, this is Ponce Delgado. He has some information you should consider."

"Mr. Delgado. Sit. Please," she said calmly.

"Thank you Mrs. Barbieri," Ponce replied and quickly sat in the other chair.

"What is it you want to tell me?" she asked. "Does this have something to do with my meeting with your cousin?"

"You have done your homework."

"I always know who I am dealing with."

"I have worked with my cousin for many years and we have done many things I, myself, am not proud of. This is an extremely unforgiving business we are in and when stakes are high, people find themselves doing things they never imagined they were ever capable of actually doing. Montez Carrillo wants you dead, Mrs. Barbieri. He no longer wants an American woman in charge of his operations once they are established in your country."

"Why are you telling me this?" she asked.

"Two reasons, Mrs. Barbieri. First, I think killing you is a major mistake."

"That's refreshing," she said.

"A beautiful woman such as yourself, if she is smart and ruthless as she is beautiful, which I happen to believe you are, is a major asset to this business, not a liability. Not by any means. Your family has worked very hard over these past years and has suffered dearly. You have paid your dues as they say and I personally think you should now be rewarded for those efforts and those sacrifices, not tossed aside because my cousin has suddenly become paranoid, blinded by greed, and with his own distorted views on how to run an enterprise such as ours. This business has taught me that one person cannot be in total control. Ever. A business such as ours is a group effort. A group that trusts each and every person involved and is safe in the knowledge that each and every person will also do what is expected of them to keep the enterprise profitable and running smoothly."

"And you are one of those people?" she asked calmly sipping her tea.

"As of today and right now? Yes. I am. We can forge a new partnership here and now. If you will trust me, I will make certain our futures together will be secured. My word on it."

"Your word?"

"Si, senora."

"How will you do this?"

"You must first go to the scheduled meeting with my cousin as planned."

"And be eliminated?" she said. "I don't think so."

"If you don't go? If you cancel now? It will only fuel his original plan and he will send people here to find you and eliminate you. Eliminate all of you. But if you do go? Arrive as planned? Montez will think he is still in control. It will be the edge we need and also be his unfortunate undoing. I will guarantee your safety, Mrs. Barbieri. Be assured no harm will come to you and afterwards we can all move forward, together. This I swear to you."

Rachel looked up at Luis.

"Can this man be trusted, Luis?"

"I think so. Yes."

A wide smile slowly formed across Ponce's face but quickly disappeared as Luis suddenly placed his large right hand on Ponce's shoulder.

"Make no mistake, Senor Delgado, I too am a man of his word and if any harm, whatsoever, should befall this woman, I will hold you and your entire family, man, woman, and child, personally responsible. Do you understand?"

"Completely," he answered. "I would expect nothing less."

Rachel looked at the three other men.

"And your other three friends here?" she asked. "Are they also members of this new partnership you speak of or do their loyalties align with Montez Carrillo?"

Ponce looked at Rachel until they were eye-to-eye.

"Those men are here to protect me, senora, and now they will most certainly protect you."

Ponce smiled and put out his right hand.

"Do I have your word, Mr. Delgado?

"My word? Si. You have my word."

Rachel stared hard into Ponce's eyes.

"To our new future, senora?" he asked.

"Yes. To our new future," she answered and shook his hand.

CHAPTER TWENTY THREE

Gunfire echoed loudly throughout the room as Special Agent Edwards watched Detective Munoz, Detective Blaine, and myself fire rounds at our respective targets. We had become the four undercover Musketeers, but because we were under the scrutiny and employ of the FBI we each had to pass several physical and mental tests including our third and final day at the private indoor shooting range.

This particular range was located in a specially built basement room in the home of a famous silent film director who never once showed his face the entire time we were there. The house was used by the FBI for special assignment training and for testing any new spy equipment such as hidden cameras and microphones.

Agent Edwards turned a switch on the basement wall and all three targets rolled their way back to our shooting lines. We eagerly inspected each other's bullet patterns like three high school jocks looking for the coach's approval.

"How did we do?" asked Detective Munoz. "Are we FBI material?"

"These are all good marks," said Agent Edwards.

"Who's the best shot?" I asked although I already knew the answer to my question.

"Detective Blaine is our shooter of the hour, gentlemen," said Agent Edwards. "A very nice grouping. Three shots are directly on top of one another. That is impressive. I have never seen shooting like that. Not ever. Nicely done, detective."

"Thank you," he replied and stared at his target. "I used to go hunting with my father when I was a boy and he always told me I had an eagle's eye when it came to shooting."

"You have a good eye and a very steady hand, Detective," said Agent Edwards. "But it's another kettle of fish when your target is moving and also firing back at you."

"I'll try to keep that in mind if and when the situation arises," he said.

"Where we are going there is no if, believe me. Situations will arise and all four of us have to be focused, watch each other's backs, and get the job done."

"We can do that. Right, guys?" I asked.

Both Detective Blaine and Detective Munoz nodded their agreement.

"We're ready for this," said Detective Munoz. "Does the FBI think we're ready?"

"That's what I'm going to put in my report," said Agent Edwards. "All three of you passed every test with flying colors. All three of you are also excellent shots. How are you feeling physically, Patrick?"

"A bit stiff and I won't lie, my bullet wounds are healing nicely but they are somewhat annoyingly sore still, but I also feel stronger with every passing day. I'm as ready and able as the rest of you. On that I can assure you. When push comes to shove? I'll push and I'll shove just like the rest of the bunch. Guaranteed."

"Good to hear," said Agent Edwards.

"When do we go," asked Detective Blaine.

"All four of you are flying out tomorrow night," said a voice from the opposite end of the room.

A small well-dressed man in a three-piece suit seemed to suddenly appear at the bottom of the basement stairs.

"Who's the little guy in the gray suit?" asked Detective Munoz. "Is that your older brother?"

"No. That's not my brother. I don't have a brother."

"Is he your dad?" asked Detective Blaine.

"Gentlemen, please say hello to the Director of the FBI, J. Edgar Hoover," said Agent Edwards.

"Oh shit," blurted Detective Blaine and took a quick step back.

Hoover approached and shook Agent Edward's hand.

"Hello, Agent Edwards. How are the men doing?" asked Hoover.

"Very well sir," he answered.

Hoover shook hands with Detective Munoz and Detective Blaine.

"Are you boys ready to go into harm's way?" he asked.

"Yes sir," said Detective Munoz.

"Absolutely," said Detective Blaine.

"You're Atwater," Hoover asked as he shook my hand.

"Yes sir," I answered.

"Are your wounds healing well?" he asked.

"Yes sir."

"Feeling ready and able?"

"Yes sir," I answered.

"Glad to hear it. I apologize for showing up unannounced, gentlemen, but I wanted to meet all of you face-to-face before you headed out. The Bureau is asking much of you and I know you will meet this challenge head on and do what you feel is necessary. The drug trade has reached our borders and you four are the immediate front line. These people you will be facing are smart, ruthless, and extremely dangerous. The four of you will have to become their equal in these matters and know full well that you are also on your own. These people have spies everywhere so trust no one except each other and if things become ugly or distressed, any future communications with the Bureau are to be made directly to me and only to me. Is that understood?"

"Yes sir," we answered in unison.

Hoover took out some cards and handed them to us.

"This is my direct access number. If you call you will first use the code word, magenta, I will respond with the word, dairy. Magenta dairy. Then and only then will we both know who we are actually speaking with. Memorize my number, gentlemen and only call if it is absolutely imperative you speak with me."

Hoover sees three target results, picks them up and looks them over.

"Well done, boys. Why am I only seeing three?" asked Hoover.

"I didn't do one, sir," Agent Edwards replied.

"You are part of this team. Are you not?"

"Yes, sir," said Agent Edwards.

Hoover placed a fresh target on the hook and sent it down.

"Let's see what you've got, Agent Edwards."

Agent Edwards pulled out his hand gun, pointed it at the target, and fired off six fast rounds.

Detective Munoz hit the switch sending the target back to the shooting line.

"Three in the head and three in the heart," said Hoover. "Well done, Agent Edwards."

"Thank you, sir."

Hoover nodded to each of us and shook our hands a second time.

"Good hunting, gentlemen."

Hoover turned and walked up the stairs. Agent Edwards placed his gun back into its holster.

"We still have a lot of information to go over. Let's get to it," said Agent Edwards.

We all nodded, took several deep breaths, and walked up the stairs.

CHAPTER TWENTY FOUR

The young boy ran quickly through the old cobbled streets. He had run many such errands as this over the last three years and had proven himself in Montez Carrillo's eyes to be a trusted soldier, even at such a young age. He followed every instruction he was told, to the letter, and never faltered from his expected duties.

Not even once.

Rain or shine, wind or cold, any hour of the day or night, little Miguel Esperanza would be summoned to the small cafe called the Dumont, given his secret instructions personally by Montez Carrillo, and would always, without any doubt deliver every communication given to him on small pieces of paper. He never asked for more money or special favors for himself or his two older sisters, who worked in one of the six brothels run by Carrillo's extensive operations on the small island called Aruba where the young boy had lived his entire life.

Miguel knew the particular communique he held today was a very special delivery. Every note he had carried previously for

Mr. Carrillo was always extremely important, and always delivered to a man of some importance. Usually these men were very well-dressed, men of very few words, wearing white linen suits, colorful ties and fancy straw hats, hiding their faces from the daylight sun. Or even more, hiding from people who might be trying to seek them out and gain information concerning his benefactor.

Dark people who might secretly wish to become competitors.

Or maybe any one of the eleven policemen who did their best to keep the people of the tiny island safe and protected.

Miguel was well versed as to what was expected of him and had never disappointed Carrillo or drawn any unwanted attention to himself.

Not ever.

This day communique was completely different.

"You will give this message to a woman, a beautiful well-dressed woman at the Hotel Paradise. Use the usual code words and you will receive a generous tip from her. You are expected to act politely with a gentleman's bowing motion and a sincere show of appreciation, and never, under any circumstances, read what is written in any communiques I give you," Carrillo told the young boy in his deep-throated whispers with his lips almost touching the boy's ear. "Do you understand?"

"Si, I understand," said Miguel.

"Use your English."

"Yes. I understand."

Little Miguel always did what he was told.

This time the note he held in his hand was going to a woman, a beautiful woman, and Miguel kept thinking about that thought as he raced through the streets.

A beautiful woman, he was told.

She was a beautiful American woman.

Montez Carrillo had also given him four times his usual fee, twenty dollars American, with a promise of doubling that amount if he reached her before the clock tower near the Hotel Paradise struck the ten o'clock morning hour.

"This must be a woman of much importance," he thought.

He slowed his pace to catch his breath and stared up at the nearby tower in the square. He looked at the clock and realized he had almost eleven minutes before the tall gray tower would sound out the hour. He knew he was only a short walk away, a quick sprint across the square before he would be standing in the hotel bar, face-to-face with this beautiful American woman, his mission accomplished, the secret note placed in her hand, and his handsome tip from her tucked safely in his pocket.

The extra bonus from Montez Carrillo made him smile. His short walk was all he had left to do. But now, for some odd unexplainable reason, he boldly broke the most important rule instructed by Carrillo as he quickly looked around the entire square to make certain no one was watching, Miguel slowly opened the note and read its contents.

It was an address and a name he did not recognize.

The address read 402 North Terrace Avenue, Nogales, Arizona and the name at the top of the note read Samuel Porter 25th Reg.

Although Miguel could read and write English and Spanish equally well thanks to his two older sisters and their home schooling efforts on his behalf, the information in his small hand made no sense to him whatsoever.

He stood in the moment staring up at the tower clock, quickly closing the note back into its original folds and suddenly understood exactly why Carrillo never wanted him to read the contents of the notes he carried.

By reading the note, he was now a liability instead of an asset. He knew something he shouldn't know, and although he didn't understand the significance of the note he was now vulnerable to the dark people always lurking about in mysterious places, and the uniformed police that were always asking the street people questions.

He was angry with himself, and made a solemn promise to never again unfold another note handed to him and read its contents.

Never ever.

As his anger began to fade and he took a deep breath, he looked down and was satisfied to see the folded note returned to its original position, and walked across the cobbled square.

The bar was nearly empty except for two waiters prepping a long table for the usual small lunch crowd that came to nosh on the free buffet, in an effort by the hotel to boost their sparse afternoon traffic.

Miguel looked around the entire bar but didn't see anyone. He took a few more steps towards the rear of the room near the small bandstand, and that's when he saw her.

He had never seen a woman as beautiful or as well-dressed in his entire life, and as he approached while she sat alone in a booth sipping coffee from a large white cup, the scent of vanilla suddenly filled his nostrils, bringing a small gasp to his breathing. Miguel walked up slowly and stood by her table.

"Senora?" he asked. "The sun is very hot today."

"The sun is always hot in times like these," she replied.

Miguel's statement and her correct reply told him he had found his contact.

Miguel was well-schooled.

"This is for you," he said and held out the folded communique.

"Thank you, young man," was all she said as she quickly took the note, opened it, and read the contents.

Rachel Stone Barbieri, dressed in summer white like some wealthy tourist on holiday, casually folded the note and tore it up into several small pieces.

"Here," she said. "You take this and throw it away for me."

Rachel placed all the pieces into Miguel's right hand, smiled at him, and opened her matching white purse.

"And?" she added. "Take this too for your trouble."

Rachel held up a fifty dollar bill like it was a long lit cigarette. Miguel reached out with his left, took the bill and quickly stuffed the torn note and the bill into his pants pocket.

"Thank you, senora," said Miguel and did his gracious bow as he was always instructed.

"What is your name?"

"I am called Miguel, Senora."

"Room number eighteen," she said.

Miguel stared down at her but didn't understand.

"Room number eighteen," she repeated and looked around the now empty room. "Tell your boss. Room number eighteen."

"Si, senora," he answered. "Room number eighteen. I will tell him."

The clock tower suddenly began to ring out the morning ten o'clock hour.

"I have to run. I have a massage I'm already late for," said Rachel.

"Si, senora," repeated Miguel.

Rachel quickly finished the last of her coffee, left a few dollars on the table, politely smiled once more at Miguel, and walked away.

Miguel stood speechless until the clock tower's sudden silence brought him back to where he was and what he needed to do. He turned, ran quickly out to the street, and across the cobbled square.

Miguel reached the Dumont Cafe in a few minutes and the tall man behind the counter pushed a small button and nodded to the door at the rear. Miguel walked slowly and quietly up to the door, turned the knob and went inside.

The room was small with two leather chairs facing a large wooden desk, and another leather chair sitting behind it. Everything sat at a slight angle on a large square handmade Egyptian carpet expertly woven in various shades of blue and green. Montez Carrillo sat behind the desk looking over some papers. Miguel stood at the doorway.

"Sit down, Miguel," he said.

Miguel sat down and noticed his feet could touch the floor for the first time since he had first started working as a runner for Carrillo.

"Did you deliver my note?" Carrillo asked without looking up from his papers.

"Yes. I did," he answered. "And I got there before the tower clock sounded."

Carrillo looked up and stared at Miguel.

"Did you?"

"Yes. I did," he said.

"Then you are expecting a bonus. Yes?"

"Yes. It is what you promised me."

"I am a man of my word."

Carrillo took out a huge wad of American cash and peeled off a twenty dollar bill and slid it across the desk.

"Take your reward."

Miguel had to get out of the chair to reach the bill. He smiled, grabbed it up quickly and put the money in his pocket.

"Thank you," said Miguel and sat back down.

"Do you have something to tell me?" Carrillo asked.

Miguel nodded.

"There is a message," he said. "From the woman."

Carrillo stared at Miguel and waited.

"What is the message?"

"She said room number eighteen."

"That was all the woman said?" Carrillo asked.

"Yes," he answered.

Carrillo looked through some more papers sitting on his desk and after a few moments of silence he stared down at Miguel.

"Should I go now?" Miguel asked.

"No. Not just yet."

A large black man, wearing casual clothes and a tan jacket walked in, closed the door and stood behind Miguel. Miguel turned and stared at the man for a moment and looked back at Carrillo.

"Well?" asked Carrillo.

The big man nodded yes. Carrillo sighed and stared coldly at Miguel.

"What?" asked Miguel. "I told you what she said. Why are you looking at me like that?"

"My look is not about what the woman said, Miguel. Do you know this man? Do you know who he is?"

Miguel turned and looked up at the big man a second time.

"This man? No," said the boy. "I do not know him."

"This is Alphonse. He works for me. Like you. And like many others."

"Hello, Alphonse," Miguel said.

Alphonse did not reply and stared at Carrillo.

"Do you know what Alphonse has just told me?" asked Carrillo.

"No," said Miguel.

"He has told me something about you without saying a word. He told me something very important with just a simple, silent, nod of his head."

"What did he say about me?" asked Miguel

"He has told me that I can no longer trust you to do your job!"

"Trust me? But I do my job. I do."

"You are paid to run messages, Miguel. Run important messages!"

"I do run. I run quickly! I do as you ask! Always!"

"Is that so?"

"Yes! That is so!" said Miguel.

Carrillo got up from his chair, walked to Miguel, bent down and whispered into his ear.

"Do you think I am a fool, Miguel?"

"A fool? No, senor. I would never think that!"

"Silence!" screamed Carrillo and slammed his right hand hard and flat onto his desk, bouncing several pencils onto his paperwork.

"I have told you numerous times. I see everything, Miguel. Everything! I am here at this desk most of any given day but I always have eyes on everyone who works for me. I make certain that the people who work for me do exactly as they are told. Always and in every case. And? In every situation. No exceptions!"

Miguel suddenly noticed his hands and face were sweating and quickly wiped his mouth with his wrist.

"What have I done to anger you?"

Miguel looked pleadingly but Carrillo's anger only intensified.

"You read my fucking note! Didn't you?"

Miguel stared down at the floor afraid to speak.

"Well? I want you to tell the truth, Miguel. Did you read my note or did you not read my note?"

Miguel looked up and spoke softly.

"Yes. I did. I read it."

"Speak up!" shouted Carrillo.

"Yes. I did. I read it but I don't know what it means. I don't even know why I read this one note. I never did it before! Never! I swear!" pleaded Miguel.

"You disobeyed my orders. Disobeyed, Miguel."

Fear came over Miguel suddenly like a huge ocean wave blocking the sun, and as he began to breathe harder and faster, he realized he had made a terrible mistake.

"Forgive me this one time. Please? I will never do it again. I swear!"

"You have broken a trust, Miguel. And in this business? This business can only run smoothly and effectively because of one very important thing! One. Thing. Trust! Complete trust! Do you not understand the meaning of this?"

Miguel felt a tear run down his cheek. "Yes. I understand." he answered.

More tears began to well in Miguel's eyes as he stared up at Carrillo.

"I understand completely. Forgive me, please? This one time?" Miguel pleaded.

"I do my job well! I speak and say only what you tell me! Always."

Carrillo leaned in again and whispered into Miguel's ear.

"I will forgive you this one time, Miguel, but your actions have a price."

"A price?" Miguel asked.

"Yes," he whispered. "Give all your cash now in your pockets to Alphonse."

"My cash? All of my cash?"

"In your pockets. Yes. Now. Give it to him."

Miguel dug into his pockets and handed over all the cash he had made for the day. Carrillo stood up and pointed at his desk.

"Now put your foot here. On my desk," said Carrillo.

"My foot?" he asked and quickly wiped another tear from his other eye.

"Yes! Your foot! Here! On my desk! Do it!"

Miguel stretched out his right leg and placed his foot up on the desk. Carrillo suddenly grabbed a baseball bat leaning next to his desk and slammed the bat down hard onto Miguel's shin, snapping the lower bone with a loud dull cracking sound. Miguel screamed in pain as he fell to the floor.

Carrillo grabbed Miguel by the hair and pulled back his face to look directly into his eyes.

"Consider yourself forgiven but you will never run for me again. Now you will limp everywhere I send you!"

Miguel stopped screaming and stared up at Carrillo with tears streaming down his face. Carrillo looked over at Alphonse.

"Take him out the back and go to the clinic. They will reset the leg."

"I will need the car keys," said Alphonse.

Carrillo opened his desk drawer, took out the keys to his silver Mercedes, and handed them to Alphonse.

"Get your leg fixed and go home, Miguel. Wait until I call for you. Do you understand?"

"Yes. I understand," Miguel responded tearfully.

Alphonse nodded to Carrillo and lifted Miguel off the floor with one arm, carrying him down the long hallway leading out to the back door.

Carrillo calmly replaced the bat against the desk, sighed, and went back to reading the papers that were sitting on his desk. He shook his head no as he heard the Mercedes drive away.

CHAPTER TWENTY FIVE

The private plane hummed loudly, constantly dipping up and down as Agent Edwards, Detective Munoz, Detective Blaine, and Yours Truly, Special Agent Temporary Patrick Miles Atwater, traveled through the night sky to a small secluded landing area at the north end of the tiny island of Aruba.

The area was built specifically for the travel convenience of the numerous white collar Standard Oil engineers and executives and staff who visited regularly to maintain watch on the drilling operations based on most of the island for the last ten years.

Along for the ride was a tall, handsome black man named Rockwell, a fifteen year veteran engineer working exclusively for Standard Oil. Rockwell had made this particular flight numerous times, knew the island and its inhabitants well, and was our sole contact responsible for providing whatever it was we required for however long we stayed in Aruba.

Rockwell wore a wrinkled gray suit, carried a .45 pistol under his jacket, drank bourbon constantly, didn't speak much to us the entire flight, and was the only other person on board who knew we were working a sensitive case with the FBI, using Standard Oil Company's presence on the island as our cover and excuse for spending time there.

The two pilots and one stewardess, a pretty young Asian girl named May Lee, believed us to be Standard Oil personnel and treated us as such the entire flight.

Secrecy was paramount to the success of the entire operation. Hoover's words of warning, trust no one, echoed in my head.

We had to assume that there were eyes and ears everywhere and we did not want to blow our cover or spook Carrillo into suddenly cancelling this one and possibly only face-to-face meeting with a Standard Oil engineer that Carrillo believed he had in his pocket.

Carrillo had a hooker named Flora work her magic on Rockwell and after several meetings with her a deal was struck, money changed hands, and the meeting in Aruba was set.

Rockwell knew he was being set up and contacted the FBI.

The plane shuddered and dipped again, waking both Detective Munoz and Detective Blaine from their slumber.

"Are we close?" asked Detective Blaine.

"Landing in a few minutes, gentlemen," said May Lee. "Please fasten your safety belts."

We buckled up and the plane began to slowly descend.

The island of Aruba is small and for the most part, the people living there are hard-working and conscientious. When a large man named Alphonse casually approached Rockwell drinking with Flora at one of the local night spots, he asked if Rockwell would be interested to build a tunnel for a wealthy industrialist. Offered a king's ransom for his efforts and his silence, Rockwell said he would consider it, and quickly contacted the FBI.

Rockwell knew immediately he was being approached by one of the new wave of European and South American entrepreneurs apparently using the island as an operations base, and was told to meet with a wealthy Spanish man to discuss the project. The date and time had been set for tomorrow evening at the Paradise Hotel bar, and the man's name was Montez Carrillo. Rockwell was told that Carrillo was a wealthy industrialist with very deep pockets, and had something to do with the Mexican railway system.

When Agent Edwards got this information from Hoover himself and related the details to us, our secret plan was set in motion, and the last conversation I had with Rachel Stone Barbieri finally made sense to me. I had asked her to tell me the motive that got her husband Enzo and the accountant Hollowell killed and she said it was as simple as ABC, with the accent on the A.

I didn't connect that until Rockwell gave us the quick history of the area.

Aruba is part of a three island group called the ABC islands. Aruba. Bonaire. And Curacao. Like many Caribbean islands, history of the ABCs included slave trafficking, then with the assistance of wealthy American and European investors, moved on to shipping oil out of Venezuela.

Since Standard Oil had taken over that enterprise, a new commodity was emerging. A commodity where a simple man could create his own destiny. If he was willing to put his own life on the line, willing to stop anyone from getting in his way, and willing to use any means possible, a simple man could become notorious and make an enormous amount of cash in a very short amount of time.

That new commodity was illegal drugs, heroin, and the man presently in charge of all Caribbean distribution was Montez Carrillo.

During the flight I had read Agent Edwards' case profile and had to admit it all made complete sense to me. We each had small pieces of information which individually did not mean much, but when linked together, became obvious they precisely fit into a bigger puzzle. The meeting with Rockwell would put the entire picture into focus.

Aruba was the island of choice where many private deals with wealthy world class entrepreneurs earning their returns in illegal activities could easily meet, set up deals, and then put them into motion. Offshore accounts were being established and becoming more common. Americans and Europeans wishing to conceal large cash profits or hidden tax money flew in to the ABCs and for a price, their money could be protected.

With the ending of the war, Carrillo was planning to bring his enterprise into the United States on a much bigger scale. He needed a strong silent partner living in the United States with a large family fortune, major contacts with political powers, and numerous real estate holdings across the country.

That profile fit the potential new partner Enzo Barbieri.

But Carrillo didn't trust Enzo, nor did he care for his pompous attitude. And after the death of Jonas Stone, Enzo Barbieri began placing certain restrictions that seemed to put more money into Barbieri's pockets and less into Carrillo's. Carrillo wanted Enzo out, but couldn't afford to jeopardize his organization, and began wondering how to deal with it.

Then completely by chance, Carrillo met Rachel Stone Barbieri, and he found the opportunity for everything to fall into place.

They had met in London shortly after her marriage to Enzo, mutual avarice culminated into a long weekend affair, and Carrillo realized she was the perfect candidate for his purpose. Rachel made it clear that if he was moving forward, she and her money wanted in. She knew exactly how her late father had made his fortune and when the reins were unfairly handed over to Enzo, instead of herself, she was not happy.

But any partnership with Montez Carrillo always came with a price.

Rachel had to prove she could be trusted. Enzo's loyalties were still cemented in Europe, and Carrillo had never trusted old European money lenders.

"Get rid of Enzo and we have a deal," he must have told her.

So it made sense that Rachel enrolled Quentin, probably offering him a huge return of cash if he helped her in addition to the usual sexual favors she was bestowing upon him, and most likely it was Quentin again who found Danielle, bringing her aboard with a three way plan to get rich.

Or richer.

What was not in anyone's scenario was that the one man Carrillo chose to assist in constructing a much needed secret tunnel, was a person who would not be swayed by any illegal financial promises, and who would immediately contact the proper authorities. This allowed for a short, stubborn FBI Special Agent checking into Barbieri, two of LAPD's finest and honest detectives attempting to solve a double homicide, and me, a lone gumshoe named Atwater hired by the woman in the yellow dress to take the fall on her ticket into high finance, combined with international intrigue and the kind of danger that always accompanies real power. Four men dedicated to justice and seeking the truth, now flying in to their clandestine meeting designed to stopping all the players cold.

The best laid plans of mice and men.

May Lee kept us primed with black coffee and turkey sandwiches, staying amazingly calm and attentive throughout the bumpy flight. She knew Rockwell by name and it was obvious that she had made this flight several times and knew what was expected of her. For some reason Rockwell didn't fully trust her or the pilots, and cautioned us to keep a low profile.

It was decided that none of us would speak about what we were planning, or even discuss our pretend jobs at Standard Oil. The five of us mostly just slept, ate, and drank in complete male silence until it was time to touch down.

When our plane finally landed, Rockwell and Agent Edwards reviewed the game plan. Rockwell gave us all official looking Standard Oil ID cards, a map of the entire island, and a quick history of Aruba and the people who worked and lived there. Rockwell loaded us into a cab bound for the hotel, and finally gave Agent Edwards a private phone number to call if we ran into problems, met unexpected trouble, or suddenly found ourselves needing back-up assistance.

We were all very aware that the people we were about to meet had a long history of extreme violence and were accustomed to getting whatever it was they wanted or needed from anyone. We were briefed, we were prepared, and we were ready, and we were not about to go home empty handed.

Not this time.

Over the years Rockwell had made many friends on the island and was well liked and well respected by the locals.

We all shook his hand and headed out to the Fairmount Hotel, an upscale establishment where visiting Standard Oil personnel always stayed. Rockwell had a small apartment he kept nearby and told us he would call with the exact time for the meeting.

Before showing our passports and Standard Oil IDs to the hotel manager, a tall thin Dutch man named Sven, Rockwell had wanted us to be very careful about any conversations we had with Smiling Sven, as he called him. Apparently, Sven was known to drop a dime on anyone he felt could possibly put some money in his pocket.

We were given keys to two adjoining rooms, and when Smiling Sven hit a bell on the counter, two young bellhops dressed in blue jumped to our assistance and carried our bags up to the rooms.

Snatching one of the local papers sitting on the counter, the large front page headline took me by surprise.

The death of Quentin Thayer had become a global event, and every newspaper around the world was carrying the sordid but highly false story stating his demise. It was publicly ruled a murder suicide, perpetrated by a single crazed unknown female fan he unfortunately befriended and invited to a rented cabin high up in the mountain community of Big Bear, California.

I had gotten a full pass from any wrong doing in both deaths thanks to Agent Edwards and the FBI, and my name and Rachel's name were both conveniently left out of the entire storyline.

We wanted Rachel feeling very secure in the deluded fact that she had gotten away cleanly and could now move about freely. It was a tricky yet necessary part of our plan.

I did feel bad about Quentin, but I blamed his death on his relationships with the secretive Rachel Stone Barbieri and the evil Danielle, now known to the world as the crazed killer of one of Hollywood's favorite actors. Quentin seemed to have everything in life a man could want, and why he got himself involved with all this cloak and dagger business was a complete mystery to me. It was so out of character for the man I once called my friend. A tribute for the fallen actor was set for the following Thursday at the Pantages Theater in Hollywood and I promised myself to attend if we returned before then.

I suppose the lure of large amounts of drugs, sex, power, and money are the four real things that make certain people of this crazy world go a little off kilter from time to time, but it almost always finally found them placed on some cold slab in an unfamiliar basement morgue, way before their allotted time.

The elevator doors opened and as prepared as we thought we were, we really had no idea what would happen next.

CHAPTER TWENTY SIX

Room number eighteen was situated on the second floor of the Paradise Hotel just across from the single elevator. Each time the elevator bell rang announcing an arrival on the floor, Rachel Stone Barbieri's heart jumped a little, both with anticipation and a slight hint of fear.

She was somewhat frightened remained steadfast, justifying all the facts racing through her brain and reminding her of what she did, what she was about to do, and why. Rachel's entire life had been a long string of selfish men who either used her or tried to control her, and she was about to break away from all of that and take complete control of her new life. She had made this decision completely on her own, from seeing an opportunity and grabbing it with both hands. She'd proven her loyalty and trust to Carrillo, the one man she felt truly loved and cared for her but she didn't love him, and she had made a clean getaway from the entire California fiasco. Using the fake passport provided by her new lover and partner, she had made her way to Aruba by ship and as requested, had not spoken to anyone, except for the small boy Miguel, for almost an entire day. She also brought along the two million dollars in cash as her good faith first payment in their new enterprise.

Rachel poured more Scotch into her glass, and as she took a quick calming sip there was a knock at the door.

Rachel opened the door to Montez Carrillo and Alphonse standing in the hall.

"Wait here," said Carrillo.

Alphonse stood by as Carrillo entered the room and shut the door. Carrillo was looking extremely serious and uptight, a look she had never seen on him before. Instead of greeting Rachel with a kiss, he went straight to the window and looked down to the street.

"Who knows you are here?" he asked.

"What? No kiss? No hello?" she asked.

"I asked you a question. I want an answer."

"What is wrong with you, Monty?"

Carrillo turned quickly and slapped Rachel hard across her cheek, and she fell to her knees.

"Who knows you are here?" he questioned again much louder and stronger than before and began pacing the floor like a caged tiger.

"No one," she said in defeat.

"You are positive?"

"Yes. I am positive."

"No one?"

"No one."

Carrillo stopped pacing and looked down at her.

"Are you certain of this? Absolutely certain?"

"Certain? Yes. I am certain. No one knows I am here except you and your little errand boy, Miguel, and that big ugly black giant out in the hallway."

"His name is Alphonse."

"And ugly black Alphonse," she said.

"Did you bring the money?"

"Yes. It's there. In the suitcase."

Carrillo picked up the suitcase, placed it on the bed and opened it. Two million dollars in American currency neatly piled in wrapped stacks of one hundred dollar bills sat under a thin violet silk handkerchief covering.

Carrillo moved the handkerchief aside, picked up one of the stacks and looked through it. Then he searched through another. Then another.

"It's all there," she assured him. "What the hell is going on? What is wrong with you?"

"I apologize for my anger, my sweet, but there is a slight problem," he said.

Rachel sat on the small chair in front of the mirror and ran her hand across her reddened cheek.

"There is a problem? What is it?" she asked, reaching for her glass to sip the Scotch.

"This engineer I am meeting with today. He brought four men with him last night when he arrived. Four men no one has ever seen before."

Rachel stared up at Carrillo for a few moments, laughed, and put down her drink.

"You find this amusing?" he asked.

"Yes. I do. I find it quite amusing."

"I do not."

"Four strangers on a private airplane has the mighty Montez Carrillo spooked? So spooked you have to slap me around?"

"I said I was sorry."

"You've been watching too many Cagney movies, lover."

"Cagney movies? I do not understand. I do not watch movies. Who is this Cagney person?"

"He's a very famous actor. Like Quentin Thayer," she said.

"You mean the late Quentin Thayer?"

"Yes. Like the late Quentin Thayer."

Rachel got up, placed a few ice cubes into another glass, poured in some Scotch, walked over to Carrillo, put one of her arms on his shoulder, looked into his eyes, and kissed him deeply. She could tell his mind was completely somewhere else.

"Shake it off, baby. Standard Oil is a huge company. Huge. These men you speak of? They could be here solely for some new oil project being planned. Don't tell me four unknown men put this kind of a scare into you? Has this new venture of ours made you paranoid? You need to relax. Here. Drink this."

Carrillo took a sip.

"I'm not being paranoid. I'm just being careful," he said.

"You're not going soft on me now. Are you?" she asked and placed her right hand between his legs.

"No. I am not going soft," he said. "Not around you."

"Doesn't feel like it. Not from where I'm standing," she whispered.

"I always like to know everyone I am dealing with. You know how I am."

"I do. Yes. What time is this meeting?" she asked.

"In about an hour," he said.

"Is it far?"

"It's a few miles south of town at a small blue roof bungalow by the water. Alphonse knows the man and the place very well. But these other four men…"

Rachel placed her finger up to Carrillo's mouth.

"Silencio, lover," she cooed. "Sip your drink."

Without taking her eyes off his, she opened his belt buckle and pants, and as they dropped to the floor she sank slowly down onto her knees.

"Tell me again how much money we are going to make?" she asked as she languidly took him into her mouth and began moving her head slowly back and forth.

"We are going to start moving fifty kilos a week. Every so often we will make sure someone is arrested trying to carry one or two kilos across the border to give the patrol officers on duty a false sense of accomplishment."

"How much money?" she asked and continued her motions.

"At a combined profit of two thousand dollars per kilo that's a hundred thousand a week, four hundred thousand a month, and once we put the tunnel into place we can quadruple the delivery amounts and the profits. All cash. I have several banks here in the Caribbean and in Europe that will take the money with no questions asked."

Carrillo began to breathe faster as he felt his climax gradually building. He quickly gulped the remainder of the Scotch and gently grabbed Rachel by the back of her head as he began to moan then suddenly and passionately poured himself into her.

Rachel got to her feet, refreshed her drink, sipped and watched intently as Carrillo put his clothing back together.

"Feeling a little better now, lover?" she asked and sipped her Scotch.

"Much better now. Thank you," he said.

Suddenly, Carrillo felt dizzy and sat down on the bed. He slowly lifted his head and looked up at Rachel. She smiled at him.

"Something wrong, lover?" she asked. "Feeling a little uneasy? Out of sorts?"

Carrillo's eyes widened and he struggled to breathe.

"You bitch. You stupid, evil, cock sucking bitch. What have you done to me?"

"It's a little trick I learned with the ice," she said. "You should be feeling a little numb by now."

Carrillo opened his mouth to speak but could not utter any words. His throat made some gargling noises as the drug began to take its full effect.

Rachel stood up and slapped Carrillo hard across his face, knocking him onto his side and down onto the bed. Rachel leaned down and looked Carrillo in the eyes.

"Did you really think you and my stupid husband could play me and my family for fools? I know my dear Enzo did. But you? You were the one pulling all the strings. It was you who had my family killed you son of a bitch. Thinking what? I'm some dumb, naïve little rich girl you could use to your advantage, take our money, fuck me, and think I wouldn't see through all that and know exactly who you were, what you really had in mind, for all of us? You are a pig, Monty. A greedy, little foul smelling bastard of a pig who finally got his lying ass caught, and played, by me, in your own fucking game. You, are now the naïve one. Not me. Now you are the one getting fucked. You are the one about to pay the piper. And you are paying with your pathetic little life. You can consider the sex my little going away gift to you."

Rachel leaned into Carrillo's right ear and whispered sweetly.

"I'm going to kill you, Monty. Today. Now. In just a few moments. I know you can't move but you can hear me and I'll make this quick. I'm taking it all over, lover. The entire operation. There isn't going to be any partnership. No profit sharing between you and me. Your cousin Ponce gave you up. Told me everything you were planning for me. So I changed the game plan. I'm killing you and taking it all. I've made all the necessary arrangements and already have all of my people in place. Including big, black, ugly, Alphonse. I have production. I have delivery. And thanks to your cousin, I will now have distribution. All done. The only thing still in my way? Is you."

Rachel stood up and spit on Carrillo's chest.

"I'm not such a stupid cock-sucking bitch now. Am I?"

Carrillo's eyes widened slightly and Rachel tilted her head to the side, gently pushing a small crop of his hair away from his fear-filled eyes, and smiled at him.

"I want you to know before you go that I will get that tunnel built, too. That was a good idea you had. And? I will make sure we call it the Carrillo Tunnel. Then everyone working for me will know who you were and what I do to people who try to fuck with me or fuck with my family."

Carrillo stared back helplessly at Rachel but could not move no matter how hard he tried. Rachel walked slowly to her purse, took out a small syringe, and held it up so Carrillo could see it.

"It's interesting how a little bubble of air pushed into someone's vein? Can cause their heart to stop."

Rachel snapped her fingers in front of Carrillo's face.

"Just like that."

Rachel picked off a small piece of lint from Carrillo's shirt and tossed it to the floor. "After today I'm going to disappear. At first, everyone will think you killed me and someone new, someone like your cousin Ponce maybe, did the same thing to you. But later? Much later after you are gone? Everyone will know the truth about the death of Montez Carrillo. Everyone. I will make sure of that. Goodbye lover."

Rachel kissed Carrillo hard on the mouth and quickly jammed the needle into Carrillo's neck, just below his collar, and pushed the air down through the needle.

Rachel waited and watched as the life went out of his eyes, then wrapped the syringe into some tissue paper and put it back into her purse.

Rachel went to the closet, took out two small suitcases and set them on the floor. She took the money suitcase and placed it by the door. She took a deep breath, blew it out slowly, opened the door, and waved Alphonse into the room.

"It's done. Take those two suitcases," she said as she turned on the large radio sitting on the table.

"You know the way to this engineer?" she asked.

"I do. Yes," said Alphonse.

"Good," she replied. "You are a good man, Alphonse. I like you."

"Thank you," he said and without looking at Carrillo, picked up the two suitcases

The sound of radio static filled the room as Rachel searched for a clear station. Alphonse calmly stood waiting for Rachel. The song Manana by Peggy Lee suddenly echoed through the room and Rachel turned up the volume.

"Let's go," she said and they headed out the door.

Carrillo's dead eyes stared up at the blank wall as Peggy Lee's voice sang out Manana.

CHAPTER TWENTY SEVEN

Ocean waves were heard crashing upon the nearby beach and a soft warm breeze was wafting through three small open windows of a blue roofed cottage facing the sea. Rockwell had spent most of his free time here when he first arrived in Aruba, using the cottage numerous times over the years as a weekend rental for a little rest and relaxation with a few of his co-workers, as well as some of the local ladies who enjoyed free drinks and the company of American men with money in their pockets. He finally bought the place back in '38 and furnished the one bedroom to make it look more like a corporate meeting place than a bachelor's getaway. The main room had two large brown leather couches, a big brown leather chair with a matching ottoman, one low wooden coffee table, and a large wooden dining room table with eight comfortable chairs. Along with two standing lamps and three oval throw rugs sitting on the wood floor, the room was comfortably filled. There was a small kitchen and bathroom on one side and a small bedroom sat in the back on the opposite side.

Rockwell had chosen this particular spot for our little get together for several reasons. The cottage had good height advantage, sitting up on a small hill. Whoever came to see us would have to park their vehicle next to ours and walk up the short wooden pathway to reach the front door. There were five windows facing the road, with the sea at our back and only one entrance at the front. It was a good spot, away from any locals, isolated, and if any problems evolved, we would clearly have the advantage.

Or so we thought.

We had been waiting over two hours and I could see Agent Edwards' frustration starting to break through. He began to tap his right foot and took several deep breaths with his eyes closed.

"You set the time and the place, so why aren't they here?" he asked.

"They are only ten minutes late. They will be here," said Rockwell.

"Are you sure?"

"Yes. Carrillo needs my expertise. They said they would be here and they will be here."

No sooner had Rockwell spoken when he spotted a silver Mercedes coming up the drive.

"Here we go. That is Carrillo's car. He's here," he said.

Agent Edwards took one last deep breath, checked his weapon, and instructed us to take our positions. In an instant we all complied.

The plan was for a simple and direct arrest. Detective Munoz, Detective Blaine, and myself would hide in the bedroom with our guns ready. Rockwell and Agent Edwards would play the roles of engineer partners, setting everyone at ease, and before anyone realized what was happening, Agent Edwards would ask if they wanted something to drink and we would be on them.

Rockwell stared out one of the front windows. "Hold on. Something is not right."

Agent Edwards looked at Rockwell.

"What do you mean? What's not right?"

"The man coming up carrying the suitcase is the man who told me about Carrillo. His name is Alphonse. There's a woman walking with him. Carrillo is not here."

I quickly peeked out the bedroom doorway and saw Agent Edwards looking out the window.

"Is it her?" I asked.

"It's her," he said.

I could feel my heart beginning to pound in my chest, knowing Rachel Stone Barbieri was coming up the walk. I felt a slight grin crossing my face as I looked over at the two detectives.

"How do you want to play this?" I asked.

"I don't know just yet. Let's see what they have to say?" he said and I ducked back out of sight and stared over at Detective Munoz and Detective Blaine once again. They could tell by the look on my face I was chomping at the bit.

Rachel and the man called Alphonse stepped inside and cordially greeted Rockwell and Agent Edwards, who introduced himself as a Standard Oil engineer named Hemsley, and they all sat down at the big dining room table.

Rachel and Alphonse had their backs to the bedroom doorway.

"I thought we were meeting directly with Mr. Carrillo?" asked Rockwell.

Rachel spoke up.

"Carrillo's dead. Let's drop the charades and all the bull shit, Agent Edwards. Tell the rest of your crew to come out of the back bedroom and let's have a little talk. I have a lot to say and a short amount of time to say it."

"Excuse me?" said Agent Edwards, confused but trying to maintain the plan.

Rachel sighed heavily and looked at Agent Edwards.

"Jesus Christ. Now, Rockwell," she demanded.

Rockwell quickly pulled out a pistol, placed it squarely against the back of Agent Edwards' head, and held the back of his collar with his free hand.

"What are you doing?" asked a surprised Agent Edwards.

"Whatever she says," answered Rockwell. "So pay close attention."

"You have been had, Special Agent," she answered as Alphonse reached into Agent Edwards coat, removed his pistol, liked what he saw, and stuffed into his own belt.

"You killed Carrillo? You are in charge?" asked Agent Edwards.

"Brilliant deduction. Come on you three! Get out here! Now!" she ordered.

Detective Munoz, Detective Blaine, and myself stepped into the room with our weapons drawn and pointed directly at Rachel.

"Hello, gentlemen," she said. "Hello again, Patrick. Kindly put your weapons on the table here in front of me and sit down, please."

"I am not giving up my gun to anybody, lady" said Detective Munoz.

"If you don't do as I have just asked then Special Agent Edwards' brain matter will be spread out across this table instead. So please? Do as I have asked? I mean no harm to anyone here but if you want to come through this, alive and intact, I need your weapons placed here. Now!"

Rachel pointed at the table in front of her and one by one we put our guns down and sat down across from her.

"Thank you," she said.

Rockwell forced Agent Edwards into the chair at the head of the table and Alphonse quickly gathered up our guns and tossed them out one of the rear windows facing the ocean.

"I can appreciate all of you coming down here to Aruba just to see me," she said.

"I am flattered. I had a little bit of business I needed to take care of and got wind yesterday that you boys were in town thanks to my new business associate here, Mr. Rockwell."

"What did she offer you?" asked Agent Edwards.

"I'll just say it was substantial," said Rockwell.

"She'll put you in the ground too once she's done with you," said Detective Munoz.

"Excuse me, Detective but this is my meeting and I will do all the talking, thank you," said Rachel. "I'm sure you gentlemen had a great plan put together here with a much different outcome than the one you find yourselves presently engaged in, but let me be perfectly clear. This business venture of mine is huge, a scale far beyond your reach, and it's growing larger every day. Believe me, when I tell you, the enterprise is bigger than your FBI and a thousand times stronger, because it is. Do not fuck with us. This meeting today is my one and only warning to each and every one of you. I can and I should, kill all of you right now. Today. But things are falling into place rather nicely right now, which puts me in a favorable mood towards all of you and as you are all fully aware, Mr. Atwater and myself do have a small but insignificant history together."

"You put two holes in me, sweetheart. I'm not going to take that lightly," said Patrick

"You and your boy scouts crew here will take whatever it is I decide to give you. So make no mistake, gentlemen. The next time we meet, if there ever is a next time, will have dire consequences as far as where your pathetic little lives are concerned. I am also softening this meetings blow to your egos by leaving you that suitcase full of cash to show you my good will."

"Your good will?" blurted Agent Edwards. "That's rich."

"Nevertheless," she replied. "I want you all to enjoy your short stay here in Aruba and all you need to do from here on in is keep as far away from me and my endeavors as humanly possible. If you or any other federal agents with dreams of grandeur cross my path you will be crushed into dust. Am I understood, gentlemen?"

Detective Munoz suddenly stood up.

"Fuck you, lady," said Detective Munoz.

Rachel reached into Alphonse's belt, took out Agent Edwards' gun, pointed it at Detective Munoz, and fired one round into his forehead.

Detective Munoz fell back and lay dead on the floor.

"There is always one sour apple in the group and I thought we were all getting along so well. This is so disappointing. I have other pressing matters needing my immediate attention so we will be leaving what's left of you now. Take their suitcase, Alphonse. They are all too stupid to listen to someone talking real sense to them." she said. "Goodbye, gentlemen."

Alphonse quickly grabbed the suitcase and walked out the door with Rachel and Rockwell close behind. We sat at the table, dumbfounded, looking at each other for a few, brief seconds, listening to their footsteps hurrying down the walk, and as the Mercedes' engine started up, we could hear the sounds of a large truck suddenly backing up to the front of the cottage.

"What the hell is that?" I asked and ran to the front window.

Agent Edwards stared in disbelief as Detective Blaine kneeled down next to his dead partner. Detective Munoz' blood and pieces of his brain and skull spattered a large section of the back wall. Detective Blaine wiped the flowing tears from his face.

I opened the front door but stopped abruptly as the back of the truck's green canopy rolled up and a tall black man wearing a dark brown jumpsuit pointed an M2 Browning .50 caliber machine gun at the front of the cottage.

"Get down!" I screamed.

We hit the floor of the cottage and the man in the truck began firing round after round, splitting the walls like they were paper instead of wood, shattering glass and pieces of plaster to rain down on us. We ducked our heads as close to the floor as possible. The barrage of gunfire lasted a good fifteen to twenty seconds, and as the dust and debris began to clear we could hear the truck driving away. I looked around, saw no one hurt, and we slowly got to our feet. I looked out at our bullet riddled car with all four tires flattened and the windows shot out. A blood curdling scream suddenly came out of Agent Edwards's mouth as he stared out a huge hole in the wall.

"Son of a fucking bitch!" said Agent Edwards. "Who does this woman think she is? And who the hell are these people she's working with? Jesus God! This was supposed to be a simple arrest. Carrillo and Stone in one surprise meeting! What the hell!"

"They're not people," cried Detective Blaine. "This is some new breed of animal."

"It's a world war all over again," I said.

"A new world war. Run by what? By who?" asked Agent Edwards.

"Ghosts," I said. "A new world war. Run by ghosts."

"She's no fucking ghost," said Agent Edwards. "She's our new enemy and we will track her down. We will shut her down. My fucking word on that!"

I nodded my agreement and looked over at Detective Blaine sobbing heavily over his fallen partner.

The new war had begun and we didn't have a clue how to face it.

CHAPTER TWENTY EIGHT

The murders of Detective Munoz and Montez Carrillo, the sudden and mysterious disappearance of the engineer Rockwell, Alphonse, Rachel Stone Barbieri and the well armed truck did not sit well with the local law enforcement on the island. Although having FBI credentials, Agent Edwards, Patrick Atwater, and Detective Blaine, after lengthy explanations, and eventually cleared of any wrong doing, were politely but firmly asked to leave Aruba immediately. Our hand guns were returned to us, as was the body of Detective Munoz. The Chief of Police, a thin lipped Dutch man named Van Der Hoven, an arrogant little person who happened to be even shorter than Agent Edwards, told the trio flat out they were never to return to Aruba.

"Our island is leaning to the tourist and hotel trade, and murder and gunfire are not conducive to that strategy," said Van Der Hoven. "You all need to leave immediately."

A private plane was quickly dispatched by the Dutch government to send us back to the states while a complete house cleaning began from one end of the small island to the other, efficiently performed under the watchful eye of Chief Van Der Hoven and his small staff of policemen.

The Dante Café was shut down by the authorities, as well as the local whore houses suspected to be owned and run by Montez Carrillo. Every shady-looking businessman or wealthy tourist exhibiting suspicious behavior, or anyone who couldn't explain to the relentless investigators their purpose for being in Aruba were politely kicked out. A complete and concise investigation was launched, looking into Montez Carrillo's comings and goings over the last several years, and anyone even remotely connected to him or his illegal enterprises.

The tiny island had decided to wipe the slate clean and concentrate solely on becoming one of the most popular vacation spots for the entire world to enjoy. Construction began immediately on several new hotels and beach resorts whose clientele was projected to be honest wealthy business men, their families, and newlyweds looking for a beautiful spot to honeymoon.

Almost overnight, Aruba seemed to transform itself from years as a dark and backward island to a new beginning as a destination jewel in the Caribbean.

While the three Americans and their fallen comrade waited at the airport for their government-sanctioned private plane to arrive, two young women in their early twenties approached them after exiting one of the local taxicabs.

"Are you Agent Edwards?" asked the taller girl, holding the local newspaper in her hand. "The Agent Edwards of the FBI that they speak of in our newspaper?"

"I am," said Agent Edwards.

The girl put the paper under her arm, reached into her small handbag and took out a torn up piece of paper covered in clear tape.

"My name is Maria. This is my sister Elena. We were forced into working for Montez Carrillo for many years in several of his houses. Our younger brother Miguel was a runner for Montez Carrillo. Our brother was handed this note to give to a beautiful, American woman, who came to see Montez Carrillo, here in Aruba. She read this piece of paper, tore it all up, and gave it back to Miguel but Mr. Carrillo did not know she had done this. We all read it and we do not know its meaning but we thought it might help you. Help the FBI catch and kill other bad men like Mr. Carrillo."

Maria smiled at Agent Edwards and handed him the taped up note.

"After the American lady tore up the note and told Miguel to throw it away he pocketed the pieces instead. We put the note back together with tape so it could be read again."

Agent Edwards looked down, read the note, and passed it to Patrick, who read it and handed it to Detective Blaine.

"Thank you, Maria," said Agent Edwards. "Where is your brother now?"

"He is at home. He has a broken leg and is healing," said Elena.

"How did he break his leg?" asked Agent Edward.

"His injury was a parting gift courtesy of the late Mr. Carrillo," said Elena and spit on the concrete floor.

"Carrillo broke your brother's leg?"

"In two places. Yes. Our little brother will walk with a limp now."

Agent Edwards reached into his pocket, took out a few twenty dollar bills and handed them to Maria.

"Here. It isn't much but I want you to have this. For all your trouble. And for bringing us this note."

Maria reached out and took the money.

"Thank you," she said. "Will this note we have given you help stop more bad men?"

"Yes," he replied. "This is very helpful to me. To us. To the FBI."

"Very helpful," said Detective Blaine and handed the note to Agent Edwards.

Large smiles appeared on both girls' faces, gratified that they had somehow assisted a few special agents of the American FBI with a simple piece of paper.

"Good. We are glad to help you. We will tell our brother Miguel," said Elena. "He will be pleased. You are all good men."

"Thank you, Maria," said Agent Edwards.

Maria touched the casket holding Detective Munoz' body.

"We are both sorry for the loss of your friend," she said.

"Thank you," said Detective Blaine.

"We will say a novena for him. What is his name?" she asked.

"His name was Munoz," said Patrick. "Special Agent Hector Munoz."

"Thank you, senors. We will keep him and all of you in our hearts. Have a safe flight," she said.

The two girls turned and walked away. After walking a few steps, Elena ran back and stared at the men.

"There are so many bad men in this world," Elena said. "It makes my heart smile inside knowing there are men like you trying to make things good and right again for people like my sister, my brother, and myself. Thank you."

Elena smiled at the men and with tears in her eyes, ran back and joined her sister.

"It's official," said Patrick. "We are the good guys."

"Remind me to get white hats for us when we get back to the States," said Detective Blaine. "How did you know my partner's name was Hector?"

"It's there on the casket. On the paperwork," he said.

Both men sighed and looked towards the sound of the arriving plane. Agent Edwards put the note in his shirt pocket.

The private plane ordered by the island officials dropped out of the blue sky and landed on the small runway. The small seventeen passenger aircraft taxied slowly to the boarding area.

"Time to go, guys," said Agent Edwards.

The two girls stood and watched as the three Americans waved their final farewells, boarded Detective Munoz' body, settled into their seats, and flew off the tiny island.

Over cocktails, the men discussed the small note covered in wrinkled clear tape.

"This little note should be good news for us, Agent Edwards," said Patrick. "Wouldn't you say?"

"Good news?" he asked. "How is this note good news?"

"We have a name and an address."

"We came down here to make an arrest. She made us look like amateurs. Fools. A taped up piece of paper isn't going to make us look good in the eyes of J. Edgar Hoover."

"Hey," replied Patrick. "We were had. We were played. But we're not done. Not by a long shot. This note is not the end. It's the beginning. This is what we call in my business, a solid lead. Our only lead but something at this juncture is better than going home facing Hoover empty-handed. Right?"

"I guess so," said Agent Edwards.

"Think about it. Rachel Stone bitch doesn't know we have this information," said Patrick. "That gives us an edge. An upper hand."

"An upper hand? To what?" replied Agent Edwards. "For all we know it's an address of some low level dealer who worked for Carrillo."

"Maybe," said Patrick. "But maybe not."

"I think it's where they're going to use Rockwell and build some kind of tunnel," said Detective Blaine. "A tunnel that will take time to build which gives us time to investigate, look into it, come up with a new plan, and nail her sorry ass and her entire crew."

A small smile crossed Agent Edwards' face.

"I would like nothing less than that," said Agent Edwards.

"We all would," said Patrick. "In spades."

"Nogales is right on 'the border of Arizona and Mexico," added Detective Blaine as he sipped his Bourbon rocks. "If you were going to build a secret tunnel? It's the perfect spot."

"I agree." said Patrick. "If I were going to build a tunnel to smuggle drugs, people, or whatever? Nogales is one, if not the perfect place to do it. It's a quiet little town. Not much activity or traffic on either side."

"You don't grab up an engineer like Rockwell, offer him big money, unless you need something done on a very large scale," said Detective Blaine.

"We still have the advantage, pal," said Patrick. "We put some eyes on this Sam Porter guy and the minute somebody gets busted in Nogales for trying to smuggle drugs across the border is when you'll know the real tunnel is built and operational."

"Patrick's right," said Detective Blaine. "Bait and switch. That's how they'll work it. They would put eyes to one place while they move product somewhere else. And like Patrick said they don't know we have that little piece of paper."

Agent Edwards drank his Scotch and stayed silent.

"Are you listening? What's eating at you?" asked Patrick.

"I agree with everything you're both saying," replied Agent Edwards. "I do. We will definitely put eyes in Nogales."

"Yes," added Detective Blaine.

"And we will check out this Porter, whoever he is? What has me thinking is the fact that Maria and Elena were whores working for Carrillo. Maybe we were given that note on purpose."

"On purpose?" asked Detective Blaine.

"Yes," said Agent Edwards. "Bait and switch, leading us to one place while they work another."

"I don't think so," said Patrick. "Those girls, whores yes, but they owed nothing to Carrillo. That son of a bitch put them and their little brother through hell. Now Rachel tells us to stay away from her or else. I don't think so. I want to finish what we started no matter what the risks. We owe that much to Munoz and to each other. This little piece of paper is our secret ticket in."

"I agree but what if we go down there, spend the next several months or so keeping eyes on Nogales and during all that time they could be building another tunnel somewhere else like San Diego or another border town in Texas or New Mexico."

"That's a good point but I don't think so," said Patrick. "I think Nogales was Carrillo's choice and that's where we'll find Rockwell, his crew, this guy Sam Porter, and hopefully Rachel Stone Barbieri."

"We can't afford any more mistakes. Not this time. Not on my watch," said Agent Edwards.

"We'll wait until they make a mistake. Someone always does and when they do? We'll be right there and take them all down," said Patrick.

Silence filled the plane, with only the drone of the prop engines as background. The men sat wordlessly sipping their drinks until Patrick looked at Agent Edwards.

"Every war has a starting point, pal. You're not going to stop it or end it solely in Nogales. Drug smuggling is too big. Nogales will just teach us the odds, and if we get extremely lucky, we will nail Rachel Stone Barbieri, that prick Rockwell and the crew, and shut her operation down, but a fight like this? It will continue for the next couple of hundred years or so, I'm afraid," added Patrick.

"A couple hundred years?" asked Agent Edwards.

"Absolutely. Yes. At least until this sort of enterprise becomes unprofitable."

"Patrick's right. Too much money to be made dealing at this level," said Detective Blaine. "That's why you run into people like Rockwell and this Nogales man, Porter. They're promised the world and paid big money by people like Carrillo and Rachel Stone. But us having one more shot at taking down that murdering smug bitch? Gets my juices flowing. I am in for the long haul. Whatever it takes."

"Me too," said Patrick.

"Looks like all I have to do now, is convince J. Edgar Hoover, and make certain we get the go ahead," said Agent Edwards.

"Get busy, pal. You're smart. You'll come up with a good plan. We're not taking no for an answer. Not when it comes to Rachel Stone Barbieri," said Patrick.

Agent Edwards stared at the men and slowly finished his drink. He picked up a pen and a legal pad and began jotting down some thoughts. Detective Blaine and Patrick looked at the casket at the rear of the plane, sat silently sipping their drinks, and the plane bounced casually through the clouds.

CHAPTER TWENTY NINE

Fourteen months had passed since our arrival back in the States. Detective Munoz was laid to rest in Los Angeles with full LAPD honors. Detective Blaine, Special Agent Edwards, and myself were all in attendance as was the Mayor, the District Attorney, and what seemed like every uniformed member of the Los Angeles police force. Detective Munoz left a wife, Sara, and one son, Roberto, who had just turned eighteen. It was a solemn service and although there was consistent rain falling for several days previously and continuing that morning, a strange moment quietly occurred at the grave site.

At the very end of the burial service the persistent rain suddenly and abruptly stopped as if someone turned off some magical sprinkler system in the sky, the dark clouds parted ever so slightly, and for a short instance a single ray of sunshine streaked down through the clouds shining directly onto Detective Munoz' casket. The moment started a muttering amongst everyone present as if God was attempting to tell us he was welcoming Detective Munoz' soul into his arms and bringing it home to some final resting place in the heavens. The moment touched all of us and brought a brief tearful smile to Sara Munoz' face and as she held onto Roberto's hand, she glanced over at us. We walked to give them our final hugs goodbye.

"You will get that bitch who did this. Yes? For my Hector," she whispered.

"We will, Sara. For Hector, and for all of us," assured Detective Blaine.

"Thank you," she said and slowly got to her feet with Roberto's help.

The clouds once again darkened, the rain began to fall, and Detective Blaine placed an umbrella over Sara, walking her and Roberto back to their waiting car.

That evening I sat in my apartment getting pissed drunk with Detective Blaine and young Butch over cold beer and tequila shots as Special Agent Edwards flew to Washington, D.C. for his face-to-face with J. Edgar Hoover.

At their private meeting the next morning, instead of receiving an anticipated demotion for his failure to arrest Montez Carrillo and Rachel Stone Barbieri, Special Agent Edwards was miraculously given another carte blanche undercover assignment. He was instructed to escalate his efforts into finding and arresting Rachel Stone Barbieri, shutting down all operations she may have put into place, and gather all intel possible connected to the manufacture and delivery of illegal narcotics coming into the United States.

"This woman, Barbieri, has simply vanished into thin air." Hoover said. "A person with her kind of resources can easily do that. We have to draw her out into the open."

"How do we do that?" asked Agent Edwards.

"Do you know that old saying? Hell hath no fury as a woman scorned?"

"I do."

"You go down to Nogales and find a way to make this woman angry. You upset this crooked apple cart of hers and she'll come running. But you'll need to be ready when she does come. Can you do that?"

"Yes sir," said Agent Edwards.

"Then I have the right man for this job," added Hoover.

Special Agent Edwards was flabbergasted and honored at his newly assigned task. Special Agent Edwards remained the man in charge, reporting directly and only to Director Hoover, and by nightfall Special Agent Edwards had once again become the front line against drug smuggling in America.

"Too many greedy bastards in this world of ours whose only bottom line is the profits they make," Hoover told him. "They don't care who gets hurt in the process nor do they give a damn about America, democracy, or the hard working people of this great country that sacrificed a great deal to keep this world of ours safe. You get out there, Special Agent Edwards, and you stop these bastards dead in their tracks. You do whatever it is you and your hand-picked crew need to do and if there is any flack about it? I'll take all the heat. I'll take every bit of it. You hear me?"

"Yes sir," replied Agent Edwards and shook Hoover's outstretched hand.

"I'm counting on you," Hoover added and handed Agent Edwards a small leather briefcase.

"What is this," he asked.

"It's your funding for this quiet war we are now engaged in," Hoover answered. "Spend it well and if you require more? Just tell me how much and I'll see you are provided for."

"Thank you, sir."

"Make these people realize that the FBI and the United States of America cannot and will not tolerate any illegal drugs corning across our borders and anyone attempting to do so will pay a heavy toll."

"Yes sir," said Agent Edwards.

Special Agent Edwards took the brief case and walked proudly out of Hoover's office.

To begin his goal, Agent Edwards hand-picked fifteen field agents he felt were up to the task and over the next four months, personally made certain they were placed in numerous undercover positions throughout Nogales, Arizona. The town itself was literally divided right down the center with the United States on one side and Mexico on the other. People living and working in the town could casually come and go across either border as they pleased without questions asked by either countries' authorities. Many American tourists came south into Nogales for the cheap cost of goods and services offered on the Mexican side. A little under six thousand people lived and worked in Nogales and the little border town was quickly growing with several new companies springing up and numerous old established businesses finally becoming financially successful.

Nogales, Arizona was beginning to grow.

The Americans and the Mexicans, for the most part, got along rather well except for the occasional arrests for petty arguments, some domestic abuse, or public drunkenness, which usually occurred on both sides. Nogales had a small but well-armed 25th Infantry Regiment of about twenty-five to thirty men acting as a border stop and sitting approximately ten miles north of town and commanded by Frederick Herman, a tall, well-built, by-the-book man of forty-five, who kept his men on a very short leash. He did his best to never show favorites, and kept a few of his best uniformed men present throughout the American side of town, acting as an armed police presence throughout the day and the night as needed to keep the peace. Captain Herman also worked hand-to-hand with the local American Mayor, a thin wisp of a gentleman named Birdwell, and the small three man police force who reported to him whenever trouble raised its ugly head, which was hardly ever.

Nogales was a quiet, safe, little border town.

On the Mexican side of Nogales, also several miles outside of town and south of the border, was a small, three building outpost and border stop where the Mexican soldados, Mexico's equivalent to the American 25th Regiment, were stationed and whose leader also positioned a few of his men in town as a precautionary measure to maintain the peace. The Mexican leader, unlike his American counterpart, was a slightly overweight man named Captain Juan Sandoval, a dedicated soldier known to be the first in line for a bet, a bribe, a free meal or drink, or a quick test run on any of the new prostitutes working the three active whore houses on the Mexican side.

Captain Herman, Captain Sandoval, and Mayor Birdwell knew each other well and would meet once or twice a month at the Cavern Cafe or the Montezuma Hotel for dinner, drinks, and to share information on any situations occurring on either side of their little border town. In the past three years of doing so, business was always as usual, quiet and non-alarming with neither side having much to report in terms of bad news.

However, several years back there had been a neatly defined cement wall, small in height, running dead center through the border town, and people coming from the Mexican side had to pass inspection at that border by American guards in order to enter the United States. One morning a deaf Mexican teenager refused to halt and be inspected as requested, and was shot and killed by an American guard. The boy's death, although tragic and deemed accidental, created tension between the two sides. To relieve that tension, Mayor Birdwell had a large obelisk placed in the center of Nogales and after that dedication day, anyone attempting to enter either country, in Nogales proper, Mexican or American, were now inspected solely by guards placed out of town several miles down the single road leading in and out of both countries.

Special Agent Edwards had his small team of Federal agents, both male and female, given paid work assignments at the volunteer fire department, the city court house, St. Joseph's hospital, the local and only bank, four hotels, a cigar factory, the foundry, the ice plant, the brick yard, a cement brick factory, several restaurants, two night clubs, and one particular cantina on the Mexican side of Nogales called Pablo's, a busy little dinner and dance place that served cheap tequila, cold Mexican beer, excellent Mexican dishes, and offered live music six nights a week.

Pablo's was known as a trouble-free, popular, night spot.

Special Agent Edwards had his best female agent, an attractive twenty-six-year-old brunette named Loretta Davis, hired on to sing with Pablo's local musicians. Her secret assignment was to get hired for her excellent vocal skills and use her feminine charms and extreme good looks to show interest and get close to the manager of Pablo's, a handsome man in his late forties named Samuel Porter, the same man whose name was written on the torn note placed in the hand of Rachel Stone Barbieri by Montez Carrillo, and the FBI's number one suspect. Porter was the key connection to Rachel Stone Barbieri in Nogales and Agent Edwards needed to know every move the man made 24/7. Agent Edwards told Loretta he wanted to know every pattern of Porter's daily routines, who were the people he spoke with, and what were the names of anyone he happened to even mention.

It was a difficult assignment for any undercover agent but Agent Edwards knew he had the right person with Agent Loretta Davis. She was bright, beautiful, and willing to do everything necessary to gain Porter's confidence and bring the entire smuggling operation down. Loretta quickly became quite popular with the locals and visiting tourists from both sides of the border, singing hit songs at Pablo's in English and in Spanish. Porter began to wine and dine Loretta almost immediately after she applied for the job. Agent Davis' cover was one of a well-dressed, newly divorced woman named Nina Douglas from El Paso, Texas, who loved music, liked the finer things in life, and had a small amount of money saved. She pretended to be a woman who just wanted to sing for a living and maybe one day find a real man, a good man, not some womanizing El Paso cowboy type, but the kind of man who could truly love her and show respect for the woman she had become.

Porter immediately fell for the phony story like a ton of bricks, doing his best to prove to Loretta he was exactly that kind of a man.

As the new singer at Pablo's, Loretta became known by everyone on both sides of the border as the sexy young singer, Lottie D, and after several months of rejecting Porter's relentless advances finally gave herself to him in her small single room at the Montezuma Hotel. The following week Porter had all her things moved into his ranch style hacienda which sat east of the border on the American side at 402 North Terrace Avenue. The house was on three acres with a large circular driveway in front, an attached two-car garage, and a large back yard overlooking an old red brick factory about a half mile away on the Mexican side of the border.

"You tell me what you need, my love, what you want or desire, and I will make certain you get it," he told her. "Whatever the cost."

"Thank you, Sam," she cooed and Porter ate it up like some starving dog being handed a juicy bone.

Porter was a very quiet man, never speaking much in public, but he knew everyone who was anyone on both sides of the border, including the Mayor, Captain Herman, who also happened to be his old commanding officer back in the day at the 25th, and Captain Sandoval, who had also became enamored by Lottie D but realized quickly that this beautiful singer had eyes only for Porter. Once she moved into Porter's house, no man would dare to go near her.

Porter ran Pablo's with a strong voice whenever he needed his cantina help to do something that catered to the local clientele or the visiting tourists. When Porter spoke the help jumped and everyone knew Porter was the man in charge. If you wanted to keep your job, you did what he asked and you did it promptly. But Porter was soft-spoken and always very gentleman-like when it came to catering to Lottie D's needs. He stocked expensive champagne, bought her a diamond brooch, and helped her pick out the outfits she wore for performing on stage. He ordered new microphones and special mood lights for the stage to give Lottie D's performances the correct ambiance for whatever tune she was about to sing.

Lottie D had clearly arrived in Nogales, with no one outside of the FBI's chosen field agents knowing her true identity. She was playing a dangerous game, but Agent Davis played to win and as far as Agent Edwards was concerned, she was doing exactly that and doing it extremely well.

I had gone back to my booth at Barney's, took on a few minor cases, visited Mrs. Clifford and her daughters in Van Nuys every now and then, and watched as Betty and Jake finally tied the knot in a small wedding ceremony on the beach in Malibu. Barney and I chipped in to send Mr. and Mrs. Jake Farnswell to Hawaii for a three week honeymoon. Jake left his brass knuckles for me in case I had another emergency.

Detective Blaine and I stayed in touch and were told by Special Agent Edwards to stand by in Los Angeles for his phone call once he had everything in place with his new team ready to make a move. After almost a year and a half's time, Agent Edwards had all of his ducks in a row. His agents were all set and reasonably entrenched into the local work place, none of his agents were even remotely suspected of being undercover, good intel was coming in on a daily basis, and his best agent, Loretta Davis, was presently sleeping alongside the man and staying at the exact address written on the late Montez Carrillo's note.

Everything was in its proper place.

All Agent Edwards needed now was someone in the smuggling operation to make a mistake. After months of patiently waiting, that one mistake was finally made and Detective Blaine and I got our anticipated phone call. We were told to say we worked for American West Construction Company if anyone asked, and were immediately flown to Phoenix, bought a used car with Arizona plates, paid for by the bureau, and drove directly down to Nogales.

The sun had been set for about three hours and we seemed to be the only vehicle on the two lane highway headed into Nogales except for two trucks and a tour bus headed in the opposite direction.

"What do you think actually happened?" asked Detective Blaine.

"What do you mean?" I replied.

"Somebody screwed up. I was just wondering what that screw-up might be?"

"Somebody made that mistake we've been waiting for," I said. "And that's all that matters to me. That, and finally taking down Rachel Stone Barbieri."

"Ten bucks says the mistake was on the Mexican side," added Detective Blaine.

"I'm not a betting man but for ten bucks I'll take that bet," I replied and pointed to the approaching border stop going into Nogales.

"Looks like we have arrived," said Detective Blaine.

Two armed soldiers waved us down as we drove to a stop. One soldier, a baby faced blonde haired kid of about twenty, leaned into the driver's side and shined his flashlight on us.

"Good evening, gentlemen. Where are we headed to this night?" he asked.

"Nogales," answered Detective Blaine.

"What is the nature of your visit, sir?"

"Cement bricks, son," Detective Blaine lied. "We understand there's a factory down there making cement bricks at an unbelievable price. We're here to check that out."

"And down a few cold beers in the process," I added.

The mention of cold beer put a smile on the young soldier's face.

"I think you will find both satisfactory, gentlemen. Enjoy your stay in Nogales."

"Thank you," replied Detective Blaine.

The young soldier waved us through and we headed slowly around the long hill winding down into Nogales.

Special Agent Edwards had purchased a small two bedroom house East of town, sitting on a small rise overlooking most of Nogales but most importantly, had a direct view south from the rear bedroom to Sam Porter's ranch-style hacienda on North Terrace Avenue. Detective Blaine and I were thoroughly impressed with the amount of effort and expertise Special Agent Edwards and his field agents had managed to apply in such a short amount of time. He had undercover agents everywhere possible, and nothing in Nogales occurred, day or night, without Special Agent Edwards hearing about it.

A drop box was set up at the local post office and every day at three o'clock Agent Edwards walked down to the post office with his leather satchel and gathered intel from his entire team. He knew who made what, how it was packaged, where it was sent, how much was sent, the time it was sent, and the names of practically every person working in Nogales that Agent Edwards felt might be a possible suspect.

Agent Edwards had a phony cover story too, going by the name Rex Carter, a single man struggling for success as a screenwriter/novelist who checked his mail daily, supposedly consisting of numerous rejection notices from motion picture producers and fake publishing companies. The cover was a good one and worked well with the locals but the full beard he had grown in the process took Detective Blaine and I completely by surprise upon our arrival.

"You look like Fuzzy Knight's cousin," I told him.

"No, he looks more like Gabby Hayes' younger brother," added Detective Blaine.

After sharing several beers, a few more much needed laughs, and a long overdue catching-up session, Special Agent Edwards finally began to lay everything out to us and what was about to happen in Nogales.

Special Agent Edwards gave us each a pair of binoculars and told us to look out the rear bedroom window.

"What do you see?" he asked.

"I see Porter's ranch," answered Detective Blaine. "It's maybe thirty years old but it's kept up well. There's a brand new Cadillac parked near the front door. That's worth a few pesos. There is a lot of empty space around the house. There are only a few bushes here and there but no shade trees in front or in back. If the plan is to surround the house to arrest him we would have no cover whatsoever except for the vehicles we arrive in."

"That's not the plan but very good observations. What else do you see?" he added.

We both scanned the area again in an attempt to answer his question.

"He does have a nice driveway and a large attached garage tall enough to put a fire truck in," I said. "That strikes me as a little odd. This entire area is dusty as hell. Why doesn't he put his new Cadillac in the garage?"

"Precisely what I thought a few weeks back," said Agent Edwards.

"This is the big mistake that brought us down here?" asked Detective Blaine. "Our number one suspect doesn't care if his new Caddy gets dusty?"

"No," said Agent Edwards. "I'll get to the mistake in a minute. Keep looking through those glasses and take a look over to the Mexican side. What do you see?"

We both saw a red brick factory about a half mile away.

"I see what looks like a red brick factory closed for the night. One single light burning on the lower east corner of the building. Is that where they make the cement bricks too?" asked Detective Blaine.

"No" answered Agent Edwards. "The cement brick factory is behind us, just north of here."

"So what's in the garage?" asked Detective Blaine.

"Nothing yet," answered Agent Edwards.

I looked through my binoculars once more and suddenly it all became clear to me.

"I see it," I said.

"See what?" asked Detective Blaine.

"Look," I said. "Look from the Porter garage to the red brick factory."

Detective Blaine looked through his binoculars a second time.

"All I see are more dry bushes, a few rocks, and a ton of desert sand. Holy shit! It's Rockwell's tunnel. Is that what we're seeing here?" asked Detective Blaine.

"That is exactly what we are looking at. The tunnel is right there," said Agent Edwards. "It stretches from the garage to the brick plant. There's a slight angle bending to the left at about the halfway mark so you can't really see from one end to the other. It's very well constructed, about five feet across and seven feet high. It's got steel rails, the kind coal miners use and it must operate from the Mexican side because there is nothing on this side except a wooden barrier at the end of the tracks."

"And you know all this, how?" asked Detective Blaine.

"Because last night I went inside it and walked it up to that halfway bend," said Agent Edwards.

"That took some balls," I said. "How did you get in?"

"There are four sets of windows on the east side of the garage. I have someone working undercover in Porter's house and she unlocked one of those windows so I could access the garage," explained Agent Edwards.

"She? An undercover? In Porter's house? Who is she?" I asked.

"Her name is Loretta Davis," said Agent Edwards. "Been with the bureau for a few years."

"What is she doing there? Is she his house maid? His cook?" questioned Detective Blaine.

"She's none of those things," replied Agent Edwards. "She's a singer at Porter's club. Goes by the stage name, Lottie D."

"A singer," I repeated. "Let me guess. Porter is crazy about her."

"Obsessed is more like it," said Agent Edwards. "He chased her for months and she kept him at arms' length. But now? She's his live-in girlfriend."

"Son of a bitch," I said. "A female undercover working under-covers. How did you make that happen?"

"I didn't. It wasn't my call. I just wanted her to get the singing gig, keep a watchful eye on the place Porter runs, a fancy cantina on the Mexican side called Pablo's, and pretend to be slightly interested in Porter. She's the one who decided to go the extra mile."

"She's sounds like one tough cookie," said Detective Blaine. "Can we get her out of there if things go south?"

"That's all part of the plan," said Agent Edwards.

"So give us all the particulars on this plan of yours," I said.

"And what the so-called mistake was," added Detective Blaine. "Did it happen here or on the Mexican side?"

"The mistake they made was washing some trucks. Here, on the American side," said Agent Edwards.

"Washing trucks on the American side," I repeated and smiled at Detective Blaine. "Interesting. Tell us more."

Before Agent Edwards could get out another word, Detective Blaine graciously handed me the ten dollars he owed me on our bet.

"Thank you," I said.

"You are welcome. What's this about? This washing trucks thing?" asked Detective Blaine.

"I have eyes all over this town," said Agent Edwards. "Last week the cement factory brought in six brand new trucks. Six. They're Chevy G 2100's. Bright shiny red. Very nice. And very clean. Two days ago three men drove one of the trucks to Porter's garage, backed it in, and washed and waxed it. They did it with the garage doors wide open, Mexican music blaring, and anyone looking at them could plainly see what it was they were doing."

"Washing a brand new truck and hiding in plain sight," I said.

"Exactly," agreed Agent Edwards.

"Why would anyone hauling cement bricks have to wash and wax their truck?" I added. "Especially new cement brick trucks? It doesn't make sense."

"It does make sense if they needed an obvious reason for the truck to be at the garage, in case anyone was putting eyes on them," said Agent Edwards.

"Like us?" I asked.

"Like us. Yes. Or anyone crazy enough to think they could become a competitor," answered Agent Edwards.

"A competitor? Is that who we're going to be? Barbieri's competitor?" I asked.

"Something like that," said Agent Edwards.

The slight smile on Agent Edwards' bearded face told me he had more to tell us. Much more.

"Is the truck still there? At the garage?" asked Detective Blaine.

"It's still there," said Agent Edwards. "The drugs come in from the red brick factory, sent through the tunnel to Porter's garage, loaded secretly onto the new red truck, and then they make their usual deliveries on Friday."

"This has been the pattern?" asked Detective Blaine.

"According to my intel it's been their pattern for the last two weeks," answered Agent Edwards. "The dope comes in on Thursday, gets loaded onto the truck around four in the morning, and then unassuming drivers take the trucks to their specific delivery spots."

"Where do these trucks deliver to?" asked Detective Blaine.

"All the trucks make deliveries to numerous construction sites throughout Arizona," said Agent Edwards. "All of the new six trucks have three specially built pallets set in the floor of the truck beds."

"So they place cement bricks on top and because of the weight nobody wants to take the time to look," said Detective Blaine. "How many pounds are they moving?"

"One hundred thirty two pounds on every run," said Agent Edwards.

"Wow," added Detective Blaine. "That's what? A hundred thousand a week?"

"Give or take. Yes," answered Agent Edwards.

"Do we know which truck or trucks are carrying the drugs?" I asked.

"We do. And. We also know which truck is scheduled for this coming Friday's delivery," said Agent Edwards. "That's a definite."

Detective Blaine looked through his binoculars and stared down at the garage.

"It's this truck? The one sitting in Porter's garage?" asked Detective Blaine.

"No," replied Agent Edwards. "Not that truck. Nor any truck. Not on this coming Friday."

Detective Blaine and I looked at each other and turned to Agent Edwards with questioned looks on our faces.

"Okay. Now I'm confused," said Detective Blaine.

"Me too," I added.

"Please? Explain. Are they doing something completely different this time?" asked Detective Blaine. "Do they know we have eyes on their operation?"

"No. No one has a clue about us. Their schedule is still the same. The drugs will come in tonight. As usual. Porter will check the load and turn in for the evening. Around four A.M. he'll get up and move the load from the miner's cart in the tunnel to the specially built floor pallets. But this go 'round? When Porter goes to move the load? There won't be any drugs to load on that truck," answered Agent Edwards.

"No drugs?" I asked. "Why's that?"

"Because tonight, gentlemen, we are going into that tunnel and we are going to steal every kilo we can carry. Hopefully every single one they've sent over," announced Agent Edwards.

"You are talking sixty kilos. Won't they also be sending over an armed guard with that shipment?" asked Detective Blaine. "I know I would."

"Anyone else moving this amount of product would definitely have guards riding along. But these people? They all think they are safe, they are untouchable, and they think they have total control over their operation with no one being the wiser," said Agent Edwards. "Tonight we are going to show them how wrong they are. We are going to create a major shit storm, a shit storm that should resonate all the way back to wherever the hell Rachel Stone Barbieri is keeping herself these days."

"A woman scorned. I like it," said Detective Blaine.

"Good plan," I added. "Instead of arresting anyone, we rip them off and watch the games begin."

"Exactly," said Agent Edwards. "Everyone in their operation will instantly become suspect and when they all come together to find out what's going on? We will also learn who the major players are, we will then move in, and we will take them all down."

We all smiled and nodded in agreement. Agent Edwards looked at his watch.

"We go in at midnight," announced Agent Edwards. "That gives us about three hours to prepare and work out all the particulars."

CHAPTER THIRTY

The full moon sat low near the horizon and lit up the night sky like some huge flashlight beaming straight across the desert. Two headlights poked into the moonlit beam as Sam Porter's dusty Cadillac came slowly down the road, parked in front of the house, and its lights and engine suddenly went dark and silent. Detective Blaine, Agent Edwards, and Patrick Atwater had taken turns watching the Porter house, knowing full well Porter's Cadillac would be arriving home shortly.

"They are here," announced Detective Blaine, on watch.

Patrick and Agent Edwards entered the room and grabbed their binoculars. As the three men watched, Sam Porter and Loretta Davis got out of the car. Loretta stood still to stare up at the stars in the night sky.

"Is that your undercover?" Patrick asked.

"That's her," answered Agent Edwards.

"Brave and beautiful," added Detective Blaine.

"Look at that sky, baby," Loretta said. "Isn't it beautiful?"

"It's a full moon and yes, the sky is very beautiful here," Sam replied, and headed for the front door.

"Sam!" she said. "You're not even looking at it."

Sam Porter stopped, took a deep breath, and looked up at the stars.

"Two flashes on my command," said Agent Edwards staring through his binoculars.

"Got it," said Patrick as he stood holding a large flashlight.

"Now!" said Agent Edwards and Patrick gave the signal.

Loretta looked up towards Agent Edwards' house and saw the signal she was anticipating. Two quick flashes of light sparked in the darkness from the rear bedroom window and Loretta knew what needed to be done. She turned her attention back to Porter.

"It is a beautiful moon," he said and his eyes moved from the moonlit sky to Loretta's face, sensing her slight disappointment for not giving her his full attention.

He walked slowly towards her and placed his hands on her waist.

"Those shining stars up there are the same sparkles I see in your eyes just before I kiss you," Porter said.

"Sparkles?" she asked. "My eyes have sparkles?"

"Yes. Thousands of tiny little sparkles."

"That is so sweet, baby."

"It's true," he added and smiled as he looked into her eyes.

"Well?" she asked.

"Well what?" he repeated.

"Kiss me, you dope."

Porter kissed Loretta deeply and looked into her eyes.

"See? There they are. Just like I said. Little tiny sparkles. Beautiful."

Porter leaned in and kissed her deeply a second time. Loretta responded in kind but in the back of her mind she was thinking only of what she had to do and how much Agent Edwards and the rest of the team were counting on her.

"I love you, Lottie D," he whispered.

"I love you, too, baby," she sighed. "Let's go in the house, take a nice hot shower, pour us a little champagne, pour us a little more champagne, and make love before turning in. How does that sound?"

A large smile crossed Porter's face.

"I have some work to do early in the morning but that sounds like an excellent idea," he agreed and kissed her hand.

Loretta smiled, knowing never to question Porter on his so-called work, whenever it needed to be done. She had made the mistake of asking too many questions early in their relationship and Porter told her never to question what he did or when he did it. Loretta obediently agreed and nothing more was ever said.

The house was dark and quiet as Porter turned on the living room lamp and tossed his keys onto the small shelf hanging by the front door. Loretta started to unbutton her blouse.

"Shall I get us some champagne," she asked.

"I'll get it," he said and Loretta walked down the long hallway to the bedroom.

From the refrigerator, Porter grabbed a bottle of champagne from the stash he always kept cold, placed it in a silver ice bucket sitting on the kitchen counter, poured some ice into the bucket from one of the three bags in the freezer, selected two glasses, and headed for the bedroom. He entered to find Loretta standing naked in front of the full length mirror and brushing her hair. Porter put the champagne bucket and glasses on the nightstand and looked at her.

"Let me do that," he said, taking the brush from her hand. Standing behind her, he slowly and gently stroked her hair.

"Like this?" he asked.

"Yes," she replied. "It's very nice."

He leaned in, lightly placed his hand on her right breast, and kissed her neck. Loretta playfully pushed him away.

"What's the matter?" he asked.

"You need a shave. A close one," she said. "And if we're going to drink champagne I want to drink my bubbly in a champagne glass. Not those."

"A glass is a glass. No?" he asked.

"Not where I come from," she said.

Loretta grabbed up the two glasses and kissed Porter lightly on the cheek.

"Ow. Go shave. I'll get the proper glasses."

"All right, my sweet," he replied, and walked into the bathroom.

Porter removed his shirt, looked into the mirror and rubbed his chin.

"You are right, I do need a shave," he said.

"Nice and close honey," she answered, leaving the room. "Nice and close."

Porter smiled, grabbed a new razor blade, popped it in his razor and ran the hot water in his sink.

"Maybe I should grow a moustache like Clark Gable," he announced. "A nice soft thick moustache. What do you think? Would you like that?"

Porter's words fell on deaf ears because Loretta had already run out of the bedroom.

"Lottie? Lottie D?" he called, sticking his head out of the bathroom and realizing she was no longer in the room.

Porter returned to the mirror and lathered his face.

Naked, Loretta raced into the garage, ran around the parked red truck, and went to the first window where Agent Edwards, Detective Blaine, and Patrick were standing outside, waiting in the dark. Loretta saw them, unlocked the window, held up one finger, and ran quickly back into the house.

"She's going to need a minute before we go in," said Agent Edwards.

"She seems to have everything under her control," said Detective Blaine.

"Definitely," added Patrick. "Most definitely."

The minute ticked slowly by and Agent Edwards quietly opened the window and climbed into the garage. Detective Blaine passed six dark blue gym bags through to Agent Edwards before he and Patrick climbed in, shutting and locking the window behind him. Each man took two bags and Agent Edwards led them to the tunnel entrance located in the rear bathroom.

"This is it," whispered Agent Edwards and lifted the false shower stall floor revealing a three foot wide wooden stairway leading down into the tunnel. All three men went quietly down the stairs.

The tunnel was dark although there were small single lights every twenty feet on one side of the track. As Patrick and Detective Blaine looked down the rails they could barely see the turn where Agent Edwards said he had walked to. Covered by a canvas tarp, a flat cart sat in the shadows of the small wooden wall at the end of the track. Detective Blaine touched the wooden walls.

"This is excellent work," he whispered. "That son of a bitch Rockwell did do a nice job. Where's the stuff?"

"It's here," answered Agent Edwards.

Patrick and Detective Blaine looked down at the cart as Agent Edwards pulled back the tarp to reveal sixty neatly packed kilos of high grade heroin.

"Holy shit," said Detective Blaine.

"Stay focused and let's get to work," said Agent Edwards.

All three men immediately went into action, placing ten kilos in each of the bags. In less than thirty seconds, the canvas tarp was replaced over the cart and the men went back the wooden stairs carrying all sixty kilos, the entire load, with a street value of over one million dollars.

Agent Edwards' raid had placed the FBI officially and illegally into the drug trade business but Agent Edwards, Detective Blaine, Patrick Atwater, and Special Agent Loretta Davis, had also successfully just pulled off the robbery of the century, a robbery Agent Edwards was certain would never see the public light of day.

Not if they stuck to their plan.

The three men quietly replaced the shower floor. As they headed for the window, a sudden popping sound echoed through the garage and all three froze in their tracks.

"What the hell was that?" whispered Detective Blaine.

Laughter was heard coming from the back bedroom.

"Champagne," answered Agent Edwards. "They're drinking champagne."

Detective Blaine breathed a sigh of relief and they headed for the window.

"You are right, my sweet," said Porter. "Champagne should be savored from a champagne glass. To tonight and to us."

"To us," said Loretta as she and Porter clinked glasses, sipped their champagne, and sat naked and slightly wet on the bed.

"Feel my face now, my sweet. Is it to your satisfaction and your liking?" he asked.

Loretta reached out and touched Porter's cheek.

"Very nice," she replied. "And I know just the place for that smooth face of yours to be."

"And where is that?" he asked.

Loretta put her glass on the night stand, put one of the pillows behind the small of her back, leaned back against the soft velvet headboard and smiled at him.

"Right over here, baby" she said and pointed to her cheek with her index finger. "Right over here."

Porter smiled, put his empty glass on the night stand next to hers, and climbed into bed next to her. He kissed her cheek, her neck, and kissed her warmly on the lips as he slowly dropped his left hand down between her legs. Loretta sighed deeply, pretending to enjoy his awkward pawing.

"That's it, baby," she lied. "Right there. Just. Like. That."

Porter moaned slightly and kept up his motions as Loretta looked over at the bedroom door and hoped everything Agent Edwards had worked out went exactly as planned. She knew what still had to be done, and also knew the following morning would turn everything that had happened up to now completely upside down.

She hoped she was ready to weather the coming storm.

Agent Edwards, Detective Blaine, and Patrick felt like three young children suddenly getting away with some Halloween neighborhood prank as they ran unseen up the hill and carrying a king's ransom in six blue duffle bags. They also knew there was no turning back. Agent Edwards' plan was now in motion in real time and everyone on their side was at great risk.

The line in the sand had been drawn and the silent war was about to ignite.

A half hour had passed, and Porter appeared to be sleeping soundly. Still naked, Loretta quietly climbed out of bed and walked quickly to the garage. She opened the Dutch door leading out to the garage and reached for the unlocked window. Seeing Porter's naked reflection in the window's glass, standing in the doorway, she stifled her surprise and instinctively pretended to unlock the window, quickly opened it, and began taking in several deep breaths of the fresh night air, pretending not to notice Porter standing there.

"What are you doing?" he asked.

Loretta turned and professionally faked surprise. Porter seemed to buy the pretense.

"I wanted to see the full moon one last time tonight," she lied.

"The full moon?"

"Yes," she said. "I didn't mean to wake you. I'm sorry if I did."

"It's all right. How does it look?" he asked. "Is it as beautiful and bright as before?"

A pang of fear ran through her body as she wondered if she was about to be caught in her phony excuse for being in the garage at this hour, or, for that matter, in the garage at all.

"Yes it is," she said and looked out the window. "Or it was. Some nasty clouds have moved in and spoiled everything."

Porter walked to the window and looked at her.

"These windows of mine must always be locked," he told her. "Too many sticky-handed people live here in Nogales. On both sides of the border. We have to be mindful. Always."

"I understand. I would have locked it again. I would have. I just wanted to breathe some real fresh air. Back in Texas the air never smells like this. In El Paso the night air usually smells like the inside of a cow."

Porter laughed at her little joke, shut the window, and turned the lock.

"Always locked. Okay?" he reiterated.

"Okay," she replied.

Loretta smiled, kissed his cheek, calmly walked past him, and headed for the bedroom. Porter watched her naked body as she walked away and sighed heavily.

"I am a lucky man," he said.

"Yes, you are," she pretended to agree and blew out a huge sigh of relief knowing she had just dodged a possible bullet.

Porter looked out at the night sky. Clouds had moved in and the full moon was no longer visible. Porter took another deep breath and walked slowly back to the bedroom. Loretta lay on the bed with her back to him as Porter climbed in, pulled the covers over them, and held her close in his arms.

Loretta lay quietly in the darkened room, still hoping she hadn't made a costly mistake.

Meanwhile, Agent Edwards, Detective Blaine, and Patrick put the six bags in the bedroom closet and decided to take turns keeping a close eye on Porter's house. Around five-thirty in the morning, Patrick entered the room to relieve a bleary-eyed Detective Blaine.

"You're early," said Detective Blaine.

"You look like you could use some sleep," Patrick said.

"I'm getting there," replied Detective Blaine and looked through his binoculars.

"Anything shaking down there?" Patrick asked.

"There is now," said Detective Blaine.

An old weathered pick-up truck arrived and parked next to Porter's Cadillac.

"Better wake up Edwards. Porter has company," Patrick said.

"Will do," said Detective Blaine and went to the other bedroom.

Three men got out of the truck and knocked on the front door. Patrick looked at his watch to note the time as Detective Blaine and Agent Edwards returned to the back bedroom and grabbed their binoculars, focusing on the house.

"We have some movement?" asked Agent Edwards.

"Three men," Patrick said. "Nobody I recognize."

"I do. It's the cement truck loading crew," said Agent Edwards. "They are about to get the surprise of their lives."

A fully dressed Porter opened the front door of the house and let the three men inside.

"What time is it?" asked Agent Edwards.

"Five-thirty six," Patrick answered.

"They're late," said Agent Edwards.

"Is that a good thing?" asked Patrick.

"It gives us daylight to observe, a good thing for us," said Agent Edwards. "One of you pick up that camera over there and start taking pictures of anyone going in or out."

"I got it," said Patrick.

Patrick picked up the camera and looked it over.

"I never saw one like this before," said Patrick. "Is it a Kodak?"

"No. It's a Contax-S. German made," said Agent Edwards. "It will get us what we need."

Patrick focused the camera on Porter's house.

"Very clear picture. Nice camera," said Patrick, snapping his first photo of the two vehicles parked in front of the house.

"What do we do now?" asked Detective Blaine.

"We keep our weapons handy, our eyes on the house and our little stash of goodies, and for now, keep taking pictures, sit back, and watch the show," said Agent Edwards.

"I'll make some coffee," said Detective Blaine, heading for the kitchen.

CHAPTER THIRTY ONE

Throughout the day and early evening, all the players on Porter's side of the fence assembled quickly once the discovery of the missing precious cargo was made. We were certain Porter had been on the phone most of the day with everyone connected with their enterprise, furiously seeking information as to who could possibly have had the guts to pull off the heist with such precision and bravado. Agent Edwards was receiving intel hourly from each of his agents throughout Nogales, but word of the heist was kept completely in house and under wraps with no one outside of Porter's inner circle knowing anything about a heist or missing heroin.

Agent Edwards might have been short in stature, but his plan was anything short of brilliant. He had orchestrated everything, with no harm or incidents occurring to us or any of his field agents. He struck right to the heart of Barbieri's new venture with no one knowing the how or the why. Each of us had executed their duties, avoided harm's way, and been accounted for.

Everyone had reported in to Agent Edwards except for Agent Loretta Davis. It was the only glitch so far but Agent Edwards kept a strong front and we all knew he was hoping for the right outcome.

All we could do now was watch, wait, and pray she was okay.

As we watched, the first car to arrive was a brand new black Hudson Commodore. Detective Blaine, Agent Edwards, and myself were surprised to see Captain Sandoval step out of his vehicle and walk to Porter's front door with apparent urgency. His uniform was somewhat disheveled and the fact that it was seven-thirty in the morning had us assume he was likely coming from one of the whore houses he regularly frequented when he got Porter's call. We were highly disappointed that a top ranking Mexican official like Captain Sandoval would be part of Barbieri's operation but after much discussion it made sense to have someone of his stature on her books. Their product and large amounts of cash would have no problems moving in and out of Nogales from either side of the border. Any illegal movements would go completely unnoticed with a man like Captain Sandoval in charge being paid to look the other way. If something were to go wrong, it would also be to their advantage to have Captain Sandoval simply step in with his soldiers and calm the situation. I snapped his photograph with the Contax-S and Agent Edwards wrote the Captain's name down on his list, right under Sam Porter's name.

"So much for border control on the Mexican side," I said. "They must be paying him a pretty penny to look the other way."

"Let's hope his American counterpart, Captain Herman, isn't on the take, too," said Agent Edwards. "That would create some very big problems with the plan."

"Nothing you couldn't handle," added Detective Blaine. "If Captain Herman is part of this he's going down with the rest. Maybe not as easy but he's still going down."

"We'll know soon enough," said Agent Edwards.

"Got another car coming up the road," I said and quickly adjusted the focus on the camera.

The next arrival was a young handsome Mexican man, driving an old beat up Ford coupe with a cracked windshield, known by Agent Edwards' intel as one of the cement factory truck drivers named Angel.

Angel was added to the list.

By nightfall there were only five vehicles left on Porter's front driveway. Besides Porter's Cadillac and the worn out pick-up truck was Sandoval's Hudson, Angel's beat up Ford, and a brand new Packard Touring Sedan with four men inside that none of us could identify. Around seven-thirty, Agent Edwards had another of his undercover agents, a young Italian kid named Vincent Correlli, stop in with sandwiches and coffees for us, and promptly took all my film to get processed without saying a word to Detective Blaine or myself. We could sense that the months of planning, working undercover, being unaware of Agent Davis' situation, and many sleepless nights were all beginning to take its toll and instigating tension in all of us. Getting down to the wire and knowing that we were almost to the end of Agent Edwards' plan, we still did not have one sign of Rachel Stone Barbieri or the traitor engineer Rockwell. Over dinner, we talked about different scenarios and wondered if Rachel was actually ever going to show. Even Agent Edwards was beginning to have doubts when we suddenly could hear another car driving up to the house. Dropping our food, we grabbed our binoculars, and stared out the bedroom windows.

"What do you think?" asked Agent Edwards.

"It's a Chrysler New Yorker. Brand new," said Detective Blaine. "Some big black guy is at the wheel."

"I can see the black guy," said Agent Edwards. "Do you see her?"

"I can't tell," said Detective Blaine.

"I see her," I said. "It's her. She's in the back seat."

"Are you sure?" asked Agent Edwards. "I can't tell from this angle."

I lowered my binoculars and looked at Agent Edwards.

"I can," I answered. "It's her. And that son of a bitch, Rockwell. He's sitting right next to her in the back seat."

Agent Edwards and Detective Blaine lowered their binoculars and we looked at each other as if Betty Grable had just asked all three of us to spend the weekend with her at some fancy New York hotel.

"She must have been close by to get here so quickly," I said.

"She's here," said Agent Edwards. "That's all that matters now. Get that camera!"

I grabbed the Contax-S, quickly peered through the window, and focused the lens. Detective Blaine and Agent Edwards stared through their binoculars and watched the New Yorker come to a stop, parking in front of the house. I snapped several shots of the tall black driver as he stepped out of the car and opened the rear door. Rockwell got out from the opposite side and I quickly took a shot of him as he turned and looked up directly at me. I kept taking more photos, knowing we could not be seen from their position in the dark.

There was a loud knock at the front door.

"Who the hell is that," asked Detective Blaine.

"It must be Vincent with more photos and intel," said Agent Edwards. "I'll answer it but I have to see her first before I do another thing."

"I hear that," said Detective Blaine.

We peered down at the house while Rachel Stone Barbieri slowly emerged from the Chrysler New Yorker as if she was attending a luncheon at some swank hotel. She wore black leather heels and carried a small black purse under her arm. Her outfit was pale yellow pants and a top with a matching attached hood. The entire ensemble draped her body in such a way that the fabric appeared like running water passing over every smooth curve of her body.

"There she is," I said. "She might be dressed to the nines but look at that face. Does that look like a happy individual?"

"That little bitch is beside herself," added Detective Blaine. "I say let's go down there right now and put a few rounds in her forehead."

"As much as I would love to do exactly that, Detective, we will restrain ourselves and keep to the plan," said Agent Edwards. "We have already broken several laws by stealing her entire shipment. I'm not about to add murder to our list of crimes. We are still the good guys. Remember?"

"I remember," said Detective Blaine. "But seeing her now makes me want to forget everything and go down there and end her."

"Patience, Detective," said Agent Edwards. "Time is on our side for the moment. We need to use that time to our advantage."

"She still looks the same," I said. "Still working those good looks of hers but she sure as hell is not smiling. At least we got that much going for us, too."

I took several more shots with the camera as Rachel, Rockwell, and the large black man approached the house.

"We haven't seen one smiling face down there all day," said Agent Edwards. "I like that. I like that very much."

"We're smiling," added Detective Blaine and grinned broadly.

"I like that too," added Agent Edwards.

Another loud knock pounded at the front door as I quickly snapped a few more photos.

"I'll get that," said Detective Blaine. "You two keep your eyes on our little angry miss. What's the Agent's name again?"

"Correlli. Agent Vincent Correlli," said Agent Edwards.

"Vincent Corelli. Got it," said Detective Blaine and left the room.

"Detective Blaine is becoming a bit anxious," replied Agent Edwards.

"He'll be fine," I said. "We will all be fine. Especially when this is over and done."

"We are close," added Agent Edwards.

"Phase two of your plan has come together nicely," I said.

"So far, so good," answered Agent Edwards. "Phase three will be a bit more difficult."

"Difficult yes, but clearly more fun for us," I said.

Agent Edwards put down his binoculars and looked at me.

"You and Detective Blaine are enjoying this. Aren't you?"

"Damn right," I said. "Rachel Stone Barbieri and her entire crew deserve everything we are going to give them. And doing this? Acting like undercover pirates and thieves sure beats being shot at by the Nazis. And look. I know Detective Blaine and I, as well as you, are never going to rest or do anything else that's worth a damn until we shut this down and give them what they got coming. In spades."

Agent Edwards nodded his agreement and put his binoculars up to his face. Rachel, Rockwell, and the tall black man were greeted at the door by a very serious looking Sam Porter and everyone went inside.

"They all look like they're attending somebody's wake," said Agent Edwards.

"They are," I added. "Their own. They just don't know it yet."

"I wish I could be down there right now listening to their conversation," said Agent Edwards.

"Agent Davis will give you the updates you want when she reports in," I said.

"Let's hope so," replied Agent Edwards.

I could see the worry in Agent Edwards' eyes but I said nothing. We put our binoculars down and tried to relax. Agent Edwards sat down on a chair and rolled his head and neck.

"She's a good agent," he said. "She'll do okay."

"Yes, she will," I said. "She'll come out of this all right. How could she not? She has us, all your other undercover agents, and the entire backing of the FBI including Hoover himself, in her corner. Right?"

"Right," he added.

I sat down near him but said nothing more about Agent Davis. She was right in the thick of it and we all knew the risks she took and the possible consequences if something went wrong. I took a deep breath and tried to change the subject.

"I would think this guy Porter, his three truck drivers, or maybe even Captain Sandoval are going to be their prime suspects as this plays out," I suggested. "They all had the most and the easiest access."

Agent Edwards sat silently for a few moments and looked up at me.

"I agree," said Agent Edwards. "If I were in Barbieri's shoes that is exactly who I would be looking into."

"That conversation is not going to be pretty," I said.

"I know," he agreed again.

Another long silence came over the room and I could see the dread on his face taking over Agent Edwards' thoughts. I tried to reassure him.

"Once they start asking questions, she'll land on her feet."

"I'm hoping so," replied Agent Edwards. "Maybe we should make our call right now?"

"No," I said. "We can't do that. Not yet."

"Why not?" he asked. "The call will put her in the clear."

"The call will put her in the clear but doing it right now wouldn't be good. The timing would be off and it would only raise red flags. A call this soon? It's too coincidental. Too pat. Barbieri just got here. We have to let them stew. Let them talk. Make them think. Probe around with some scenarios of their own. When the call comes we are the ones who have to sound impatient. It plays out better that way. Remember? Those were your words. Not mine. And you were right. It's a good plan but we have to let some time pass. Let's stick to it."

Agent Edwards looked at me and took a deep breath.

"You're right. I just don't like waiting"

"No one does," I said.

"Okay. We'll stick to the plan and wait two more hours to make the phone call."

"Good," I said.

"I just hope she'll be okay until we do," he added.

"I get it. You're worried for her. We all are. And I'm telling you. We'll come out of this all right. You, me, Detective Blaine, and every last one of your agents. The people who should be worrying are down there in Porter's house. And we are going to get them. All of them. Just like we said we would."

A slight smile crossed Agent Edwards' face.

"Thanks," he said.

"You're welcome," I replied.

"It is a good plan. Isn't it?" Agent Edwards asked.

"The best," I said. "On the surface it's illegal as hell. But it will still play out nicely. So don't go second guessing yourself. Not now. Stay positive. Focused."

"I will."

"Have you decided which one it's going to be?" I asked.

"No. Not yet. Let's look at what Vincent has brought us and then we'll all decide. Together," said Agent Edwards.

"Another good plan," I said. "The only down side is we have to drink Detective Blaine's lousy coffee."

"A small price to pay," added Agent Edwards. "Let's get the new photos processed immediately."

"Absolutely," I said.

I popped the film from the camera, following Agent Edwards out of the room. Detective Blaine was pouring fresh coffee. Agent

Correlli was placing newly developed photographs on the kitchen table, with Agent Edwards gazing down at them.

"Let's get this last batch of film processed, Agent Correlli, and then I think we should have all the players down there accounted for," said Agent Edwards.

"Yes, sir," answered Agent Correlli, taking the roll of film from me and walking out the front door.

Detective Blaine handed us coffees.

"That kid don't talk much," said Detective Blaine. "Does he?"

"He's doing an outstanding job with these photos," said Agent Edwards. "Whose turn is it at the window?"

"I'll take it," I said.

The two of them sifted through the photos and the intel as I reloaded the camera and headed back to the window.

CHAPTER THIRTY TWO

Casually smoking a cigarette, Ponce Delgado sat calmly on the stairs at the bottom of the tunnel entrance. Rachel Stone Barbieri, Sam Porter, and Rockwell stood in the tunnel watching the three men, earlier arrivals in the pick-up truck, slowly walking the tunnel tracks. All three had flashlights and were searching every inch of the tunnel, hoping to find some answers about how Friday's heroin shipment was stolen out from under their very noses. A single lit oil lantern was set on the empty cart.

"This tunnel search is a waste of time," said Rachel. "What do you think they are going to find out there?"

"I don't know," said Porter. "Maybe they'll find foot prints. A tossed cigarette, maybe. Something."

Ponce ground his cigarette out on the stair and threw it on the ground.

"I'll tell you what they will find," he said as he stood up and walked to the cart sitting on the track. "They will find nothing! And I will tell you why. Look here."

Ponce pointed to the ground below the small wooden deck near the tracks.

"This is where the cart always sits. Yes?" he asked.

"Yes," replied Porter.

"And the only way this cart moves is operated from the Mexican side. Correct?"

"Correct. That was how Mrs. Barbieri wanted it. Captain Sandoval moves the cart and then locks his entrance. What's your point?" asked Porter.

"My point is this" replied Ponce. "Sixty kilos. Five high. Four across. Three deep. You tell us maybe two or maybe even four men stood right here last night or early this morning and walked all sixty kilos up these stairs and out through your electric garage doors while you and the girlfriend were in your bedroom doing, how shall I say this nicely? Fucking each other's brains out."

"That's what I said. That's how I think it occurred," answered Porter. "Yes."

"I disagree and I will tell you why," said Ponce. "Look here. Rockwell? Shine that light of yours down here by my feet."

Rockwell turned on his flashlight and stepped closer to the cart.

"Tell me what you see?"

Rockwell moved his light as Porter and Rachel stepped in closer to take a better look.

"I see your footprints but nothing else," said Rockwell.

"That's right. These thieves, whoever they were, either covered up their tracks when they left. Or."

"Or what?" asked Rockwell.

"Or they were never here and moved the cart somehow down the tracks and back to the Mexican side. Never using these stairs to come in or go out."

"That makes sense," said Rachel. "But why? The money to be made is here in the states. Not back in Mexico."

"They are most likely sitting on the product as we speak. You can steal what was here but no one can sell sixty kilos without us hearing about it. No one. They must have some other plan in mind."

"Some other plan? A ransom?" asked Rachel.

"Possibly," said Ponce. "Turn a quick dollar and return everything with no questions asked."

"That will never happen," Rachel added. "Whoever did this will pay with their lives."

"I agree. We will have to make an example of these fools," said Ponce. "Every last one of them."

"If I did this? If I stole sixty kilos? I would definitely want to take the product to the states side," said Rockwell. "Not back to Mexico."

"If?" said Ponce, lighting another cigarette.

"What?" asked Rockwell. "You think I did this?"

Ponce blew out the smoke with a slight turn of his head and spit a small piece of tobacco on the ground.

"Did you?" asked Ponce.

"No. I didn't," replied Rockwell.

"You are building what? Seven tunnels for us including this one. Lukeville. Cowlic. Sasabe. Lochiel. Naco. Douglas. It would be easy for a man like you to move sixty kilos anywhere and anytime you choose. Even on the Mexican side of the border."

"That is true but it is also absurd," said Rockwell and stared at Rachel. "I was only speaking about a possible scenario."

"A scenario?" asked Ponce. "I have a scenario. Maybe you have grown tired of building tunnels for Mrs. Barbieri and myself and maybe, just maybe, you started thinking sixty kilos of prime grade white boy could make a nice final pay day for you! Maybe you have some secret hiding place built somewhere along here where you and maybe Porter and his Mexican workers could help you move it down the tracks, store it for a little while, and then make, as they say in those American westerns, the clean get away. Once the coast was clear. Huh? What do you have to say to that scenario?"

"That is a nice story but it is crazy talk," said Rockwell. "Whoever did this is a dead man. Everyone here knows that. Maybe they don't know that yet but I sure as hell do. And so do you. I also enjoy breathing and I like building these tunnels. That's what I do. I have also been paid exceptionally well for my expertise, my assistance, and my loyalty. I am and always have been loyal to you and to Mrs. Barbieri. I want to know who did this just as much as you do. And I don't go putting secret hiding places in any tunnel unless I'm asked to do so. And no one has asked."

Ponce took another drag on his cigarette, slowly blew the smoke out once again, and quickly turned his attention over to Porter.

"What about you, Porter," Ponce asked. "What do you have to say for yourself?"

"Me? I didn't do this," answered Porter. "I have always been loyal. Always. I did everything I have been asked. And I deeply resent your accusations. The only people that even know about any of the tunnels and what goes through them, are standing here right now."

"Except for Captain Sandoval sitting upstairs," said Rockwell. "He has more access to this tunnel than any of us here. Maybe you should be pointing your fingers at the good Captain!"

"I will vouch for the Captain," said Ponce. "Sandoval is many things but being this stupid is not in his nature. But you, Porter? You and my deceased cousin were partners in crime long before Rachel and I took over. Maybe his untimely death left some bad feelings for you towards the rest of us."

"You are way off. None of us here would ever dream of stealing. That's a certain death sentence and we all know that," said Porter. "It's a stupid play."

"Is it?" asked Ponce.

"Yes!" yelled Porter.

Both men stared hard at each other.

"All right, boys," said Rachel. "Let's stop this macho pissing contest, agree that none of us had anything to do with this, and look at the facts. Sixty kilos are gone. Vanished. That's one hundred and thirty two pounds. Not easy for one person to grab up and run off somewhere. This had to be accomplished by more than one person. Agreed?"

The three men nodded their agreement.

"Agreed," said Rockwell.

"And? Some knowledgeable person or persons," she added. "They knew where and they knew when. Now our product is gone and I want it back. Someone outside of our little circle here found out somehow, some way, when and where these kilos would be and snatched them all up. Quickly. Quietly. Effectively. Completely under our radar. Think. Somebody tell me. How the hell did this happen? Who could make this happen?"

Porter, Rockwell, and Ponce stood silently for a few moments and Rachel could tell by the looks on their faces no concrete answers would be forthcoming. Rachel looked into Porter's eyes.

"What about this girlfriend of yours," she asked. "How much do you really know about this Nina Douglas everyone calls Miss Lottie D?"

"She's just a club singer from El Paso. A good singer. We have grown quite fond of one another over the last few months. The clientele at Pablo's absolutely love her."

"I get it. She's highly entertaining. She's never been down here? With you?"

"Here? No. Never."

"She doesn't ask you a lot of questions?"

"Questions? No. I'm telling you. She's not part of this."

"Does she have any friends in Pablo's? People she talks to besides you?"

"No," said Porter. "She stayed at the hotel in town, alone, worked at the club, we started dating and then she moved in with me. We are together all the time. I already told you this."

"Does she ever make any demands on you?"

"Demands? No. I have given Lottie many things but she has never asked for them. I have done that because we are a couple. She is very appreciative of how I take care of her. The woman loves me. And I love her."

"Montez Carrillo loved me," said Rachel. "So did Quentin Thayer. Trust me. Love between men and women is highly over-rated. Have you ever caught her snooping around the garage? Playing with the electric doors? Seeing how they worked? Going through your closets or your bedroom drawers?"

"No. Never! Nothing like that. Not ever."

"Think! Tell me something she might have done lately that seemed odd to you."

Porter suddenly remembered the other night. Rachel immediately picked up on the defined look in his eyes and on his face.

"What?" Rachel pressed. "Spit it out!"

"I wouldn't call it odd," said Porter.

"You wouldn't call what odd?" she asked.

"The night of the robbery. She was out here. In the garage. Looking up at the full moon from one of the side windows."

Rachel and Ponce looked at each other.

"Son of a bitch!" squealed Rachel.

"It was nothing! I'm telling you! She was out there bare assed naked. Looking at the God damn moon!" Porter screamed defiantly. "That was all!"

"Looking at the God damn moon? You saw her looking at the moon because that's what she wanted you to see!"

"No! She was trying to get me to appreciate the beauty in nature!" he added. "That's all!"

"Come on, Porter. This woman is in your garage just before sixty kilos go missing and you didn't think that might be suspicious behavior on her part?"

"No. I didn't. You don't know this girl like I do. She likes the moon and the stars. And she likes me. A lot. I am telling you. Lottie D knows nothing about our business. Nor has she ever asked. And she doesn't know about this tunnel. Right now she thinks you are my business partners and we're all in the garage discussing a problem we have at Pablo's!"

"A problem at Pablo's? That's what you told her?" asked Ponce.

"I had to tell her something! Lottie and I are either here, alone together, or we are at the club. We are not used to all this kind of company. I told her some money is missing and we are trying to figure out what happened."

"And she believed you?" said Rachel.

"Yes!" he replied. "She knows nothing."

"You are absolutely certain?" asked Ponce.

"Yes. Lottie doesn't know a thing. I would bet my life on it," said Porter.

Ponce suddenly turned and looked directly at Rachel and smiled slightly.

"He bets his life he says," said Ponce.

Porter calmed himself with a few deep breaths and looked at Rachel.

"You have to believe me," he said calmly. "She's just a kid singer fresh from a bad marriage to some shit heel cowboy back in Texas. That's it. She has nothing to do with this."

"I hope for her sake you're right, Porter," added Rachel. "She loves you. You love her. She loves the moon and all the stars. She's an artistic type."

"Yes," said Porter.

"I understand. Completely."

"Thank you," he said.

"I'm still going upstairs and have a talk with Miss Lottie D."

"Please? Don't hurt her," begged Porter.

Rachel turned to quickly catch Ponce's eye and slowly stepped closer until she was face to face with Porter.

"I didn't say I was going to hurt her. I said I was going to talk to her. And I am going to do whatever I feel is necessary to get the answers I need to have. Do not get in my way over this. Do you hear me?" she said.

"I would never get in your way. Ever. And yes. I hear you," answered Porter. "Do what you need to do."

"I will. Now I'm going upstairs and have a little girl to girl chat," added Rachel.

"Wait," said Ponce. "Hold up."

"What?" asked Rachel.

Ponce looked down the tunnel at the three men still searching and looked at Rachel.

"This other man upstairs, Angel, he works with these three men?" asked Ponce. "Yes?"

"Yes," replied Porter. "My god, have you all gone completely paranoid? Lottie D knows nothing and these men, and Angel? They are all good men. Trustworthy people. Loyal to a fault. They were hand-picked by me and are all well taken care of. Paid nicely for their assistance and most importantly for their silence. They would not do something like this."

Ponce lit another cigarette and looked at Rachel.

"What are you thinking?" asked Rachel.

"I think you need to go speak with the girlfriend and Porter and I should have a little talk of our own with these three gentlemen."

"I'm telling you that is not necessary," said Porter. "Mrs. Barbieri? Please? These are good men! Loyal men."

"I'm sure they are," said Rachel. "Especially if you are vouching for them."

"I am."

"Then you should stay here, Porter," she said. "Talk to them."

"Just talk?" he asked.

"Yes. Talk. Talk to your men. See what they have to tell you."

"I would rather be upstairs when you talk to Lottie."

"You can talk to her after she's answered my questions. Right now? You stay down here with Ponce until we hear what your men have to say for themselves. All right?"

"I can do that," he said. "We are all telling you the truth, Mrs. Barbieri. I swear to you."

"I believe you," replied Rachel. "Stay here until all these questions become answers. Yes?"

Porter nervously shook his head yes and took a deep breath.

"Okay. Sure." said Porter. "Whatever you say?"

"It's best this way," said Rachel as she gave Ponce a quick glance. "Be your diplomatic self, Ponce. No need to hurt these men to get what we came here for. Agreed?"

"Absolutely," replied Ponce.

"Good," she added. "Get this done. Do it correctly."

"I will," Ponce answered.

Ponce smiled at Porter and slowly blew out more smoke from his cigarette. Rachel and Rockwell walked up the stairs.

"These men, and Angel, and my Lottie D, are not involved," said Porter. "You have to believe me."

"We will know soon enough," said Ponce. "Wave them all back here."

Porter grabbed the lit lantern from the cart, stepped out onto the tracks and waved to the men. Ponce took one last drag on his cigarette, tossed it to the ground, casually drew a silencer from his pocket and quietly attached it to the handgun he had holstered in his jacket.

"Two of those men down there have families," said Porter as he continued waving the lantern and looking down the tracks. "They know the risks they take. The risks we all take in this dirty business."

"It is that my friend," said Ponce. "It is that."

"It is what?" asked Porter.

"A dirty business," replied Ponce.

A sudden popping sound was the last thing Porter heard as Ponce pointed his gun, fired, and watched his bullet blow out the back of Porter's skull. Blood and portions of Porter's brain matter splattered onto both sides of the tunnel walls as Porter's body thumped forward onto the ground. The sound of the smashing glass from the broken lantern falling onto the steel rail startled the three approaching men and they stopped dead in their tracks.

"Shit!" muttered Ponce and stomped his foot at the burning oil pouring out and onto one of the railroad ties.

Realizing what had occurred, the three men quickly turned and began running in the opposite direction. Ponce stepped onto the tracks, stared down the tunnel and took careful aim using two hands to steady his weapon. Three more pops burst from Ponce's weapon and, one by one, all three men went down. Ponce gazed down the tracks and waited silently for any sounds or any movement.

None came.

Ponce slowly removed the silencer from his gun, kicked some dirt onto the last flickering flames of the spilled lamp oil, turned, and went up the stairs.

CHAPTER THIRTY THREE

Phase three of Agent Edwards' plan had finally gone into high gear. Everyone was where they needed to be and Detective Blaine and myself were eager to close down Rachel Stone Barbieri's entire operation once and for all. Agent Correlli was manning the bedroom window to keep a close eye on Sam Porter's house, Detective Blaine checked his handgun for the tenth time, and I stared at the photos Agent Correlli had developed and placed on the small kitchen table. Each face had a name written on pieces of tape across the bottom and federal arrest warrants were all neatly typed and ready to go.

"Looking at all those faces makes me feel like it is Christmas in Nogales," said Detective Blaine. "What do you say?"

I picked up the photo of Rachel Stone Barbieri, held it up, and looked at Detective Blaine.

"Just taking down this one would be Christmas enough for me," I answered. "But yeah, the night does have a kind of festive feel. What time have you got?"

Detective Blaine looked at his watch and smiled.

"This is a little ironic. It is twelve twenty-five."

"Happy birthday, Jesus," I said. "Where's the man?"

"The man is here," said a clean-shaven Agent Edwards as he walked into the room from the hallway bathroom. "Everybody ready?"

"Me and Atwater are definitely ready and set," said Detective Blaine.

"Well, look at you," I said. "Got yourself all cleaned up for the final count down. Are you expecting the press or do you just want to look pretty for Mrs. Barbieri?"

"No press," said Agent Edwards. "There won't be any press or any photos. Not tonight. Tonight we are going to get this done quickly, quietly, and hopefully without incident."

"And if there is?" I asked.

"Then we will handle that issue as well."

Agent Correlli's voice suddenly filled the room.

"Hey out there? We have a winner!" he announced with a loud whispering voice.

Agent Edwards walked swiftly to the back bedroom and Detective Blaine and I followed him in. The room was completely dark and the night air gave off a slight hint of eucalyptus as Agent Correlli sat on a small wooden stool peering through binoculars out the opened window.

"Who is it?" asked Agent Edwards.

Agent Correlli lowered his binoculars.

"It's Captain Sandoval and he's moving as if his ass was on fire," said Agent Correlli.

"It's about to be," said Agent Edwards. "Things must be getting extremely tense down there."

"Any other movements?" asked Agent Edwards.

"None as yet," said Agent Correlli. "Is everyone in place and ready to do this?"

"Everyone is set," said Agent Edwards.

We all stood and watched as Captain Sandoval got into his Hudson, started up the engine, and pulled quickly out of the driveway, heading down the street towards town.

"Okay, gentlemen. This is it. Time for us to make the call? Are you ready, Agent Correlli?"

"Yes sir. Whenever you say?"

"I say let's do this now. Patrick? You and Detective Blaine keep your eyes on the house."

"Will do," said Detective Blaine and took the binoculars from Agent Correlli.

"Go get 'em, kid," said Detective Blaine.

"Thanks," answered Agent Correlli and gave Detective Blaine a reassuring nod.

I moved the stool away from the window and watched Agent Edwards pick up the large black phone.

"Are you good to go?" asked Agent Edwards.

"Yes sir," said Agent Correlli and took several quick deep breaths. "I'm good."

Agent Edwards dialed the phone and handed the receiver to Agent Corelli, who held the receiver out so we could hear who and what was said on the other end. He stood patiently as the phone made a few clicking noises and began to ring. On the fourth ring a man's voice answered.

"Hello," the voice said.

Agent Correlli spoke English into the phone and used a faked Mexican accent.

"This is Randy," he said. "I want to speak with Captain Sandoval."

"Hold on," said the voice.

Detective Blaine and I were very impressed with Agent Correlli's sudden voice change and complete character transition. A woman's voice suddenly came on the line.

"Captain Sandoval is not here at the moment, Randy," the woman's voice replied politely.

"Not there?" repeated Agent Correlli staying in his Randy character. "I need to speak with him. Now. Immediately."

"I am terribly sorry but the Captain has stepped out for the moment. Would you like to leave a message of some kind?" she asked.

"A message? Yes. I would like to leave a message," he said. "You tell that fat fuck my men have grown tired of waiting and if he doesn't bring us our money right now we will be gone and so will every bit of his fucking merchandise."

"His merchandise?" she asked.

"Yes. That is what I said. Maybe I should speak more clearly so you can understand me. Tell Sandoval if we are not paid, every pound of his merchandise will no longer be available."

Agent Edwards smiled and nodded his head.

"We don't want that to happen, Randy," the woman replied.

"Who am I talking to?" he asked.

"My name is not important, Randy. What is important is that you and your men get the money you were promised. I can make that happen."

"You can, huh?"

"Yes, Randy. I can. I will personally bring you and your men all of your money straight away."

"You can do that for us?" he asked.

"Yes, I can," she said. "Where are you?"

"Didn't that fat fuck tell you where we would be?"

"No. He did not," she said. "He obviously wasn't expecting you to call him this soon."

"This soon?" interrupted Agent Correlli. "We have been waiting much too long already, bitch! We want our money and we want it now! Comprende?"

"I understand completely," she said. "We have your money. Your money is right here. I am looking at it as we speak."

"Jesus fucking Christ! What kind of games are you running here? We had a fucking deal with Sandoval and now he is dragging his feet!"

"My sincerest apologies, Randy," she said calmly. "Would you like to come here and pick up your money?"

"That wasn't the deal, woman! Sandoval was to bring our money here! To us!"

"All right. Tell me where you are and I promise, you will have your money within the hour."

"You will bring this to me personally? Alone?" he asked. "No tricks?"

"No tricks," she said. "My promise to you. And yes. I will do that."

Agent Correlli suddenly stopped talking, held up one finger, and took a long deep breath. Agent Edwards stared into Agent Correlli's eyes trying to understand what he was doing.

"No," he finally uttered. "Here is what you will do. You will do this. I do not know who you are. But I do know the singer named Lottie D. You send that woman, alone, with my money or there is no deal. You can tell that fascist bastard Porter I will guarantee her safety. No harm will come to her. That is my promise to you. Are we in agreement?"

Another long pause hung over the phone conversation. The silence became deafening as we looked at one another and waited for the response.

"Yes," she replied. "Lottie D is here and we will send her to you."

"Alone!" he demanded.

"Yes! Alone," she said as she calmed her voice. "Where and when?"

"The Hotel Santiago. Room 531. You have thirty minutes," Agent Correlli said and hung up the phone.

"How did I do?" asked Agent Correlli. "Do you think she bought it?"

"Hell," said Detective Blaine. "I watched you do it and I believed it!"

"That was very believable," I added. "Nicely done."

"Thank you," said Agent Correlli and plopped himself down on the wooden stool.

"Very well done, Agent Correlli, but we all need to get moving and I mean right now," announced Agent Edwards. "Up and at 'em!"

I took the phone from Agent Correlli's hands, placed it on the night stand and quickly followed everyone out of the room. The trap was set and all we could do now was wait with the hope our prey would blindly oblige us and willingly step in.

Time was finally in our favor. Or so we thought.

CHAPTER THIRTY FOUR

Rachel Stone Barbieri was livid.

The conversation with Agent Correlli, aka Randy, had given her the answers she was so desperately searching for but had left a bad taste in her mouth. She hung up the phone and began slowly pacing the living room floor.

"What is it?" asked Ponce. "What is wrong?"

"Everything!" she replied. "We find people we think we can trust. We pay them well. They respond to us, in kind, pledge their loyalty, and the first opportunity they get to screw us over? They try to screw us over!"

Rachel kept pacing attempting to calm herself down but the betrayal she was feeling was too overwhelming.

"I blame myself for this," she said. "You were right. I have been too soft. Too kind. And this is the result of that kindness. Give me a cigarette."

Ponce took out his cigarette pack, handed Rachel the last smoke in the pack, and gave her a light. She took a deep drag and blew the inhaled smoke up to the ceiling.

"You were wrong about Sandoval," she said. "We both were."

"Sandoval is responsible for this?" asked Ponce.

Rachel kept pacing the floor.

"Yes," she replied. "This hard-nosed Randy just gave him up because evidently he and his whoever crew haven't been paid for their services."

"This Randy has our merchandise?" Ponce asked.

"So he says. He'll give it back if he gets paid."

Ponce stopped Rachel from pacing and looked directly at her.

"We are not paying these fools," he asked. "Are we?"

"Hell no. They're going to be paid. Each and every one of them, including Sandoval. But not with cash. And not with our merchandise! They are going to pay with their heads for this betrayal!"

Ponce smiled.

"What?" she asked.

"You should stay angry more often. I like you like this. Say the word and I will kill them all."

Rachel smiled, leaned down, and crushed out her cigarette.

"We will do exactly that, in time. But for right now we have to back away from our original approach in this."

"What do you mean?" asked Rockwell.

"I mean we can't kill everyone. Not yet. At this stage? I have to go pretend to be nice. But it's the last time. Believe me. The last time. The both of you just follow my lead."

Rachel turned and headed to the back bedroom. Rockwell and Ponce looked at each other and quickly followed.

Lottie D and Angel had been sitting quietly in the back bedroom along with Ponce's three men and the large black man, Alphonse. The four men had been standing watch, not giving them answers as to what was going on and why they were being detained in such a manner. Lottie D was doing her best to maintain her cover and hold it together, but her thoughts kept telling her that everything could all go south in the next few minutes. She began to search the room for some possible survival options in case her thoughts rang true.

Suddenly Rachel burst into the room and walked directly up to where Lottie D was sitting.

"My sincerest apologies for all this unbearable waiting we have put you both through and please excuse my being blunt in this moment, Miss D, but there is a critical time factor present that needs to be addressed in a timely manner so please, tell me this. Who the hell is Randy?" Rachel asked.

Lottie D breathed a huge sigh of relief somewhere deep inside herself and instantly knew she was relatively safe for the time being. The call had worked and the fish had taken the bait.

For now.

"Randy?" Lottie asked and doing her best to lie into the face of unspeakable evil. "I don't know any Randy. Who the hell are you? And what is going on here? I have a show to do tonight. Where's Sam?"

Rachel took a deep breath and remained as calm as she could.

"I will ask you again," said Rachel. "Who is Randy? And where is the Santiago Hotel?"

Rachel's questions to Lottie D made Angel chuckle. Rachel turned to him immediately.

"Did I say something funny to you?" she asked.

"Por favor," said Angel. "With all due respect, Senora. The Hotel Santiago? It is not a hotel. It is the name of a whorehouse."

"A whorehouse?"

"Si," he replied politely. "It is the poor man's whorehouse. The women there are very old and very tired."

"Do you know where this place is?" she calmly asked.

"Si, Senora. It is on the edge of town on the Mexican side of Nogales. Near the river."

"You have been to this place?" Rachel asked.

"Yes. Many times. The tequila is very reasonably priced, as are the senoritas."

"Where is Sam?" asked Lottie D wondering for real where he was and if he was still alive. "He may be able to tell you who this Randy person is."

Rachel looked at Ponce and smiled.

"Sam went to meet up with Captain Sandoval and some of his people," said Ponce.

"I may know this Randy person you speak of," said Angel.

"You do?" asked Rachel.

"Yes. I have seen him at Pablo's a few times and the Hotel Santiago many times. His real name is Rudolpho Zapeta but everyone calls him Randy. He's a complete asshole. Always running his mouth and acting like he's some kind of big time gangster. Sam threw him out of Pablo's a month ago for coming on to one of the cocktail waitresses a little too strong if you know what I mean."

Lottie D quickly jumped in to enhance Angel's story.

"That Randy?" Lottie D added in. "I do remember him and he is an asshole. I always saw him with Captain Sandoval, drinking and whispering to each other in that rear booth at the back of the club."

Rachel bit her bottom lip, took a deep breath, and sat down next to Lottie D.

"This is true? You saw this Randy and Captain Sandoval talking together?"

"Yes," Lottie D lied. "I did. But if he walked in here right now I really don't think I would recognize him. It's been some time since I've seen him."

"That's all right. I need a favor from you. From the both of you," Rachel said. "I need you, Lottie, to bring this Randy person a little gift from me and I need you, Angel, to make certain this gift is given to the same Randy you are both speaking of. Could you do that for me?"

"I know what he looks like," said Angel. "I will do as you ask."

"Is he the one who stole the money from the club?" asked Lottie keeping up the façade.

"Yes," said Rachel. "Once we do this the police are going to arrest him."

"The police need our help," added Rockwell.

"Will you help us?" begged Ponce. "Please?"

Lottie paused to answer and stared into Rachel and Ponce's eyes.

"I'll do it," said Lottie D, "As long as I'm back in time for my evening show? The band starts at nine. Sharp. They get upset if I'm late."

"There'll be plenty of time for you to do your show," said Rachel.

"Okay then. I'll do it. What's the gift?" Lottie asked hoping it might be a weapon of some kind she could use later on if need be.

"It's a small attaché case," Rachel replied. "It's empty. Very nice expensive leather. All you have to do is hand it to him and walk away."

"At this whorehouse place?"

"Yes," replied Rachel.

"I can do that," Lottie answered and began to run newer survival options across her mind. She knew if she made it to the car her odds of surviving would be largely in her favor.

"Wonderful," said Rachel. "Rockwell? Grab that attaché in the living room. Angel? You ride with Ponce and these gentlemen and Lottie D? You ride with the rest of us in my car and let's go see this Randy person. It won't take long. I promise."

"Okay," Lottie D agreed pretending to go along. "I want to get my purse before I go. If that is all right with you?"

"Certainly," said Rachel. "Alphonse? Help Lottie D get her purse."

The tension in the room became quite obvious but Lottie D kept her composure and pretense intact. She went calmly to the walk-in closet to get her purse but knew she couldn't grab the one holding her small handgun, not with Alphonse so close by. She decided on another and as she took it down, Alphonse quickly checked it and handed it back to her.

"Thank you," she said pretending not to be bothered by the big man's arrogance.

Another near fatal mistake avoided as Lottie D left the walk-in closet.

Rachel got up, leaned in to Ponce, and whispered in his ear.

"When this is done? Kill the kid and this singing bitch and put their heads with the rest."

"With pleasure," said Ponce and turned to Angel. "Let's go young man."

Rachel, her crew, Lottie D and Angel all walked out and headed to their respective vehicles. The night air gave Lottie D a new sense of hope as she slipped into the back seat next to Rachel. Rockwell sat in front with the attaché in hand and Alphonse sat at the wheel.

"Let's go," announced Rachel and Alphonse started the big Chrysler engine and waited for Ponce's Packard to swing by and lead the way down North Terrace Avenue.

The two cars reached the corner and Ponce noticed one side of the street was cordoned off by military soldiers. A young private carrying a rifle pointed the only way left to travel and Ponce made the turn and headed slowly out.

"What's going on?" asked Lottie D knowing full well the trap set and executed by Agent Edwards and his team was quickly closing in.

"It looks like a traffic accident," said Rockwell. "There are lights up ahead and a car pulled over."

"I think it's some military exercise," said Rachel. "They're out here every now and then pretending to be real soldiers. Just drive slowly and do whatever they ask."

Alphonse nodded, looked in his rear view mirror, and noticed the soldiers moving their roadblocks up to the next corner. A line of a dozen or so armed soldiers took positions across the street.

Rockwell noticed Ponce's car being directed to the side of the road. As Ponce parked his vehicle, he was suddenly surrounded by five soldiers pointing their rifles at him and the other men.

"If this is some faked exercise they are really going to some extremes here," Rockwell announced. "Look at this."

Rachel sat up in her seat and looked out the front windshield. Another blockade was set about ten feet ahead of Ponce's car. Several military jeeps and four spotlights were set along the blockade and Rachel had to shield her eyes to see.

"This is ridiculous," she said calmly. "Captain Herman and Mayor Birdwell are going to hear about this."

A slight smile crossed Lottie D's face as another soldier stepped in front of Rachel's vehicle and ordered it to stop.

"Please shut off your engine and exit your vehicle," he ordered. "That includes everyone!"

"What do you want me to do?" asked Alphonse.

"Do what they say," said a highly annoyed Rachel. "The faster we co-operate the faster we can get out of here."

Alphonse shut off the engine and everyone stepped out of the vehicle. Eight armed soldiers pointed their rifles as one young sergeant walked casually up to the car.

"Really?" asked Rachel. "Rifles? Are they really necessary?"

"Good evening, everyone. Kindly place both your hands on the vehicle, please."

"We have a very important meeting to attend to, soldier boy," said Rachel. "We do not have time for any of this nonsense and we do not appreciate being part of your military exercises this evening. I am going to report this to Mayor Birdwell and to my lawyers."

"You're going to need a lawyer, sweetheart," said Patrick as he stepped into the light of the car's headlights. He wiped his lip with his right hand and smiled. Rachel's face immediately went pale as she realized what was actually going on.

"And this is no exercise," announced Agent Edwards as he and Agent Correlli also stepped into the light.

"Place your hands on the vehicle! Now!" barked the young sergeant with a much needed authoritative tone. "I will not repeat it a third time!"

Everyone from the car placed their hands on the front hood, including Lottie D.

"This is a fucking joke and a complete waste of time," said Rachel quietly to herself.

"Confiscate any weapons and you, open it up," said Detective Blaine as he stepped up to Alphonse.

"Open what up?" asked Alphonse.

"Your trunk, Einstein," said Detective Blaine as he stared across the hood of the car, took a hand gun from Alphonse's jacket, and smiled at Rachel.

Alphonse looked at Rachel and she nodded yes and took a deep breath. Alphonse opened the trunk and stepped back. The sergeant shined his flashlight into the trunk, pulled back a gray wool blanket, and discovered a blue gym bag. He quickly opened the zipper and looked inside.

"Same as the others," the sergeant said as he pulled the bag from the trunk and walked to Agent Edwards.

"Others?" asked Rachel. "What others?"

The sergeant held the opened bag down into the headlights so Rachel could see the contents.

"It appears each of these vehicles contain blue gym bags with ten kilos of high quality heroin," said Agent Edwards. "White boy, as it's known in the trade."

"Those aren't my bags," said Rachel. "The bags belong to Captain Sandoval."

"Not according to the law," said a smiling Agent Edwards. "Your car. Your bag. Sandoval's car. Sandoval's bag. Ponce's car. Ponce's bag. And when we find Sam Porter and his three drivers? Well, they will be coming along too. With all of you."

Agent Edwards looked to the left and pointed at Ponce's car. Ponce and his men, along with Captain Sandoval, were all handcuffed and being led away under the direction of Captain Frederick Herman and several other FBI agents. Angel walked up to the car and put his arm around Agent Correlli.

"Mrs. Barbieri," Angel announced. "I see him!"

"Who?" she asked.

"This is Randy. The man you were looking for. Turns out he, like myself, work for J. Edgar Hoover and the FBI. Randy? Say goodbye to Mrs. Barbieri and her friends."

"Goodbye, Mrs. Barbieri. I hope you and that fat fuck enjoy your federal prison time," said Agent Correlli in his Randy voice. "It's going to be a long one. Believe me."

If looks could actually kill, Rachel's face and burning stare would have executed everyone on Agent Edwards' team immediately.

"May I?" asked Agent Davis, no longer needing to pretend to be Lottie D.

"Be my guest," answered Agent Edwards, as Detective Blaine handed her a pair of handcuffs.

Agent Davis pulled Rachel's arms behind her back and placed her in handcuffs.

"You pulled out all the stops on this one," said Rachel. "Didn't you, little man?"

"Yes I did," answered Agent Edwards. "We all did. And there was nothing little about this operation."

"It will never stick," said Rachel. "And each and every one of you? You are all dead men. My word on that."

"Rachel Stone Barbieri," said Agent Davis. "I am Special Agent Loretta Davis with the FBI and I am placing you and your associates under arrest for drug trafficking, smuggling, and murder."

"And dead women," she added. "I'll make your demise extra special, honey."

"Make all the threats you want, ma'am," said Agent Davis. "You are going to have a lot of time to think. A lot of time. Unless, of course, they give you the gas. Step to the front of the vehicle, please?"

Agent Davis led Mrs. Barbieri to the front of the car as Detective Blaine placed Rockwell and Alphonse in handcuffs.

"That's too tight," Rockwell protested.

"I know," answered Detective Blaine. "Get these people out of here."

Several Agents took Rockwell, Alphonse, and a very calm and cool Rachel Stone Barbieri to a waiting van, placed them inside, and drove off into the night. Patrick, Agent Edwards, Detective Blaine, and the other agents all watched the van drive away.

Captain Herman's soldiers quickly dismantled their makeshift road blocks, placed them into two waiting trucks and within a matter of minutes every vehicle, jeep, truck, and spot light was nowhere to be seen. The area had once again become dark and quiet as Agent Edwards, Detective Blaine, and Patrick watched Agents Davis, Correlli, and the young man, Angel, run up towards Sam Porter's house, guns in hand.

"Looks like you two can go back to your private citizen status now that we're wrapping this all up," said Agent Edwards.

"Do you think Hoover will miss us?" asked Detective Blaine.

"Not for a second," answered Agent Edwards. "You both will receive a hefty bonus, compliments of J. Edgar Hoover and the Federal Bureau of Investigation for all of your hard work."

"This operation was all you, Edwards," said Detective Blaine. "But we'll gladly take the government's money. Right, Patrick?"

Agent Edwards and Detective Blaine noticed Patrick deep in thought. Agent Edwards broke the silence.

"What's on your mind over there? Are you seeing something we missed?"

Patrick turned and looked at Agent Edwards.

"It's what I didn't see," said Patrick.

"What do you mean?" asked Detective Blaine.

"When I got the drop on Barbieri up at Big Bear and she had this sense that it might all be over for her because she couldn't buy me off, her face began to twitch. Tonight we got them all. They are all going over. No escape. But her face didn't twitch. Not one little bit. She was calm as a cucumber. That bothers me."

"That bitch is done," said Detective Blaine. "I hope they gas the lot of them."

"She acted like she knows something we don't," added Patrick.

"Don't give it another thought, my friend," said Agent Edwards. "They are all going down and I'm sure when dear Mrs. Barbieri hears what her sentence is going to be, her face will start twitching and probably never stop. She is not going to like federal prison. Believe me. And if they do give her the gas? We'll be there to say our goodbyes."

"You mean good riddance," said Detective Blaine.

"I hope you're right," added Patrick. "She deserves every ounce of unhappiness and misery for who that woman is and what she's done."

"Let's get to Porter's place. We still have one more player to deal with," said Agent Edwards.

Patrick nodded yes and walked up the road with Agent Edwards and Detective Blaine, not yet realizing Operation Nogales had finally come to a highly successful close.

CHAPTER THIRTY FIVE

The office space looked to me like some fancy new hotel room where rich people stayed while on vacation in Florida or Acapulco. The entire rear walls were all glass from ceiling to floor and the view of the Pacific Ocean gave the three rooms a sense of warmth and tranquility. It had a large bright waiting area. Betty had taken on the role of interior decorator and placed four leather chairs at the entrance, hung a huge framed photograph of old Santa Monica as it was in the early nineteen hundreds, and on the south wall she placed a large black framed mirror.

"People coming to see private eyes are nervous," she told me. "People seeing themselves in this mirror will relax them. Help them feel at ease."

"I shave in a mirror almost every day and it doesn't relax me or make me feel at ease."

"Trust me on this, Miles," she said. "You also need to hire an attractive secretary with great legs who is as efficient as she is attractive, but she also needs to make your new clients feel safe. Secure."

"Can't I just hang up another mirror somewhere?"

"No," she demanded. "You gave me your budget on this and you need to have all the necessary items in place if this new business space is going to be successful. That includes a secretary. I will find you one. The right one. The perfect one."

Betty had a small coffee maker set up in one corner with an array of fresh doughnuts made available, day or night.

The entrance door was half glass and I had the maintenance super, an older Italian man named Angelo, known by everyone in the building as the Mighty A, hand-paint Patrick Miles Atwater, Private Investigations across the beveled glass. I was officially opened for business. The office costs set me back some, but I knew it was the right move and with Betty's help it all came together relatively quickly and painlessly. The new place sat on the top floor in the heart of Santa Monica, an easy drive from my apartment or from Barney's By The Sea. The rent was a little more than I wanted to pay but again, Betty convinced me that the space and the furnishings were imperative to my new success as a private investigator. Betty had desks delivered and set in each office, both with two matching leather chairs that sat in front, a fancy swiveled leather chair behind each desk and two floor lamps. To maintain her theme, as she described it, two more large black and white photos of old Hollywood and downtown Los Angeles hung on the walls. I took the old Hollywood office because it was in the corner and had an extra window on the adjoining wall. The secretary's desk was all wood with an extra side car, as I called it, attached to the right and Betty had it placed in the center of the waiting room. We had three phone lines put in, a recording unit, a brand new electric typewriter, two tall filing cabinets, and a green colored banker's lamp. The only thing missing was that special secretary Betty promised me.

But it didn't take long for Betty to come through.

It was early Friday morning. I had been in the new digs for only three days and I sat at the secretary's desk downing my second donut and third cup of coffee as this shy and highly attractive young girl entered the office.

"Hello, are you Mr. Atwater?" she asked.

"I'm Patrick Atwater. You must be Phyllis."

"Yes sir. Phyllis Gardener. Betty Farnswell told me you were looking for a new secretary and I should come and speak with you."

"Would you like a donut and a cup of coffee, Miss Gardener?"

"May I?"

"Please do."

Phyllis appeared nervous but as she poured herself some black coffee and took a large bite of her chocolate donut she became more relaxed. I got up from the desk, grabbed one of the leather chairs, pulled it closer to the desk and sat down.

"Please? Have a seat, Miss Gardener," I said and motioned her to the secretary's chair.

"Here?" she asked.

"Please," I repeated.

Phyllis sat down still holding her coffee and donut and smiled at me. She was dressed in a brown tweed skirt with a matching vest, a pale pink blouse buttoned to the top, and on her feet, at the bottom of her long legs, she wore a pair of expensive-looking crème colored heels. She had dark brown shoulder length hair, a peach-like complexion and wore very little makeup. To my eyes, Phyllis was the spitting image of the secretary Betty had described for me. I could see she was just a kid but her energy added to the brightness in the room and I liked that.

"How does it feel?" I asked.

"Feel?"

"The chair? The desk? The surroundings?"

She gazed around the room.

"It feels quite comfortable here," she replied. "This is a very nice office. It smells brand new."

"It is brand new. Compliments of Mrs. Farnsworth's expertise. Tell me a little about yourself."

Phyllis put her coffee and donut down carefully and took a deep breath.

"Well," she said. "This coming February I will be turning twenty-one. I'm single. I graduated third in my class at Manhattan Secretarial School here in Los Angeles, that's where I met Betty. I live alone in a small house in Woodland Hills that was left to me by my deceased grandmother, Hattie. It was supposed to go to my older brother, Eddie, but he was killed in the Pacific. He was on the ship that delivered the atom bomb that was dropped on Japan. My parents live up in Santa Barbara, where I grew up, and my father is a District Court Judge. He's been on the bench for fifteen years now. I don't smoke. I don't drink, and I don't have any acting aspirations of becoming the next Bette Davis or Lauren Bacall. So many young girls come here for that sort of thing."

"But not you?" I asked.

"No sir. I am more practical in nature. I enjoy secretarial work and hope to have a secretarial service school of my own someday."

"Can you type?" I asked.

"Ninety words a minute, sir."

"Do you own a car?"

"Yes sir. It's an old Hudson but it gets me where I need to be."

"Nothing wrong with a Hudson. Can you live on forty dollars a week?"

She suddenly gasped slightly and her face froze for a moment. She looked like she wanted to speak but couldn't utter any words. She finally broke out of her thought and looked directly at me.

"Forty dollars a week? Holy cow. That is very generous of you."

"I'll expect you to be here from nine to five, Monday through Friday, take an hour for lunch, and you may get a phone call or two from me on some weekends when I'm working a case. You can call me Mr. Atwater whenever we're in the office around clients but anywhere else you just call me Patrick. Agreed?"

"Agreed. And you can call me Phil. My nickname. From my brother. If that's okay with you?"

"Agreed," I said and we both smiled. "The job is yours if you want it, Phil."

"I very much do want it, Mr. Atwater. Patrick. Sir."

"Then let's shake on it."

Phil stood up quickly and vigorously shook my hand.

"Thank you," she said.

We no sooner shook hands and the phone on the desk rang. Phil looked at me, tossed her hair back, and picked up the receiver.

"Patrick Atwater's office," she said in her most professional tone.

She listened intently and slowly sat down.

"Yes he is," she stated. "Can you hold, please? Thank you."

Phil put the call on hold and looked at me.

"It's a Detective Blaine of the LAPD," she announced.

"Punch me through," I said and headed to my office.

Phil waited until I was situated in my chair and transferred the call. I picked up the phone and looked out at the ocean below.

"Patrick Atwater, at your service. You are my first call in the new digs."

"I heard you were finally getting a real office space. Down by the beach somewhere, right?"

"Santa Monica. What's shaking up in Los Angeles? Any word from Agent Edwards or J Edgar on the Barbieri crew?"

"I heard through the grapevine that Rockwell was rolling over on all of them, hoping to get a deal."

"Edwards won't go for that. Keep me in the know."

"Will do," he said. "Let me tell you why I called. This just came over the wire. Remember that big mug Stanley Clifford?"

"Sure. I remember Clifford. They gave him twenty years for beating his wife and molesting his two daughters."

"He's dead."

"Dead," I repeated. "How? What happened?"

"Van Nuys police just shot and killed him and his accomplice."

"His accomplice? They shot them in stir?"

"No. At his house."

My heart began to sink deep in my chest and a dark veil of dread washed over my entire body. The face of Mrs. Clifford and her two daughters suddenly stared at me in my mind and I froze in my chair for a few moments.

"Are you still there, Patrick?"

"I'm here. What happened?"

"Clifford and some other crazy named Skibo broke out of county while they were waiting to be transported up state. Some guard and his lawyer girlfriend helped them do it and they killed them both once they were out and then stole a car. I was waiting to get the make and model and when this other news came out I thought you should hear this from me."

"I'm listening," I said.

"Clifford and Skibo raped the two girls and then they beat them to death. They made Mrs. Clifford watch."

"Jesus. And then?" I asked.

"Then Clifford beat his wife to death with a baseball bat."

My brain went into a mental tailspin as Detective Blaine explained how the police arrived and shot and killed both men but his words sounded like they were echoing from several galaxies away. My head seemed to implode and everything I thought to be true, real, honest, virtuous, or even beautiful immediately vanished into some gigantic unexplainable red explosion of bitter hot smoke and a foul haze began to permeate somewhere deep behind my eyes, forcing my face to tighten and my eyes to squint. A huge knot of pain ran down my entire body and I placed both hands on the desk and tried forcing myself to breathe. I slowly put the phone back to my ear.

"I promised that woman and her two girls he would never hurt them ever again," I said and realized my next thoughts were being spoken the instant I thought of them. "I looked in their eyes and promised them safety. I gave them my word, Detective. My word."

"This is not your fault, Patrick."

I heard the words but my grief and my anger wouldn't allow a response.

"I'll come down your way tomorrow, Patrick and you can show me the new place. Maybe have a few beers at Barney's By the Sea. Okay?" he asked.

"Sure," I said. "Thanks for the call."

I slowly hung up the phone, put my head in my hands, and could not hold back my grief. I sobbed uncontrollably for a few minutes and when I sat up and took a deep breath I saw Phil standing in the doorway.

"Can I get you anything?" she asked.

"No, but thanks for asking."

"I'll see you on Monday? Nine o'clock?"

"Yes. Nine o'clock."

Phil stared at me and I could tell she was hoping I would be all right. I raised my hand and nodded yes to her and she headed out the front entrance.

I locked the place up, jumped into the coupe, and headed out to Van Nuys. When I arrived, the coroner was putting Mrs. Clifford's body into their vehicle. There were six police cars, three news trucks, and it seemed like the entire neighborhood was gathered on one end of the small street, rubbernecking to see what was going on.

I knew the policeman at the perimeter and when I told him my relationship to the situation, he let me through and I walked inside.

The house was a total wreck.

It looked like Stanley and this other man, Skibo, had destroyed everything they could get their hands on, with pieces scattered everywhere. There was shattered glass, stuffing from pillows and chairs, and freshly splintered wood. So many broken pieces of furniture and framed pictures strewn about the entire living room, it looked as if a herd of cattle had just run through the house.

And there was blood. Blood was everywhere. The walls and floors were covered in it. I shuddered to myself trying to imagine the horror and the pain Mrs. Clifford and her two girls, Elizabeth and Sandra, must have suffered trying to defend themselves from such a horrific attack.

I stood there trying to maintain my composure as Officer Kramer entered the room from the hallway and saw me.

"Hey, Patrick. He said he'd come back and do this. I just wish I had gotten here sooner."

"You and your partner took them down?" I asked.

"We came in with our guns drawn and both men, covered in blood, were smiling and sitting on the couch drinking beers like they were at a ball game. Clifford raises his two arms and says, "We surrender!" and the two of them start laughing. Mrs. Clifford's naked body was all battered and bloody, lying face up on the dining room floor but you couldn't really see a face. My partner kept them covered and I went into the back bedroom."

Officer Kramer took a long deep breath and leaned in close to me and whispered.

"When I saw those girls? And seen what they had done? I walked out here and without a word or a warning I shot them both dead where they sat."

"Is that what you are going to put in your report?" I asked.

"Yes. Only my partner and I are going to say they pointed their weapons at us and I had no choice but to fire."

"They had weapons?"

"We made sure they did after I shot them."

Officer Kramer and I exchanged glances and he walked to the rear of the house. I took a deep breath and walked slowly back to my car.

I decided to hit the Beverly for a much needed drink and tossed my keys to Freddie. He must have sensed the tremendous pain I was feeling because he silently took the keys and opened the front door with a slight smile and a complimentary nod. I walked across the entrance through the double doors and sat down at the end of the bar, ordering up a double Scotch.

Neat.

One Scotch turned into two. And then a third. I had a quick bite to eat but kept drinking, alone at the bar, until I knew it was time to have Bobby the bartender call a cab and send me home to a much needed sleep. Bobby gave me a container of coffee for the ride home. As he picked up the phone to call the cab, a group of about four or five women, all dressed to the nines and laughing to themselves, passed by and I suddenly detected a familiar slight hint of vanilla.

I put some cash on the bar to cover my bill, grabbed my coffee, and quickly headed for the cab stand out front.

I walked out into the night air just as the women from the bar were piling into a long black limousine. I focused my eyes into the vehicle and I saw her.

Rachel Stone Barbieri.

She looked me straight in the eye and smiled as if we were old friends who hadn't seen each other for years and now just happened to bump into each other again at the Beverly.

I was stunned.

A million questions began racing across my mind and I convinced myself I was only seeing things because of all the alcohol I had consumed. The cab arrived, I got in, and as Freddie told the driver my address and shut the door, the big yellow cab headed to my apartment. My head began to spin and I leaned back and fell asleep.

"Hey pal? Wake up!" said a loud voice as I slowly came awake.

I paid the fare, stepped out of the cab, and realized I had left my keys with Freddie. I sat on the small wall in the front of my apartment and took in the night air. Suddenly my Ford coupe arrived with some young-looking college kid at the wheel. He jumped out quickly and asked the cabbie I was with to wait for him. He walked up to me.

"Here are your keys, Mr. Atwater," he said and placed them in my hand.

"Do I know you, kid?" I asked. "Are you a friend of Freddie's?"

"No sir," he said. "I'm a bar back at the Beverly. My name is Everett."

Everett headed towards the cab.

"Then how do you know my name, have my keys, and my car?"

"She told me," he said and stepped into the cab.

I quickly went to the cab, opened the door, and leaned down to look at him.

"She told you? Who told you?" I asked.

"The woman. At the Beverly. The woman in the yellow dress. She gave me your keys, and a hundred bucks to drive your coupe here. A real looker, that one. Here, see? She even wrote down the address."

He took a piece of paper from his shirt pocket and handed it to me.

I stood there holding the piece of paper as the cab drove away. I slowly brought the paper up to my nose and again detected that all too familiar scent of fresh-cut flowers with the slightest hint of vanilla.

"Son of a bitch," I said and crumpled the paper in my hand.

I staggered slowly to my apartment, went inside, and sat by the phone. I picked up the receiver and dialed carefully. The phone rang five times and someone picked up.

A long silence hung in the air like some thick cloud passing over me.

I took a deep breath and let it out slowly.

"Magenta," I said.

The phone on the other end went dead.

I dialed again and after two rings an operator came on the line.

"The number you are dialing is not a working number," she said.

I hung up the phone and noticed my hands beginning to shake. I clasped my hands together, took another deep breath, and stared at the floor.

The war of ghosts was trying to create another casualty.

I would not allow that to happen.

The time had come to declare a war of my own.